There'd been a time when she wasn't afraid of anything.

Now, everything, everyone, every action needed to be thought over, accepted or rejected, and it fell on her shoulders. Maybe it was the pregnancy playing havoc with her thoughts as well as her hormones. She hoped so. Because then, after her little girl was born, things would go back to normal.

No, they'd never go back to normal, but she'd at least be able to make good decisions again.

"Peeve likes kids." Oscar's voice was deep, his smile broad.

So were his shoulders. He was tall, with a square jaw and black hair cut short. There'd been a time when Shelley might have added gorgeous to her assessment. Now she was looking for a flaw.

Not his eyes. They were so deep a brown they bordered on black. And they spoke to her. They hinted at safety, yet...she wasn't sure she could trust him with her secret.

Dear Reader,

I'm never short on story ideas because my life is a situation comedy without the thirty-minute time constraint and/or the perfect clothes, hair and body. The new point of humor in my life is a puppy named Lucy.

Regimented me, who likes lists and research, decided the family needed a dog. I have a ten-year-old son, and every boy needs a dog, right? My husband wasn't sure. The cat voted no. I decided on an Australian shepherd, male, between one and three, a rescue that would already be housebroken and like cats. Maybe they exist. I'm not sure. I took the first puppy I saw.

Our little family now has a GIANT German husky who is still a puppy but looks like a full-grown dog. Oh, it's a girl. She wasn't housebroken because she was only eight weeks.

The cat's not talking to me. The husband *is* talking to me but most of our conversations are about what the dog is eating: toothbrushes, socks, books (never a Harlequin Heartwarming!) and every dog toy (we get two days' use max).

I walk Lucy every morning and night. One morning, I met a mother and her one-year-old. The one-year-old ran to Lucy (twice her size!), who took it with good grace and slobbering tongue, and the mother and I got to talking. Meanwhile, the one-year-old toddles to the closest house and peeks through the window. Her mother was aghast. Me? I got a whole story idea. You're about to read it.

Thank you so much for delving into Harlequin Heartwarming books! If you'd like to know more about me, please visit www.pamelatracy.com.

Pamela

HEARTWARMING

Holding Out for a Hero

———

USA TODAY Bestselling Author

Pamela Tracy

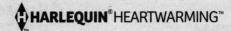

Recycling programs
for this product may
not exist in your area.

ISBN-13: 978-0-373-36832-7

Holding Out for a Hero

Copyright © 2017 by Pamela Tracy Osback

All rights reserved. Except for use in any review, the reproduction or
utilization of this work in whole or in part in any form by any electronic,
mechanical or other means, now known or hereinafter invented, including
xerography, photocopying and recording, or in any information storage
or retrieval system, is forbidden without the written permission of the
publisher, Harlequin Enterprises Limited, 225 Duncan Mill Road,
Don Mills, Ontario M3B 3K9, Canada.

This is a work of fiction. Names, characters, places and incidents are
either the product of the author's imagination or are used fictitiously,
and any resemblance to actual persons, living or dead, business
establishments, events or locales is entirely coincidental.

This edition published by arrangement with Harlequin Books S.A.

For questions and comments about the quality of this book,
please contact us at CustomerService@Harlequin.com.

® and TM are trademarks of Harlequin Enterprises Limited or its
corporate affiliates. Trademarks indicated with ® are registered in the
United States Patent and Trademark Office, the Canadian Intellectual
Property Office and in other countries.

Printed in U.S.A.

Pamela Tracy is a *USA TODAY* bestselling author who lives with her husband (the inspiration for most of her heroes) and son (the interference for most of her writing time). Since 1999, she has published more than twenty-five books and sold more than a million copies. She's a RITA® Award finalist and a winner of the American Christian Fiction Writers' Book of the Year Award.

Books by Pamela Tracy

Harlequin Heartwarming

Love Inspired

The Rancher's Daughters

Love Inspired Suspense

To my wonderful editor Adrienne Macintosh,
who will soon be out taking walks with a baby
of her own. Enjoy every moment.

CHAPTER ONE

"IF YOU HAVE enough money for your son to be in the only private preschool in Sarasota Falls, you have enough money to pay me back. You owe me." The anger behind the words was palpable. Shelley Brubaker disconnected the call.

Sarasota Falls, New Mexico, was a small town, and while Shelley didn't know everyone by name or voice, she knew almost all by face.

They all—thanks to social media—knew *her* face.

So many people hurting, and her ex-husband was to blame.

In a few minutes, she would take her son to preschool—late, because the baby kicked most of the night and Abigail Simms's dog kept barking, keeping Shelley awake. And echoes of the unpleasant phone call would follow her.

Shelley was never late. It bothered her.

Ryan could attend preschool only because she'd been awarded one of their benevolence tuitions. Mostly because of all the years her father had donated fund-raiser items from the grocery store he managed.

"Phone!" Ryan had the endearing habit of announcing a phone call well after all conversation ended. His words jarred her from her reverie.

"Thanks for letting me know." She scooped the three-year-old up and did a half twirl. She used to do five of them, quickly, making Ryan scream with delight.

As she gave Ryan a quick sponge bath and dressed him, she figured it was time to change her number again. She couldn't count how many people had demanded she pay them back these past six months, since Larry Wagner, aka lousy ex-husband, disappeared into thin air the first week in December. Most calls were local, but some were from as far away as Maine. Never mind that her ex-husband had robbed her of every penny she had.

At first, she'd attempted to explain. The callers weren't interested. After explanations, she'd tried apologies, especially to the people she'd recommended her husband to. When the dust settled and she realized the extent of her ex-husband's crimes, she'd almost had a breakdown—which she neither had the time nor the money for.

"Mommy, play." Ryan, the spitting image of Larry with slightly curling golden hair and dimples, collapsed against her knee, all clean and dressed for fun, and looked up at her with a brown-eyed expression of glee.

There'd been a time when Ryan's requests to play were met with enthusiasm. Shelley really wanted to say, "Yes! You can jump on my bed, and I'll throw a ball to you." But now her bed pulled out from the sofa, and at eight months pregnant, it was all she could do to play his second-favorite game of chasing him around the one-room apartment while he wore a mask and pretended to be a monster.

Shelley tried not to analyze why he was a monster being chased by a nonscary but very pregnant woman.

Right now, though, the caller's raspy voice kept playing over and over in her head—*you owe me, you owe me, you owe me*—until Shelley couldn't breathe.

Ryan took matters into his own hands by heading to his toy box, grabbing his Thomas the Train hat and saying, "Let's walk."

He mimicked her tone exactly. At least three

times a day, she suggested, "Let's walk." Anything to get out of the tiny garage apartment, out into the air. This part of Sarasota Falls, on the edge of town, was a mixture of old and new. If she looked to the right, from the large picture window she could see a block of fairly new homes with a bed-and-breakfast—one of the oldest buildings in town—on the cul-de-sac. To her left, an established subdivision that led to the center of town.

"Okay, let me use the restroom first and then we'll eat and head to your preschool." This, her first pregnancy—as Ryan was her stepson—was a study in "Always go to the bathroom first," and "Eat or you'll soon feel nauseated," as well as, "You will feel nauseated no matter what you do."

Ryan was patient. He'd learned to be during the course of the investigation after his father disappeared. He'd done a lot of waiting for her, sitting on hard chairs in strange rooms with authority figures as Shelley'd been questioned. It had felt weird because some of the people asking her questions, especially the local chief of police, knew her well. Tom Riley knew the answers to the questions he was asking, but still he asked them.

It had been the other agencies, though, state

and federal, that truly scared her. They tried to press her into admitting she knew where Larry was.

She didn't know, didn't even care where he was. She never wanted to see the man again.

Finally she and Ryan were ready. She opened the front door and went ahead of him. He could go down the stairs by himself, but if he tripped, she wanted him to fall into her instead of down to the ground.

Their new place was over the garage of Robert Tellmaster's house. He'd been hesitant to rent to her. After all, most of the town had fallen victim to her husband's crimes, but in the end, because he knew her mother, he'd relented. He was a computer geek who rarely left his house and had been alone since his mother died many years ago. He never so much as smiled at Ryan or offered a kind word to her.

There was no traffic on the street. At nine in the morning, most people had already left for work. Shelley had lived in the apartment only two weeks, and during that time the parking lot at Bianca's Bed-and-Breakfast had been pretty much empty except for an oversize motorcycle. So far, Shelley hadn't figured out who the motorcycle's owner was, just that he worked strange hours. Bianca was one of the few in town who still nodded to Shelley when they passed each other. She'd even brought over some diapers and a crocheted blanket for the "little one."

Speaking of little ones. "We're going to be a tad late." Shelley awkwardly bent to tie Ryan's shoe. "But you'll be there in time for play."

Ryan didn't seem to care. He was watching a bird fly across the street and land in a tree in front of the house belonging to the newlyweds.

They had to be newlyweds; they seemed so happy.

Shelley turned to the left. She'd pass the cul-de-sac that Bianca shared with Abigail Simms. Abigail was in her fifties and gardened but always much earlier than nine. Her son was unemployed and in and out, but he'd never be up this early. She also had a tiny white poodle that barked constantly.

Shelley knew most of her neighbors, thanks to her mother and all the years Shelley had helped deliver baked goods to parties and such. The only family in the neighborhood— besides the newlyweds—who weren't Sarasota Falls natives were the Duponts, living farther down from Bianca. They had a special-needs son who kept Mrs. Dupont busy.

Shelley didn't think too much of Mr. Dupont. The first week she'd been in the garage apartment, he'd approached her, and she'd gotten the idea he was trying—in a smarmy way—to figure out how desperate for company she was.

Not that desperate. If she'd learned one thing from her ex-husband, it was that love could be an illusion. She intended never to let her guard down again, not with a man who promised the moon but delivered only heartache.

Her distrust of relationships grew as her pregnancy progressed and her responsibilities to her father, Ryan and now the little one fell on her shoulders alone.

She'd expected a love like the newlyweds had. Thanks to her picture window, Shelley had seen them together fairly often. The woman was probably a few years younger than Shelley. She left in the morning carrying a tote bag. The husband worked for Little's Supermarket, the grocery store Shelley's father had managed before he got too sick to work.

The husband was gone long hours.

Yeah, Shelley knew about husbands being

gone for long hours. Hers used those hours to steal and cheat. Yet when the young husband came home, he always seemed happy and rushed inside, often with flowers in hand.

The wife had family who'd already come to visit twice since Shelley'd moved in. An older man—probably the woman's father—came once bringing a kitchen table and chairs and a second time with food. A woman came, too, probably a sister.

Interesting.

Shelley took a deep breath, hoping to ease some of her back pain, and hurried to keep up with Ryan as he sped down the sidewalk. Today it appeared Ryan had places to go, people to meet, things to do. His Thomas the Train engineer's cap bounced up and down with each step he took. Yup, preschool was the social event of his season.

Shelley wished she had a place to go, anyplace other than here. A place where she could start a new life, make new friends, and where people might not remember that she was the hometown girl who'd married Larry Wagner, the villain who brought a small town to its knees. Thanks to social media, for a few days there her long jet-black hair and six-foot frame were the focus of a lot of attention.

The only thing she was thankful for was that her parents hadn't witnessed her fall from grace. Her dad, thanks to his job, had known almost everyone. Beyond that, he'd been the guy who could fix anything. Right now, he couldn't fix himself. Alzheimer's was like that.

Her mother had, at one time, been in charge of the store's bakery. When Shelley came along, her mom had started her own business and baked from home. For twenty-some years, she'd made the town's wedding cakes, baby-shower cakes and designer cupcakes. She'd wanted Shelley to take over the business.

But Shelley'd been a dreamer and thought the big city offered something small towns didn't. She'd been college-bound and career-ready. Now she was garage apartment–bound and unsteady.

She shouldn't have to hide. After all, she hadn't really been married to Larry Wagner because Larry Wagner hadn't been his real name. She'd found that out too late. It was a name—one of many—he'd used to con people, and he'd certainly pulled the wool over her eyes during the lowest, most vulnerable point of her life.

Now she was too busy and too angry to

let anyone take advantage. Or help. She had to take care of Ryan and get ready for baby Isabelle's entrance into the world. So far, it felt like she was carrying a quarterback or trapeze artist in her belly. As if to prove the point, Isabelle kicked and Shelley whistled.

"I see dog," Ryan said happily, and before Shelley had time to focus, he was in the street, crossing to the other side.

Large dog, Shelley noted as she sped up, putting a hand on her stomach and hoping the animal had a big heart, because no way was Ryan not going to pet it.

"Honey, wait a minute…"

The dog's owner paused, seemed to realize he couldn't get out of the way in time and, to Shelley's surprise, stopped and calmly said, "Sit, Peeve."

The dog obeyed, tongue lolling, just as Ryan wrapped his arms around the animal's neck. Peeve looked like a stoic old man—er, old dog—resigned to the attention of small beings who tugged on his collar and gave hugs.

Shelley slowed, disaster averted. There'd been a time when she wasn't afraid of anything. Now everything, everyone, every action needed to be thought over, accepted or rejected, and it all fell to her. Maybe it was just the pregnancy. She hoped so. Because then, after the baby was born, things would go back to normal.

Normal? She wondered if she'd ever see normal again.

"Peeve likes kids." The voice was deep, the smile broad.

So were the shoulders. He was tall, taller than her, square-chinned, with black hair cut short but still managing to look somewhat shaggy. Shelley might have added *gorgeous* to her assessment. Instead, thanks to Larry, she looked for a flaw.

Not his eyes. They were so deep a brown they bordered on black. Bushy eyebrows. Yes, that was it. His eyebrows were too bushy. He reminded her of someone; she couldn't place who.

"You have kids?" she asked. Maybe he was the dad of one of Ryan's preschool peers.

"No, just the dog. He's enough."

"I want dog," Ryan said, letting go of Peeve's collar. "Big one."

"Not until after the baby's born," Shelley said, silently adding the words *years after*. By her best estimate, if she were careful, she had enough money to support her, her children and her father for a few months. Now was not the best time to put in job applications.

"Soon," the dog's owner said to Ryan with a quick glance to her stomach, "you'll have someone to play with who's even better than a puppy."

Ryan didn't look convinced.

"Boy or girl?" the man asked.

"Girl."

"Must be an exciting time for you," he observed. Shelley had no response, just an empty, festering feeling that took her breath away—right when she needed it most. The back pain had her closing her eyes. She squelched the tears. She wasn't even sure which of her many messes she wanted to cry about this time: her ex-husband, missing and wanted by the police, her father's worsening Alzheimer's or the loneliness that dogged her steps.

After a minute, she opened her eyes and cleared her throat, her mind scrambling for a response. She didn't need to bother. Tall, dark and bushy knew a messed-up female when he saw one. He took about three steps back, his eyes guarded. "There's such a thing as too much excitement. You all right?"

"I'm fine. We're running late. Ryan, come on. Time to go."

Ryan, however, had left the sidewalk and was hurrying toward the large front window of the house whose sidewalk they were standing on: the newlyweds'. Shelley'd waved a brief hello a time or two but never stopped to chat. If you didn't count Mr. Dupont, tall, dark and bushy was the first neighbor she'd spoken more than a greeting to, apart from Bianca.

Not really a successful encounter for either of them. The man and his pet were already at the next house. Not looking back.

"Ryan, wait!" She skipped the walkway and rushed across the grass and around the back of the red Prius in the carport.

Ryan peered inside the house—a short, unafraid Peeping Tom—and asked, "Asleep?"

Great—just what Shelley needed. She didn't want to deal with the woman waking up and seeing two people looking in the window as if they were spying. "Come on, Ryan. We need to get to your school. Then you can have something to drink."

Shelley carefully bent down, her hands cupping Ryan under his arms, and started to scoop him up. Since his father disappeared,

Ryan spent half his time being clingy and the other half being angry. She was doing her best to deal with both, but she'd had only a little over a year to practice. Ryan was Larry's son, but Larry had gotten full custody when Ryan's mother went to prison.

So many secrets in her ex's life.

Ryan, giggling, struggled and pulled away. She understood. The mommy in her wanted to swing him high, tickle his stomach, get him laughing, maybe laugh herself. Ryan escaped her fingers and turned back to the window.

Shelley followed and stepped closer to the window. Judging by the blood and open, unblinking eyes, the woman who lay on the floor wasn't asleep. She was dead.

Worst of all, Shelley recognized the man standing behind the woman.

Larry Wagner, her ex-husband.

CHAPTER TWO

"I JUST MET Shelley Wagner face-to-face."
Oscar Guzman sat on his bed, Peeve content and panting at his feet, and spoke via phone to Lieutenant Colonel Lionel Townley. Currently, Townley was Oscar's boss at the Federal Bureau of Investigation. Before that, during Oscar's military service, Townley had been the second lieutenant who'd given Oscar most of his orders. Of all the men Oscar had served with, he respected Townley the most. So much so that when Townley requested Oscar be pulled from a long-term assignment for this under-the-radar case in small-dot-on-a-map, New Mexico, Oscar said yes before he'd known the specifics.

Of course, Oscar had spent a summer of his childhood in this small dot and had an aunt here. He had contacts in Sarasota Falls and could get close to Shelley Wagner without her suspecting who he worked for and what he wanted: her ex-husband, Larry Wagner.

"She was walking her son to preschool."
No surprise there. Since his arrival, Oscar
had tracked her routine. Two weeks ago she'd
made things amazingly easy by moving into a
garage apartment just five houses away from
his aunt's bed-and-breakfast.

"I thought we were going to avoid contact
for now," Townley said.

Oscar thought about Shelley and just how
hard, in the flesh, she'd been to avoid. For a
moment, when he realized she was heading
his way but also her son was doing a nosedive
aimed at Peeve, he'd been unable to move.

She'd been wearing white capris, a huge red
shirt and sandals. Her toes had been painted
the same red as her shirt. Cops noticed things
like that.

Even more, red-blooded men noticed things
like that.

Pregnancy, if anything, only made her
more beautiful.

But he'd not been in his cop persona. He'd
been an overtired dog walker thinking about
a big breakfast and his bed. "She must have
been running late. Usually she's gone when
I walk Peeve."

"Anything unusual happen?"

"No, not really. Ryan wanted to pet Peeve.

She and I exchanged pleasantries. I acted like I didn't have time. She acted like she wanted to get away. After a moment, I watched her hightail it back to her apartment. Funny, I thought she was taking the kid to preschool. Maybe she forgot something. Anyway, it was bound to happen, us meeting. We're living so close."

Townley waited a couple of beats before saying, "You're right. Do you think there was something unusual about her being late?"

"I do. Before this, she left at the same time every morning with a variation of only three minutes."

Anyone else would have laughed. Not Townley. He'd taught his soldiers about punctuality. "Okay, let me know if anything changes."

Punching the off button, Oscar lay down on his bed, sweats still on. He stared at his police uniform over the chair by the window. He was bone-tired and intrigued. He was still amazed that he worked for one law-enforcement agency and was undercover for another one.

The graveyard shift was a tough one, but he'd done worse.

Shelley Wagner wasn't what he remembered or expected.

He'd known her briefly as a kid, but he'd

not seen her in sixteen years. Nor had he kept
track of her, so reading about her and studying her photos from before Larry Wagner's
departure had been informative. Ten years
ago, she'd been a driven high school student;
six years ago, she'd been accepted into every
college she'd applied to; and two years ago,
she'd come home to spend one more summer
with her family.

From what he could tell, nothing had de-
railed her until her parents' illnesses and her
misfortune of meeting LeRoy Saunders, also
known as Larry Wagner, and by a few other
names—some even the FBI probably didn't
know.

He wasn't sure why this morning's encounter had him on edge. He'd never hesitated
to think the worst of people; military intelligence had a way of wringing empathy and
sympathy out of a man. He stretched out on
the bed. He'd reported the encounter, knew
where she was, and needed sleep. Still, his
mind continued going over the scene and
what was happening in the neighborhood.
There'd been a black cat sleeping on the top of
one of the parked cars. A child's scooter had
been tossed carelessly in one yard. A white
car had driven down the road, not in a hurry.

Hours later, a light knock on the door woke him. The sun still brightened his windows, and he was due back to work in an hour. Peeve was long gone, no doubt given freedom the first time he whimpered at the door. Oscar was going to have a hard time separating Peeve from Aunt Bianca. Or would it be Aunt Bianca from Peeve?

"Oscar! Get up," she yelled from downstairs. Aunt Bianca didn't know how to whisper. She'd not been in the military, but she could take on any drill sergeant when it came to giving orders.

He headed for the hallway bathroom, and after splashing water on his face, he went down the stairs to the kitchen, where Aunt Bianca waited.

"I have chicken on the table."

It was never that simple. Aunt Bianca usually had some household maintenance detail she'd like him to attend to, or worse. Tonight was the *or worse*.

"Abigail Simms's granddaughter will be in town this weekend." Bianca sounded very matter-of-fact.

Oscar didn't take the bait. Instead, he finished his first helping of chicken.

Aunt Bianca was patient. She gave him a

second helping before adding, "She's here for Abigail's birthday."

"That's nice," Oscar said.

"I told Abigail that you had some free time Saturday and that you might be convinced to take her granddaughter for a ride on that bike of yours."

Funny, when Oscar first arrived on his aunt's doorstep, she'd hated the motorcycle.

"Death machine," she'd called it.

Now it seemed the death machine was okay as long as she could connect it to a little matchmaking.

"I'm doing some undercover work this weekend," he said, heading to the pantry to look for dessert.

Aunt Bianca placed an elbow on the table, crooked her hand and placed her chin in it, looking at him and waiting. His mother did the same thing when she wanted an answer.

Bianca loved that he'd joined the police department, never dreaming that strings had been pulled and procedures ignored. Even chief of police Tom Riley had no clue his new rookie wasn't a rookie at all.

Somehow the deception felt wrong. He tried to blame it on keeping secrets from his aunt, but he'd grown to respect Riley and wished the man was privy to all the details.

His FBI boss, Townley, insisted on the assignment. "This legitimately gives you access not only to the files but also to the people who wrote them. If we can prevent Larry Wagner from conning even one more person, your role will have made a difference."

Townley had that right. So far, Larry Wagner, Saunders, Templeton, whatever name he was working under, had conned a lot of people. He was an equal opportunity crook and didn't care who he was taking advantage of.

That he'd married Shelley and left her pregnant without any remorse said it all. He was a man without a conscience, and his crimes were escalating. Sarasota Falls—a town with two squad cars and six officers—had been taken, from face-to-face fraud to account hacking. If acting as an officer, low man on the totem pole, working eight at night until eight in the morning, was what it took to bring Wagner down, Oscar would willingly do it.

Chocolate-chip cookies discovered, he headed back to the kitchen.

"You're not working the whole weekend," his aunt protested. "You need some time to play."

"I'll play when I've closed a few of these cases."

Mainly Shelley Wagner's, a woman who operated alone and who appeared to be a good—albeit hovering—mother.

"But—" Aunt Bianca started.

He put his plate in the sink and gave his aunt a kiss on the cheek. "I'll let you know when and if I need a date, but believe me, I can find my own girl."

"By the time you go looking," Aunt Bianca muttered, "you'll be too old to do more than watch television and complain about your health."

"You've been talking to my mother again," Oscar accused her.

THE NEXT DAY, he sat at his desk, finishing up his last report when his phone rang.

"Hi, Mom," he answered, earning a few smirks from other officers in the room.

His mother filled him in on his sister's latest antics as well as his brothers' accomplishments. She segued to a funny story about his uncle Rudy's garage, and finished by saying how excited she was that he had a date this weekend with a neighbor's granddaughter.

Ah, the phone call was the result of a joint effort between his aunt and his mother.

"I'm at work, Mom, and need to finish up." Since his return stateside a year ago, his mother had been trying to make up for lost time. She continued a moment more about family matters and then signed off. Oscar had just a few more things to do before he could go. Just as Oscar was closing up the last open file on his computer, thinking about getting to his aunt's place and sleep, Lucas Stillwater came in, a Snickers bar in hand. On the small Sarasota Falls police roster, he was long-term, having been with the department for over twenty years, and he hadn't been young when he joined.

Lucas now worked the day desk and no longer patrolled. The most pressing job he had was visiting schools and discussing Stranger Danger. He paused by Oscar's desk to say, "Hey! Riley just called. We found a DB, and you'll never guess where."

Oscar waited. Lucas liked to play guessing games, which Oscar didn't have time for. Stillwater talked too much and worked too little. It hadn't always been that way. At least, that was what Oscar had heard. According to Chief Riley, Stillwater's retirement was merely months away, and his goal was keeping alive and out of trouble. Oscar squinted at the computer screen and responded, "Where?"

"Vine Street. Right down from where you are."

Oscar's fingers stilled. His aunt had a few older neighbors. He hoped it wasn't Abigail Simms from across the street. But…

"That young couple fairly new to the town," Stillwater continued. "She's a schoolteacher. Her husband manages Little's Supermarket."

Something heavy formed in Oscar's chest. It moved to his stomach, started to churn. This wasn't good.

"The last name's Livingston. She…"

The chair squealed against the floor as Oscar scooted away from his desk. Candace indeed lived three houses down from him and had hung around with his little sister when they were in school. Candace and her husband, Cody, had moved here nine months ago when she secured a teaching job. Cody managed Little's Supermarket, a chain owned by Candace's father. Oscar stood, reaching for his badge and touching the sidearm already secure in his holster.

Lucas let out a low whistle and bemoaned,

"We still haven't gotten over the excitement of Larry Wagner and making the national news. Now this. Chief Riley's not going to be happy."

Oscar didn't care.

Candace murdered?

She represented what was good and right in the world.

He had to pause a moment, get his bearings and ask the right questions. "Who reported this?"

"We got a call from Crime Stoppers."

Anger, white-hot and immediate, sent Oscar to the door.

"Bailey and Riley are already on site."

Officer Leann Bailey was all the help Oscar needed. Right now Chief Riley thought Oscar was wet behind the ears, good only for traffic stops and petty crimes…but this was different. Personal. Riley might take lead investigator, but Oscar would be alongside him for this, never mind the hours. He'd known Candace most of his life, and she was all of twenty-three and had been married just over a year. Who would take her life? She and her husband, Cody, didn't seem to own anything of real value. True, her dad was a millionaire a few times over, but Candace and

Cody preferred to make it on their own. Before taking the assignment here, he'd even driven up and joined her and her husband for a couple of barbecues in their backyard. Twice she'd tried to fix him up with a co-worker. He should have gone, just once, to make her happy. Now...

Oscar paused as he opened the door. "They know time of death?"

"Just that it was yesterday morning," Stillwater said.

"What was the cause of death?"

"Head trauma. Some sign of a struggle. Husband probably did it. Supposedly he's out of town. They haven't been able to—"

It took Oscar ten minutes to drive to his neighborhood. Already police tape cordoned off the house. He parked his motorcycle the next house down from Candace's and swung one leg over the seat. He couldn't proceed, though, because suddenly cotton billowed in his throat.

This was little Candace. He'd taken her to her first dance because the boy who'd invited her had backed out at the last minute, and Oscar's little sister, Anna, had come crying to Oscar. Oh, his brothers had teased, but in the end, Oscar'd had a great time. He and his brothers had waylaid the date-breaker a few days later and made him aware that Candace and Anna were not in his little black book unless he wanted a big black eye.

The memories made it hard to move.

It occurred to Oscar that, except for fellow soldiers, this was the first death he'd be working of someone he loved. And now he was glad his case had sent him to the Sarasota Falls Police Department.

But to make a difference here, he'd have to convince himself to walk past the cordon tape, into Candace's house, and ask Riley for the facts.

Oscar could see the facts displayed over the front yard. This was a house, cared for by two individuals building a home.

He took off his dark glasses, momentarily blinking at the sudden brightness. When his eyes adjusted, he noted a tiny lizard crawling on top of the gray block fence next to the carport. It was probably hoping for a scent of oranges, maybe the hint of an early spring breeze. No such luck. As if realizing the futility, the lizard scurried off and disappeared into a hole in the dirt.

What had it seen? Heard?

Nothing it was willing to share with law enforcement.

The neighborhood was quiet, as if nature knew there'd been a disturbance and was now withdrawing—like the lizard—leaving them to investigate the disruption.

Next to the front door, two chairs boasted bright blue cushions. They appeared new but had been used. Candace's tennis shoes were under one of them. She'd obviously been playing in the mud again, pretending to garden. She'd complained last week about "everything dying."

And now she was dead.

A tiny table was situated between the two chairs. On it, a pair of gardening shears sat with the same black, lumpy mud on its blades as on the bottom of the shoes. Maybe she'd been digging with the shears instead of using a trowel. There was also a pair of flowered gloves that surely were too big for Candace's small hands. He'd watched her one day, on her knees in the sodden yard. She'd wanted perfection, every rock moved, every weed eliminated. Her fingers had gone through the loose dirt, pushing tiny holes into sections, reinventing space and filling it back in with something that would grow: new life.

A garden hose lay in the front yard. Dripping water spread onto a small section of struggling grass. If Candace died yesterday morning, it had dripped all night. Judging by the amount of sogginess, it had.

Ornamental chimes hung overhead.

No wind today.

No sign of life, literally or figuratively.

Chief Riley exited the front door, carefully closing it behind him. He joined Oscar and gestured to the yard. "You see anything out of place?"

The cotton in Oscar's throat doubled in size, and tears threatened to spill as he shook his head. He didn't mind. He'd watched Lieutenant Colonel Townley, who Oscar considered the biggest hero America had, break down and sob over situations he had no control over.

Men he'd lost.

Riley seemed to understand and waited while the sun beat down on them and minutes ticked by.

"You call the medical examiner?" Oscar choked out.

"You think I don't know my job?" Riley queried.

It was the kind of sarcastic response Oscar

needed to snap out of his stupor. "I've known the victim all my life. She's from my hometown of Runyan, New Mexico."

"I didn't know that. And the state police who are already on their way will be interested, too."

"You know who else has a home in Runyan?"

"Who?"

"Jack Little, who owns the chain of Little's Supermarkets."

"And that concerns us because…"

"Candace is his daughter."

Riley said a bunch of words Oscar knew he would not want put in the report, ending with "No kidding. Why didn't I know that?"

"She didn't want people to know. She wanted to make friends, get established, before everyone started seeing her for her family's name and power instead of who she was."

"It's time to make some phone calls," Riley said. "Give me a few minutes."

Oscar figured it would take more than a few minutes before he was ready to go inside. Carefully he stepped over the cordon tape and stood at the front of the driveway, looking at a pair of sandals by the side gate.

They, too, were Candace's. She always preferred going barefoot.

Riley returned, but he didn't share who he'd called. "See anything?" he asked.

"Nothing out of place in the yard that I can see, except the hose has dripped all night. Candace never would have left it on."

Riley nodded, waiting.

"You need to find Shelley Wagner. She lives in—"

"Shelley Wagner," Riley interrupted. "What does she have to do with this?"

"She lives in the garage apartment across the street. I encountered her yesterday morning walking her little boy. He ran to this window and she followed. Maybe she saw something."

"I know Shelley Wagner," Riley said. "And I know where she lives. You say she's involved in this?"

"I didn't say she was involved." If she was, no way would she have been so calm—

But she hadn't been calm. Not exactly, not when she was hurrying away. Maybe it hadn't been the encounter with him.

"I don't think she is involved," Oscar started again. "She just happened to be out here, taking a walk." What he couldn't tell Riley was that she walked every morning and he knew what time she returned. Oscar couldn't share that she was paying four hundred dollars a month for her one-room apartment and that she had two thousand, three hundred dollars in her bank account.

Oscar knew because Townley via the FBI had provided the information.

"You sure it was Shelley?" Riley asked. "I wasn't aware you were acquainted with her."

"Just under six foot, very pregnant, not much older than Candace. Ran into her yesterday morning during my walk with Peeve."

She'd worn sensible shoes, Oscar remembered. They'd landed silent on the sidewalk when she'd stopped to talk to him. Peeve, his German shepherd, had sniffed at them and then been distracted by a bird fluttering in a nearby bush.

"That's our Shelley," Riley agreed.

Oscar remembered her chasing the toddler, who'd taken off across the sidewalk and tottered into Candace's yard and then to the picture window. He hadn't watched what happened next. There'd been a noise, and Peeve had barked until finally a cat scurried from its hiding place. When he'd turned back to the street, Shelley had been carrying Ryan up the apartment stairs, and Ryan had been crying. Just another day. That was what he'd figured.

He'd been wrong.

He wished more than anything he hadn't been distracted by Peeve and the cat.

"Anything else you remember about the encounter?" Riley asked. "It might be important."

"No, except something was bothering her."

"You could tell that by how she looked?" Riley smirked.

"I've a sister. She had the same look Anna gets when something is bothering her."

Speaking of Anna, Oscar needed to call her, break the news about her best friend, let her know he would do all he could to bring the killer to justice.

Riley raised an eyebrow. "I've got Bailey canvassing the neighborhood, asking if anyone noticed anything out of the ordinary yesterday. I'll have her go to Shelley's apartment. They know each other." Immediately Riley pulled out his phone, called Bailey and gave the order.

Riley managed only a few words before he stopped talking to listen. It was all Oscar could do not to snatch the phone from his chief so he could hear, too.

"You're sure?" Ending the call, Riley shook his head in disbelief. "Bailey's talking with Shelley's landlord right now. Apparently she's packed most of her stuff and fled. Shelley Wagner's gone."

Not what Oscar had expected. He glanced up at Shelley Wagner's apartment. Bailey and Shelley's landlord, Robert Tellmaster, were just coming out the door.

Oscar turned to Riley. "I need to see the… the crime scene."

Riley raised an eyebrow. "The State boys wouldn't like that. It's best—"

Oscar took a breath, opened and closed his hands a few times before balling them into fists. "Candace didn't deserve this. She's— was—a kindergarten teacher, great sense of humor, could play second base like…" Oscar was rambling, which was out of character. But he knew the victim, knew her well. Loved her like a sister.

The two men stood, sizing each other up. Oscar didn't so much as blink. He had two inches on Riley, but that didn't seem to matter. Maybe Oscar needed to check—Riley sure looked ex-military.

"One minute is all I ask," Oscar finally said. "I won't go in. I won't touch anything."

Riley's eyes narrowed.

"I've been in this house several times. You asked me about what I noticed outside. I can tell you about the inside."

Riley didn't like it, Oscar could tell, but he marched to the front door and opened it, backing out of the way. Oscar didn't hesitate.

He saw Candace first, lying belly-down on the floor. She wore a pink nylon shirt and jeans. One foot still had a sandal. The other was bare. Her brown hair was matted and her head was next to a leg of the coffee table. The table was scooted a few feet from its regular position near the middle of the room. Blood smeared a corner. The couch was bare, except for two pillows and an upended book. The television was off and a few movies were stacked next to it. Across from the couch there were a dozen antique wall clocks. All told the correct time of fifteen minutes after ten. Two easy chairs were in the room. Nothing on them. No animals—Candace's husband, Cody, was allergic. Oscar couldn't bring Peeve when he visited.

A large wedding portrait hung over the couch.

Except for Candace, nothing appeared out of place.

He stepped back, bowing his head to say a quick prayer, mostly thinking of how devastated Cody would be.

"Everything is as it should be." Oscar proceeded to fill Riley in on his and Candace's history, last time he'd seen her, family and friends. After a few minutes, he asked, "What do you know about Cody's whereabouts?"

"He's supposedly at a two-day meeting in Albuquerque. We've got the police there looking for him. He's not answering his cell, and it doesn't look like he was in his hotel room last night. No one's seen him since yesterday morning."

"I know Cody. He wouldn't kill his wife." Oscar heard the conviction in his own voice yet knew the husband was always the first suspect in a case like this.

"I'll keep that in mind," Riley said, but Oscar could tell he didn't mean it.

It was after eleven when he made it back to his office and started searching the computer for information about where Shelley might be. With Ryan, she'd need to stop. And since she was eight months pregnant, she'd likely need to stop, too. A lot.

He called Townley, who was able to tell

him that Shelley had withdrawn two hundred dollars from an automatic teller before she left town. If she used her debit card again elsewhere, she could be tracked.

Townley suggested that Oscar head for Santa Fe. It was big enough to get lost in. "She has no known relatives except her father," Townley reminded him. Oscar added the address of the father's care center to his notebook. Townley sent a file detailing Shelley's history, including names of college roommates, instructors, people she'd worked with.

Oscar printed it out and compared it to the file Sarasota Falls had on her, looking for repeated names. There weren't many, as her local file had more to do with her connection with Larry Wagner.

Wagner had stolen and scammed roughly seven hundred thousand dollars from the good people of Sarasota Falls.

Over three hundred thousand of that came from the sale of Shelley's family home and its furnishings.

Riley was good. Thorough. He'd ferreted out two women who'd had affairs with Wagner during his short marriage to Shelley. One worked at the bank. The other wasn't named, but a desk clerk at the Sarasota Falls Inn swore Wagner had checked in with a high-class blonde at least five times. The signature on file matched Wagner's handwriting. Unfortunately, the female hadn't signed any receipts, and Wagner hadn't called her anything but Sugar.

Picking up the phone, Oscar called Riley. "I'm going to head over to the care center where Shelley's dad is."

"Good idea. Wait for me. I'm coming in."

"State police arrived?" Oscar asked.

"An hour ago. A couple of pretty decent guys. They looked over our reports of what the people in the neighborhood did and didn't see. They took even more photos than I did. They think she was pushed and happened to hit her head on the table. But, based on the condition of the bedroom, they know there was a struggle. Coroner arrived right after they did."

"Struggle in the bedroom. Did…?" Oscar hated that his attempt not to contaminate the crime scene meant he'd gone no farther than the front door. There'd been more to see, more that other people might miss.

"Lead guy said he didn't think so. Seems

someone broke in and disturbed her while she was getting dressed."

"Time of death?"

"Between six and eight a.m., but only because she was dressed. The coroner says it could have been earlier. He prefers, for now, to say midnight and six."

"If she fell and hit her head, then it might not be a murder."

There was a full ten-second pause. "There are marks on the back of her shirt that could be handprints. Then, too, the way she landed implies speed and gravity. They figured this out by measuring. At the very least, it's involuntary manslaughter."

"Yes, but—"

"They're still gathering evidence, from a strand of hair they found on the floor to a drop of blood taken by swab from the edge of the coffee table."

"Have they moved her body yet?"

"Yes, but it will be a few days before we know anything."

"And you've told them about Shelley Wagner and—"

"Yes," Riley interrupted, "and they find it quite interesting that from the window of Shelley's garage apartment, you can see right

into Candace's living room and backyard.
One of Candace's coworkers said Candace
noticed the young woman across the street
watching her and was spooked about it."

CHAPTER THREE

Tell and you'll be sorry.

SHELLEY HAD ALREADY been frantically packing when the text from her ex-husband arrived. It had only made her pack faster because—just great—after Larry had taken her life savings and left her to deal with the authorities, her first communication from him was a threat.

Sorry? She was already sorry. Sorry for making such a bad decision as marrying Larry.

Unfortunately, every decision she'd made in the hours since receiving the text had been wrong, really wrong, and downright stupid.

If she could do one thing over, she'd scream for the man with the dog to come back. She'd scream as loud as she could. Scream so loud they'd hear her in the next county. There'd been a moment when she could have brought down her husband.

The memories of what he could do when

angry had stilled her voice; the memories hadn't stilled her feet. Which was why her first instinct had been to run.

She squinted at a green sign up ahead and shook her head when she could make out the town's name. One more small town she'd never heard of. She'd already put almost three hundred more miles on her old green Impala. She wasn't even sure where she was heading.

She checked the rearview mirror. Ryan slept at last. She'd not handled him well, either. It was her own fault she'd wound up traveling with a tired, confused three-year-old because she'd utterly failed during the split-second packing stage. She'd correctly grabbed his worn Thomas the Train backpack and necessary box of Legos. However, she'd undervalued the beloved Winnie-the-Pooh stuffed animal.

She'd never do that again.

The only thing she'd done right, because she couldn't leave that poor woman lying in her living room with no one knowing she was there, was stopping at a convenience store and telling the cashier that she thought she might be in labor and needed to call her husband but didn't have a phone.

Sometimes being eight months pregnant got results.

She'd called Crime Stoppers. Then she'd headed west. That had been over four hours ago and it was time to stop for gas and check her messages. She had one.

And not from her ex-husband; she'd blocked his calls.

A nurse at her dad's care center texted to say her dad was having a bad day and was restless and confused. Would she please come?

If not her, who else?

A new wave of guilt and worry overtook her. She couldn't run away from Sarasota Falls. Her dad was all she had left of her old life, and there was no one else who cared as much as she did.

And, really, where was she heading to? How would she survive? Who could she turn to?

She'd been relying on herself since Larry left. She'd continue to do so. Only now she'd need to constantly look over her shoulder.

The middle of nowhere offered the perfect turnabout, and soon, she was making her way back home. Glancing in the rearview mirror again, she made sure Ryan was still asleep.

Tears streaked his cheeks. Winnie-the-Pooh was the least of her worries. Returning to Sarasota Falls was not the safe or sane thing to do. But she couldn't leave her father alone.

Soon her cheeks looked like Ryan's.

The miles passed as one small town after another whisked by. In each, people did normal, everyday tasks. None would guess the turmoil going through her mind. She envied them, their quick trips to the store or to pick up kids. A simple day sounded heavenly.

But not for her. Her back hurt, her side had some sort of pulled muscle and all she wanted to do was walk. Maybe that wasn't what she wanted, but what the baby wanted. Sitting still this long hadn't been easy. Careful to check for traffic—none—she queried Siri and found out that Sarasota Falls was still miles ahead.

It would be an hour or so before she could check on her father. She'd called, and a nurse reported that her dad was in his room sleeping. Shelley needed to see for herself, first thing, before she returned to an apartment that would never again feel safe.

Eventually, the city limits shimmered ahead. There were no tall buildings, more a gentle sloping of a small business district surrounded by homes.

She stopped at the first light, feeling panic start to surface. Then the light changed to green. Shelley needed to turn right to get to the apartment. Instead she turned left. She wanted her father. It didn't matter that he could offer her no real advice.

A few minutes later, she pulled into a fairly deserted parking lot. She gathered her purse and rounded the car to help Ryan from his car seat. She'd just put her hand on the door handle when her phone pinged.

Don't look at it.

She took Ryan from his seat, balancing him against her. He was getting heavier, growing, and with her advancing pregnancy, she was getting bulkier. She kicked the door shut with her foot and was soon inside the building, at the front desk, saying, "Did you just call me?"

"No," said the nurse, scooting the sign-in sheet toward Shelley.

"How's my dad?"

"Better now. He was very agitated, awake several times and roaming the halls more than usual."

Shelley wrote down her name and the time of arrival on the sign-in sheet before heading down the hall. Music came from the piano room. Wheelchairs were in the hallways. Most of their owners were elderly, but not all. Alzheimer's wasn't limited to those in their twilight years.

Her dad was in his room, sitting on the edge of the bed, just staring at the closet. He had a shirt on, plus a tie, but no pants. Laying Ryan on the couch, she placed protective cushions on the floor and then—glad for something to do, something to take her mind off her troubles even for a moment—turned to help her dad with his pants.

When she finished, her dad went back to staring at the closet. On the couch, Ryan continued sleeping. She sat down next to her father, thinking about decisions she didn't know how to make.

Maybe a minute passed, maybe twenty, before her dad finally moved. He stood, rounded the bed and picked up the newspaper that waited on the bedside table. She noted how the bottom half of his shirt was unbuttoned and how he put the paper down, picked it up again and then did the same three more times until she gently removed it from his hand.

"Dad, how are you doing today?" She didn't really expect an answer. "Would you like me to read some of the articles to you?" Immediately she decided that was a bad idea. There might be something in there about the murder. Information she needed to know but couldn't stomach just ten minutes after returning to Sarasota Falls.

He sat down on the couch, one of his hands going out to pat Ryan's foot. She checked her phone. A message from her service provider, but nothing from Larry. Could he get to her father, and what should she say to the front desk to warn them? One thing was for sure—she'd made the right choice returning. It wasn't just herself and Ryan she had to consider. It was her father, too.

"So, Dad, did you hear that Abigail Simms's son got a new job? He's working at the car wash."

Her dad wasn't listening, but Ryan stirred, looked at her, turned over and went back to sleep.

Shelley kept talking, more to fill the silence than anything else. "When I picked up Ryan from preschool the other day, everyone was talking about whether or not all-day kindergarten would be offered next year at the elementary school. Guess I should be thinking about all that, huh, for the future?"

If she had a future…

Her dad started nodding at her every word—as she'd jabbered on about the weather, politics, TV shows—but he offered no response for over an hour. Just when she was about to say her goodbyes and figure out her next move, he spoke up. "I have a daughter named Shelley. She's a little younger than you."

She sat back down. "I am your daughter, Shelley. I'm here visiting you, Dad. I brought you some peppermints for your candy bowl." At a convenience store halfway home, she'd spent money she didn't have for candy he shouldn't have. Because…because she might have to leave, disappear, figure out how to keep her children safe from their father.

And in the process she'd lose contact with her own father when he needed her most.

"Shelley's in college. She's studying finance," Dad said.

"I graduated a few years ago, Dad. With a major in English and a minor in finance." Those were happier days, when she believed everyone was a friend and the world was for the taking.

He continued, "She'll finish school in a month."

Shelley shook her head. She'd worked her

way through college as a bank teller. Once she had her diploma in hand, she'd moved back to Sarasota Falls and intended to apply at the local branch. Her mother's illness, followed by her father's Alzheimer's, had changed all that.

"We're hoping she moves back home for a while," her dad said. "I wonder where my wife is. Martha? Martha!" After a moment, he surmised, "She must have gone to the grocery store."

Shelley smiled, playing along.

"You will stop by again?" her father asked. "When Martha's here. She can probably answer your questions better than I can."

Shelley wanted to tell him she'd be by again and soon. Instead, she bit back tears and patted his hand. She hadn't asked any questions. Today she'd merely filled his candy dish, watched Ryan sleep peacefully on the living room couch, chattered aimlessly and stayed close to her father, wishing more than anything that he could put his arms around her and say, "We'll get through this. Larry Wagner's not gonna touch you. Somewhere out there, someone will see to it that justice is done."

The baby kicked.

"Ow." Shelley couldn't stop the sharp intake of breath.

"Martha, we need you," her father called, waking Ryan up.

"Want Pooh," Ryan wailed.

"If Martha were here, she'd give you Pooh," Shelley's dad said.

Shelley fled the room. Right now, all she wanted was someone to help her get from today to tomorrow.

But that person didn't exist.

CHAPTER FOUR

THREE CARS DOWN from the entrance, Oscar called Riley and told him Shelley was at the care center. "Why didn't you wait for me?" Riley sputtered.

"I had the time, and we needed to find her. That's what I did. I—"

"And now," Riley said, his voice steel, "you're going to wait for me."

Oscar said, "Yes, sir," and recorded the time and date on his report.

He'd barely finished when Shelley burst out the front door, ran to her car and began frantically scrounging through the trunk. Oscar practically fell off his motorcycle in his hurry to get to her side.

"Looking for something?"

She whipped around, and when he saw the tears shimmering in her eyes, his chest tightened. He hated that she'd been hurt. And he might very well hurt her more because he was a man with a mission—hunt down her ex and no way could she avoid being caught in the cross fire.

Then her lips pursed as her eyes went up and down his uniform, recognition immediate. "A cop?" she said. "It just figures."

"One of Sarasota Falls' finest," he said. "So, what are you looking for?"

"Nothing that concerns you."

"What if I told you that the only reason I'm here is you?"

Surprise flickered on her face for a moment, but she recovered quickly. "Then I'd tell you that you have too much free time."

He didn't hesitate before responding, "I wish that were true."

She took a deep breath and then released it. Oscar waited. Finally she turned back to her trunk and said, "I'm looking for one of Ryan's toys. He's inside and upset." As if to prove it, she grabbed a coloring book that had been squished in a corner and was wrinkled from its proximity to a suitcase.

Oscar nodded and slowly walked around the car, noting the fast-food wrappers on the floorboards as well as the toys in the backseat and the suitcases and such stashed in the trunk.

"Want to tell me why you're all packed up?

Going somewhere? Returning, maybe? Does it have something to do with what you saw in your neighbor's living room?"

He watched expressions flitter across her face as she tried to compose a safe response.

"The truth always works best," he advised.

"I heard about Candace. I'm so sorry. She seemed like a nice woman. But I'd already planned on having an adventure today with Ryan. We went to Santa Fe, the children's museum there, and just got back. It's been some time since we've seen my dad, so we stopped by."

"You have a receipt from the museum?"

Riley would admonish him for interrogating without him or his permission, but Oscar didn't care. He was in Sarasota Falls partly to investigate Shelley Wagner, and that was what he was doing.

"It's none of your business." She looked back at the care center as the wind picked up, billowing her oversize shirt and emphasizing her pregnancy. She tugged at a loose strand of hair, curling it behind her ear. He remained quiet for a moment. Her hair was limp against her head and needed combing. Not once in all the time he'd been watching her had she been anything less than put together. This was a woman on the edge, and she needed to talk to him.

"I promise," he told her, "whatever you say, I will listen to and believe." It was an awkward promise, because he intended to honor his declaration, but knew, just knew, she wouldn't tell him what he really wanted to know.

She didn't respond.

"Is someone after you?" He nodded toward her suitcases.

She looked at him with a serious expression. "Everyone's after me. Because Larry Wagner was my ex-husband, I must know where he is."

"I've never seen you like this." Too late, he wanted the words back.

"I just met you yesterday. How would you know what I'm like? Oh, wait—you've been watching me?"

"Not long."

Shelley stared at the sky. He wanted to tell her that she'd find no answers there. He doubted she'd appreciate the advice. She focused on him again and shook her head—dismissing him as she closed the trunk and turned toward the entrance.

Two steps had him by her side. "Chief Riley's

on his way. He has a few questions he'd like to ask you. Why don't we go inside and sit down?"

He watched her hands fist, release, fist.

She quickly looked left and right, searching for something. He looked, too. Then she turned and marched back inside, past the front desk and down a hallway. Oscar stayed right behind her. He faltered at the door she passed through. It led to a combined bedroom and living area. An older man, her father, sat on the couch. His black hair was uncombed and unruly. The television was on, but the man wasn't watching. Ryan, who Oscar had met yesterday morning, clutched a pillow, his cheeks wet, his head on Shelley's dad's leg. Shelley's purse was on the floor at her father's feet.

"Everything okay?" Oscar asked.

"No, nothing is okay, but if you're asking if my dad and son are all right, then I think so." She sat on the edge of the bed, looking from her dad and Ryan to him. "What do you really want?"

He recognized the tone of voice. She was trying to sound brave.

"Just for you to share what you might have seen in the neighborhood yesterday," he said as he sat down.

Chief Riley appeared in the doorway.

Oscar watched as Shelley tensed. Thanks to her ex-husband, she probably knew that now started the questions, and more questions, and then a million more, and a file and reports to go in that file.

"So, Shelley," Riley began. "Looks like you found trouble again."

Actually, Oscar thought, trouble had found her. He watched as emotions danced across her face. She felt some kind of pull, a connection that he couldn't tell whether was good or bad.

Probably bad.

It resembled the longing he'd felt ten minutes ago, wanting to pull her into his arms.

Riley glanced at her father, his face softening. "Is there someplace private we can talk?"

Oscar stood. "I noticed a few vacant rooms earlier. One of them should do." He needed to ignore the connection between himself and Shelley and act like the professional that he was. He didn't blink, didn't give her a chance to say no. He stepped toward the door, expecting her to follow.

Except she didn't move. Instead she asked, "What makes you think I know anything?"

"You want us to start with you leaving the

scene of a crime and then fleeing the city?" Riley said.

She looked from Riley to Oscar, and he had to give her credit. She kept her voice steady. "I didn't flee. I took Ryan to Santa Fe for an adventure. I had nothing to do with that girl's death, nothing."

"I hope that's the case," Riley said.

Shelley looked up sharply. "It is."

"I didn't like it there," Ryan mumbled. "Mommy forgot to pack Pooh."

"I hate when that happens," Oscar told the little boy. "My mom once forgot my stuffed Spider-Man. I cried for an hour."

Ryan nodded.

"I had to hold on to a pillow." Oscar smiled. "It made it a little better."

Ryan nodded again and clutched his cushion tighter.

Oscar sat back down, facing Shelley. "We pretty much know your every step starting early yesterday morning."

"Because you knew who I was yesterday morning."

He heard accusation as well as an edge of disappointment thread through the question. "Yes, I did. But—"

Luckily Riley interrupted. "We didn't start

looking for you, Shelley, until your landlord told us you'd packed up and left. With a murder just across the street, and a witness putting you at the victim's window and looking in, you became a priority."

She grimaced. "I don't want to be a priority."

"Good," Riley said calmly. "Tell us what you know."

"I don't know anything."

"Shelley Wagner, you know plenty," Riley accused her.

"I'm Shelley Brubaker," Shelley corrected him.

"I knew a woman named Shelley Brubaker." Shelley's father spoke up from the couch. "Can't remember if she was a relative or a neighbor. But she was a good girl."

SHELLEY WANTED TO tell her father that Shelley Brubaker was no longer good, but if she did that, she'd start crying. No way, not in front of the cops. "Dad, I'm taking Ryan to Cara up front, and then I'm going to go down the hallway and talk to these gentlemen. I won't go far."

Then she looked at the two cops, the ones ready to escort her away as if she were a criminal. Bad enough to deal with Riley, but Officer Guzman was the man from yesterday, the nice one with the German shepherd. She'd thought he was just a guest at Bianca's bed-and-breakfast.

She took Ryan by the hand. He came willingly, holding the cushion and looking up at Oscar somewhat in awe.

"I 'member you," he said. "You have dog."

"Peeve," Oscar supplied.

"I like dog," Ryan said.

Shelley silently agreed. She liked the dog, too; she didn't, however, like the cop. She followed him, determined not to cry, noting how Riley brought up the rear, in essence trapping her.

She'd known Riley all her life. He was a good cop. He'd been the officer she'd called just six months ago after the first frantic phone call came from an irate friend who'd just been notified by her bank that she no longer had any money.

Shelley'd already been gathering the proof that her husband had taken her for every dime. She hadn't, however, known the full range until she'd heard the shrill voice. "I went to buy Christmas presents and my bank card was rejected!"

Shelley still remembered holding her cell phone tight, letting the truth of the words sink in and knowing the black hole of her life had just gotten blacker.

"The bank says," the caller continued, "that the money was withdrawn by your husband. The check I wrote him was for six hundred dollars, and the check he presented was for six thousand dollars. All I had!"

Shelley'd mumbled an apology, followed by a promise to find out what had happened, and then tried Larry's cell number: disconnected. Before she could move off the couch, three more calls came from friends experiencing the same thing. Then the bank president had called. Seemed Larry had been busy that morning. The bank president deemed it suspicious activity. Soon the whole town knew.

By the time Chief Riley arrived, Shelley had checked the dresser where Larry kept his things. His clothes remained, except for a few favorites. She'd have never noticed them gone if she hadn't looked.

She'd been so upset, she'd thrown up.

Once the story broke, Shelley became the scapegoat. No surprise—she'd been the one left behind with no money to start over. She'd changed her phone number and email address, but still the calls and emails came. Most were from people who wanted her to pay them back. Not possible. Riley couldn't offer any meaningful advice except that she "wasn't the only one it had happened to." Not what she needed to hear, but she'd seen it in his eyes. She was just one more victim: not a role she desired and not one she intended to keep forever.

Now here she was again, walking down the hallway with Chief Riley, curious glances aimed her way and an unsettling feeling of guilt warring with the flutter of the baby's movements.

A shout came from her father's room. "I think Shelley Wagner was a neighbor!"

Shelley blinked hard. She would not cry.

Riley offered, "Maybe it would be better if we headed to the station and—"

"Not an option, unless you've got a warrant for my arrest." She wasn't heading anywhere. Thanks to Larry and the myriad of police officers who had taken over her life six months ago, she knew her rights.

"That can be arranged," Riley said.

Shelley rolled her eyes and led them down a hall. After turning Ryan over to Cara, who worked the front desk and always had time for the little boy, Shelley headed for the piano room. On weekends sometimes it held as many as forty people: patients, staff, visitors. During the week, it was usually empty unless Mr. Vaniper was in the mood to play.

He was and doing a perfect rendition of "Send in the Clowns." If she hadn't been on the brink of tears, she'd have laughed. Who were the clowns? The cops? The people her ex-husband had ripped off? Her?

Mr. Vaniper, who had the room next to her father's, wore his black tux. He played music he no longer remembered the words to in front of an audience he didn't know wasn't there. The tune came to a crescendo and ended. Mr. Vaniper wandered from the room.

Officer Guzman stepped up to the front desk and said something to Cara while Chief Riley escorted Shelley to a beige couch, covered with roses and vines, flanked by two pink high-back chairs. A coffee table with a fake flower arrangement was in front of the couch. Shelley sat on a chair. No way did she want to be trapped between these two cops. Her innocence had dissolved almost as quickly as her trust in the system.

"We know," Riley started, taking a seat opposite her, "that you contacted me about

Candace's murder. What exactly did you see yesterday?"

Shelley swallowed back hot bile. It rose inside her like a mountain of fear. She couldn't trust the cops. Yet she had a dozen things she wanted to say. She wanted to tell them that she was almost out of money, that her father was drifting further and further away, that she'd started introducing Ryan as Ryan Brubaker but that he was legally Ryan Wagner and she was terrified that someone would figure out her name wasn't on the custody papers and take him from her. She wanted to tell them she'd seen her ex-husband standing there in that living room yesterday morning, and that she'd run home, dragging Ryan with her, and sat down on her couch, fumbling with the phone, intending to call.

She wanted to tell them that her ex-husband still had the ability to pull her puppet strings and that he'd killed Candace and had threatened Ryan and seemed to know her every step. She couldn't answer the cops' questions honestly because she knew her ex-husband would make her disappear.

It could even happen today.

CHAPTER FIVE

OSCAR COULDN'T DENY that he felt drawn to Shelley. And it made no sense when examining what was stacked against her. There was the packed car, the fact that she'd fled the crime scene and the town. No matter how he looked at it, Shelley Wagner—Brubaker, that was—was more involved in this murder than they originally suspected. Too bad. Oscar had gotten the idea that he could like this kind, determined woman.

Didn't mean she was completely innocent; he had to remind himself of that.

She was working hard to keep control, and Oscar had the feeling it wouldn't take much to get her to reveal what she knew. She kept looking past them, through the wide doorway, at the front desk, where the nurse and Ryan were playing some online game on the computer.

Riley placed an audio recording device on the coffee table in front of them. Oscar couldn't tell where he'd stashed it earlier. "Do you mind if I record this?"

"I do mind."

Riley didn't hesitate. "Then I'll take notes."

A visitor or two wandered into the piano room, seemed to sense the seriousness of the situation and quickly wandered out.

Shelley, her voice shaky, said, "Look, I got scared yesterday. Maybe I made a few bad decisions, but what's happening now, you here questioning me, is exactly why I didn't report the…the body immediately or report it in person."

Oscar watched Riley regroup and understood exactly what the other cop was doing. They needed Shelley to work with them, not against them. Riley rested his pencil on his notepad, and Oscar used the opportunity to take over.

"Right now, all we want is to know everything you saw yesterday morning. Start with the fifteen minutes before you met up with me."

She didn't answer. She sat quiet, but certainly not calm. She perched on the edge of the couch looking poised for flight.

Oscar downplayed the seriousness of her situation by sharing, "I've already told Riley what I noticed during the walk." He cleared his throat, hoping his comment would relax her. "I've told him how no one was out, not even Mrs. Simms taking care of the flowers in her front yard. I told him about seeing you, and about a white car that turned the corner."

For a moment, she was so still, he couldn't even tell if she was breathing. Then she said, "I'll tell you what I know, but it's not much. We were running late. I'd had trouble sleeping because Abigail's dog woke me up about five. Then the phone rang, and I got upset. That cost us precious time. Fifteen minutes before we encountered you, I was getting Ryan ready for preschool. I tried to hurry him. As we started I didn't see anyone out."

Oscar asked, "What got you upset?"

Shelley looked at Riley. "Someone got my number and wanted me to pay back money that Larry took."

Riley nodded. "Go on."

"It was hot outside. I was miserable. We walk to preschool. I'm watching my pennies, saving gas. Even if it makes us later, we walk. We'd just made it past the first house." She looked at Oscar. "The young couple."

"Candace and Cody," he supplied.

"We saw you, and Ryan fell in love with

your dog. Then he got distracted, and you saw him run up to the big picture window. I followed. That's when I saw her, lying on the floor. I could tell she was dead."

"Why didn't you holler for me?"

Shelley looked like Mona Lisa with her lips pressed together. His sister looked exactly the same when she felt backed into a corner and about to come out fighting. "You were already down the street." Shelley kept her words quiet, monotone.

"You could have caught me."

"I didn't want to upset Ryan."

Riley took control of the interview. "Ryan saw Candace Livingston?"

"That's her last name?" Shelley whispered.

"Candace Maria Livingston," Riley said.

Shelley shook her head. "Poor woman. Yes, Ryan saw her and thought she was sleeping. I don't think he even noticed the blood."

"How well did you know her?"

"Not at all. I'd seen her once or twice in the driveway. She'd say hi, and I'd say hi back. Nothing else."

Riley asked, "You'd never seen inside her living room?"

"No, just yesterday morning when I was looking in. I got away from there as fast as I could. I took care of my son, kept him safe, and I eventually notified the police."

"It's the *eventually* that concerns us," Oscar said.

Riley added, "Want to tell me why you packed up and left?"

Shelley rolled her eyes. "I'm not staying in the neighborhood. Not only has someone been murdered, but also I'm the one who found her. I've got enough on my plate and plenty of reasons not to trust the police. Another reason I called you and didn't leave my name. I wanted to let you know what I discovered and stay anonymous. Shouldn't I be given the courtesy of reporting a crime while remaining anonymous?"

"There are ways," Riley agreed, "to stay anonymous. You didn't choose that route."

"I was flustered," Shelley said.

"What I can't explain," Riley mused slowly, "is why you came back."

"Again, as I told Officer Guzman earlier, I came back because of my dad."

"Your dad is safe."

She glanced down the hallway. Nope, Oscar thought, this woman did not truly believe her dad was safe. That meant she didn't feel that she or Ryan was safe. Oscar needed to find out why. If it wasn't for the fact that nothing had been taken from Candace's house—not money, jewelry or electronics—Oscar might think Larry Wagner had something to do with the crime.

Oscar had to act. He was losing this argument. "Ms. Brubaker, Candace was a friend of mine. I've known her since she was in kindergarten. She was a good person who never hurt anyone. Anything you can tell us would be appreciated."

"I can't tell you any more than I already have," Shelley whispered.

"Can't or won't?" Oscar demanded, ignoring the look of reprimand Riley shot him.

"I didn't know her," Shelley protested. "I followed Ryan to the window. He said, 'She's asleep.' I took one look and knew that wasn't the case. I was terrified. It hasn't even been six months since my ex-husband took off. You called me Shelley Wagner. You've been in town, what, a month? And you already know who I am, so you must know the destruction he left and what I went through, what I'm still going through. I get calls every week from people wanting my story or wanting me to reimburse them for what my husband stole from them. If I had waltzed into the station and reported seeing a dead body, I'd have been on the five o'clock news yesterday. Ryan doesn't need the circus to begin again. He's just now sleeping through the night."

"What if your hesitation, your unwillingness to tell us everything you saw, gives the murderer an opportunity to kill again?" Riley queried.

Not the direction Oscar would have taken, but it didn't seem to faze Shelley Brubaker.

"Maybe it's the husband," Shelley responded. This time she didn't whisper, and Oscar got the idea she'd given the conclusion some thought. "I don't have much faith in husbands. Have you asked him?"

"I thought you didn't know the family," Riley countered.

"I know that the young man managed the store my dad used to manage. My window looks right down on their house. I did see enough of them to realize who they were."

"Funny thing," Riley said. "Her husband is out of town and you left town. Were you meeting up with him?"

Oscar almost slid off the chair. For a small-town cop, Riley knew how to unnerve a witness. He was unnerving Oscar. The cop in him should have been prepared. The human in him wasn't. He'd been watching Shelley for weeks. He knew she wasn't seeing Cody Livingston. The woman took care of her son and took care of her father. That was about it.

"I don't even know his name," Shelley said indignantly.

"You sure packed quickly."

"Did you see the size of my garage apartment? Everything I own will fit in a laundry basket. Oh, and take a look at what's in my car," Shelley offered. "You'll find what amounts to fifteen minutes of packing up clothes, games and food. I had no intention of putting myself, or my son, in front of the media again. Fat lot of good it did me."

"You could have done a fat lot of good yesterday," Riley stated. "We'd have found the body sooner. The first twenty-four hours are the most important. You cost us a few of those hours when you didn't report what you saw immediately."

Shelley huffed. It was the wrong reaction. It bothered Riley enough that he tossed out words like *subpoena* and *civic duty* and even mentioned that leaving the scene of an accident was a class two misdemeanor.

The last one, Oscar knew, was overkill. There'd been no accident. Candace had been murdered. Then Riley pulled out his cell phone. Oscar watched as his fingers danced over the screen, and suddenly he was swiping through photos.

He was probably going to show Shelley a close-up of Candace Livingston—go for the shock and guilt tactic. Oscar closed his eyes for a moment, steeling himself against the sudden pain in his heart.

Senseless death.

He'd seen way too much of it in Afghanistan. As a cop, he wanted to help people. Yet cops and murderers were uneasy dance partners with one always trying to lead the other.

He wished the case was all his, that he could take over the questioning, demand answers, but he was pretending to be the new kid on the block.

"Here, maybe you need to see this." Riley turned his cell phone toward Shelley, showing her a photo.

Shelley looked away. Oscar started to protest. This wasn't the time or place, but her rescue came from a different source.

"Hello, Mr. Vaniper," Shelley said. The piano player had returned. For a moment, Oscar thought Riley would continue to talk right through "Amazing Grace." Oscar'd had to "ahem" twice to get Riley's attention. Riley passed the cell phone to Shelley. She glanced at it, gave it back to Riley and announced that she'd be calling her lawyer.

Oscar saw the tears in her eyes. They barely shimmered, but they were there, and just as an hour earlier, when he'd seen the proof of her grief, he almost interfered. Oscar almost told Riley what he could do with the photo.

"Good," Riley said. "Have your lawyer meet us at the station. I'm sure you know where that is."

If looks could kill, Riley would have been a chalk line on the floor, because Shelley was now one very annoyed pregnant woman.

Shelley stood and started to leave, but her cell phone pinged. He watched as she pulled it from her pocket, checked a text or message and then turned pale.

"Everything all right?" he queried, wishing he could get a look at her phone.

"Just a typical day." The words were typical; the tone was not. An edge that hadn't been there earlier was present, a terseness.

Whatever she'd read on her phone had changed things. She'd been both angry and wary during the questioning; now she was visibly shaken.

She retrieved Ryan from the front desk, hefting him into her arms and holding him tight. She made it look easy, but the kid had to be heavy.

Oscar took one step toward her. "You need some help?"

She gave him a look that put him in his place. Alongside Riley, he was pond scum. Usually it didn't bother him. Rarely could a cop arrest a perp without being called worse than pond scum. Shelley's look, however, bothered him.

Bothered him a lot.

CHAPTER SIX

"SHE'S NOT TELLING us everything." Riley strode toward his vehicle, Oscar at his heels.

"You're absolutely right," Oscar agreed. "She just got a message on her phone and it spooked her."

"What kind of message?"

Oscar knew Riley was hoping for details. Instead all Oscar could provide was "It was an email or a text, and she didn't share."

"I'll see if I can't get her to open up," Riley said. "Usually talking to them at the station works. Doesn't matter, male or female. It's all about turf. If that doesn't help, I'll get a subpoena, make sure we can legally get to her phone messages. I can't believe that she packed up her belongings, didn't inform her landlord, was heading out of town and is unwilling to tell us where or why. Something's going on. She didn't act this hinky back when we were dogging her about her husband's whereabouts."

Riley got in his vehicle, but before he started the engine, Oscar rapped on the window until the man rolled it down.

"Everything's happened so fast today. I probably should mention that Shelley Wagner and I have met in the past."

"Really?" Riley frowned. "Where?"

"Here. I spent a summer with my aunt when I was twelve."

"Anything I should know about?"

"Not really. Look, for what it's worth, I think she's telling the truth about what she saw. It's what she's omitting that has me worried."

Riley just shook his head.

"Why is she omitting anything?" Oscar went on. "Why would she do that? What will it get her?"

It was the sixty-four-thousand-dollar question, and Oscar didn't have an answer. He pressed on. "Call it a gut feeling, and what would her motive be?" Oscar waited, hoping the other man would do a little back-and-forth, share scenarios.

Riley waved Oscar away before starting his vehicle and driving toward the station.

Oscar stood for a moment. He'd overstepped the boundaries set between new cop and seasoned cop. He'd questioned when he should have listened. He'd argued when he should have reasoned. He'd tried to lead when he needed to follow. Going undercover for the FBI meant playing the role, not risking everything because of passion.

He wanted the people who had hurt Candace. Wanted them bad. He hopped on the back of his Harley, gunned the engine and followed Riley's vehicle. It made no sense to him, this insane feeling he had for Shelley. So what if he'd been watching her with Ryan, watching her idly rub her stomach? She was alone and determined to do right by her children. No, that wasn't what had him wanting to pull her into his arms and comfort her.

But this wasn't the time to be empathetic. Catching hardened criminals was part of his day-to-day job with the FBI, and each one had a sob story. Here, in Sarasota Falls, he might run into a hardened criminal—what? Once a year? Maybe. This wasn't what he wanted, was it?

Still, Oscar hadn't expected to like Sarasota Falls so much. He hadn't been crazy about it the few times he'd visited as a kid. There hadn't been a skate park or an indoor trampoline facility. Now, though, he was interested in other things. Things that had nothing to do with his job. First of all, there was his aunt. What a tough old bird. Oscar wasn't sure, but he thought that Aunt Bianca was more angry at being ripped off by Wagner than she was hurt. When Oscar had called to say he was coming, she'd laughed, insisting she was fine. When she opened the door to invite him in, she continued to be fine. Now that he was living in one of her guest rooms, she claimed to be more than fine.

She liked his company.

Parking next to Riley, Oscar followed his boss to the station's entrance and said, "Innocent until proven guilty. I don't think Shelley Brubaker had anything to do with Candace's death."

"Here's an idea," Riley offered. "Since it doesn't appear your Ms. Brubaker is having an affair with Cody Livingston, maybe we should consider that your friend Candace was having an affair with Shelley's ex-husband. Maybe Larry Wagner—"

Oscar laughed, interrupting the chief. "Candace hasn't even been married a year. She married her high school sweetheart. Beginning of the school year, they were moving into their first house and talking about which bedroom would be for their someday baby. Not the time to stray."

"Best time, one last fling. You think you know someone…" Riley entered the station.

Oscar didn't follow but stood thinking. His first thought was that Candace was smarter than that. But from what he could tell, so was Shelley. And maybe, right now, Riley wasn't talking about either of them.

Everyone at the precinct was aware that Riley's wife had left him years ago. According to Lucas, the cop who knew the scoop on everyone and everything and shared all of it, Riley had been gone too much and available too little. It was a common enough problem. Oscar's last girlfriend had balked when he started training for the FBI. She claimed she'd have been afraid to answer the phone or door should he get a dangerous case. In retrospect, he probably shouldn't have responded with "They're all dangerous." It had taken him a whole month after the breakup to realize that since he'd picked the career over her, he must not have loved her enough.

"But I believe you're right about Shelley when you said she hadn't had an affair with Cody," Oscar said. "Trust me—"

This time, it was Riley who interrupted

with a wry laugh. "As a cop, you can't afford to trust." Then, as an afterthought, he said, "Trust me on that."

Oscar knew all about trust and its power. He could say the word even if he couldn't believe in it. He'd learned the hard way that trust was fleeting, and now he stayed away from commitments unless they were to his immediate family or his job. Most of all, he spurned serious relationships. He didn't want to marry, have a family, only to have it fall apart due to his work hours and conditions.

He never wanted to disappoint those who believed in him.

No one had been able to find his father. Now Oscar worked for an organization who not only found people but also actually made the world better.

Oscar would find Larry Wagner.

He would find Candace's killer.

Unlike the police in his hometown, he would not give up. Funny how he'd wound up on the Sarasota Falls force. It was even smaller than Runyan's.

Oscar wondered if that was why Chief Riley hadn't paid more attention to a stranger named Larry Wagner when he'd come to town. Oscar would have.

Chief Riley wasn't perfect, but he was a decent cop. Oscar hurried to keep up. "Candace wasn't someone who would cheat."

"You never know what really goes on behind closed doors."

"Why don't you let me talk to Shelley? Maybe, because I'm new and closer to her age, she'd be more likely to share."

Riley raised an eyebrow. "You do much interrogating? That badge is still pretty shiny. And she already knows you were watching her even before the Livingston woman's murder."

"Can't learn without opportunity."

Riley shook his head. "I think she'd trust you more because of that fool dog of yours, not your age, but go ahead. Shelley's car is over there. Convince her to get out of it and come in the station. She's probably got cold feet."

Oscar turned around. Sure enough, Shelley sat in her green Impala with her head leaning forward against the steering wheel. Slowly he walked toward her, trying to figure out what to say.

He thought about his job, his town, his state of mind. Maybe right now, as restless as he was, he needed to be here. Needed the ordinary before the extraordinary. He'd decided to be a cop when he was just ten years old and caught a rerun of some old cop show featuring a hero in every single episode. Oscar'd been enthralled. This cop would never run out on his wife and children. He'd wanted to protect people. Oscar figured the FBI was one step beyond that.

Extraordinary.

As much as he wanted excitement, craved it, he'd also loved how just a simple helping hand made a difference. He'd wound up changing a tire while on duty and heard later that it did indeed fall under his job description. Riley called it community policing.

He wished that was all he was doing with Shelley.

He rapped on her window. The look in her eyes as she climbed out of her vehicle told him how unhappy she was, yet she kept a smile for Ryan, who was just waking up and crawling over the seat and out of the car after her. He held a toy truck in one hand and a cookie in the other. "Want to go home. Now. Want Pooh."

"Not yet," Shelley said, pulling Ryan close to her side. "We're just stopping by to answer a few more questions."

"Don't like it here," Ryan said.

"Officer Bailey—that is, Leann—is on her way," Riley said as they escorted Shelley and Ryan into an interrogation room. "She'll be here in five minutes to watch over Ryan."

"This shouldn't take long," Shelley said, for the first time her voice soft, no edge. "Can't he stay with me?"

"Leann will keep him in the break room." Riley's tone brooked no argument. "You don't want him to see some of these pictures or hear any of the details."

Ryan was wide-awake and assured Oscar, "I like pictures."

"Then," Oscar said, "I'll make sure to get you some pictures of Peeve. Would you like that?"

"I want Peeve." Ryan looked around as if expecting to find Peeve somewhere nearby. "Can I have him?"

"Well, Peeve has a home. But he'd love for you to pet him next time you see him."

The look Shelley shot Oscar didn't promise a second encounter. Ryan didn't seem to notice. "I can have a dog," he announced.

"When we move to a house with a back-yard," Shelley promised.

"Ten years." Ryan's tone was exactly like his mother's. He also held up eight fingers.

"Ten years," Shelley agreed, holding up ten fingers and reaching over and adjusting Ryan's count.

"Ten years." Ryan's voice turned pensive, and Oscar got the idea that a dog was a hot topic in Shelley's household.

"Peeve's my best friend," Oscar said. "I've had him since my second deployment in the military."

Oscar hadn't picked Peeve from a litter or rescued him. Peeve had done a stint in search and rescue. When a ceiling collapsed, Peeve's handler was killed. Oscar saved the dog, and then he and the dog went on to save three people buried in the rubble. There'd been no time to think because the next morning, another call came in, a rural neighborhood bombed, and when Oscar arrived on the scene, someone handed him Peeve's leash.

They'd been together ever since. When Oscar exited the military, Peeve retired and went with him. Now the old dog had arthritis and was losing his sense of smell, so much so that Oscar and his aunt were warming up the dog's food just to entice him to eat more. "There's something pretty special about a dog," Oscar said softly, more for Shelley's ears than Ryan's.

"We'll get a dog. It will just take time," Shelley said.

Officer Bailey arrived and promptly bent down to give Ryan a hug. "Good to see you, buddy. It's been a while."

Ryan smiled. "Name's not Buddy."

"We might need a while longer," Shelley muttered.

Oscar looked at her, thinking that she was really, really young to be going through all this.

"I'm getting dog," Ryan told Officer Bailey as they disappeared down the hall.

Shelley closed her eyes, and Oscar thought about what Ryan had shared. "Maybe in ten years." Was that how long she thought it would be before they had a real home again?

Oscar's aunt, Bianca, was more than annoyed that she'd lost money to Larry Wagner, but other than a decrease in her savings account and an increase in how much her family worried about her, nothing had changed.

Everything had changed for Shelley.

None of it for the better.

CHAPTER SEVEN

THE POLICE STATION was overly bright, maybe to blind lawbreakers the moment they walked through the door. It also smelled of lemon cleaner, too much lemon cleaner. Either that or the pregnancy was heightening her sense of smell.

"I need to use the restroom," Shelley said.

Riley nodded, and she took off down the hall. She wasn't going to cry, act scared or do anything to let these people know how defeated she felt. After she did what needed to be done, she washed her hands and ran cold water over her face. She was tired of things happening to her. Every time she turned around, some new roadblock appeared. She pulled her phone from her purse and reread her latest text message.

One thing was for sure. Shelley wasn't going anywhere. But she was seriously thinking about no longer reading text messages, ever. First, her ex must have a dozen phone numbers because if she blocked one, he simply sent a message using a different number. Now her text messages were nothing but bad news. Like the one she'd received back at her father's care facility that made her knees weak.

Sarasota Falls Bank recently returned one of your checks, bank card purchases, or other transactions due to insufficient funds. While this was probably the result of an oversight on your part, you need to deposit funds to cover the charges shown below and any future transactions that may be presented for payment.

This morning she'd had over two thousand dollars in the account. Money she'd budgeted down to the last dime. Money meant to see her through the next few months and birth of her child. She'd withdrawn two hundred in cash yesterday morning when she'd fled. It might last her until the end of the month since she had food and her rent was paid.

Rent on a garage apartment she'd just tried to break the lease on. Ha, she had the worst kind of luck.

She was due to have a baby in three weeks and she didn't have enough money for her next bottle of prenatal vitamins.

Quickly she called the bank. The manager was a friend of her father's. He listened and promised to call her back. She felt like the floor had just been taken from underneath her.

Shelley listened to Officer Leann Bailey offer Ryan ice cream. They must keep it in the break room for all the criminals' kids.

I am not a criminal, she reminded herself.

No matter her innocence, her association with her ex-husband and his crimes had made her feel guilty, but she would get over that.

"Thank you," Ryan said, and Shelley could hear him giggling up at the deputy as if she were his preschool teacher. Sometimes Shelley thought that if she ever saw Larry again he'd regret it, not because he'd hurt her but because he'd hurt Ryan, who was old enough to remember, and the yet-to-be-born Isabelle, who would have to know the truth someday. Small towns could be long on memory and slow to forgive, at least when it came to their pocketbooks. And someday, Ryan and Isabelle would have to answer the questions their friends and their families asked them.

Riley beckoned her down another short hallway with "Come this way."

She followed him to one of two interrogation rooms. "Have a seat." Riley pulled out the chair for her. Then he surprised her by excusing himself before disappearing out the door.

The table she sat at was old, probably a relic of the seventies, with plenty of scratches. A few crumbs were scattered across its surface. Had someone eaten lunch in here? Depressing. The walls were painted a bland gray color, guaranteed to make people long to escape. The narrow fluorescent light made the room much too bright, guaranteed to create headaches. She started to stand, thinking maybe the door was unlocked and she could sneak out. In her present condition, if she got busted, she could claim another restroom emergency.

Before she even managed to scoot the chair back, Officer Guzman came in. He carried three bottles of water. He set one on the table, handed her one and opened the last one for himself.

He took a long drink, giving her the time to look him over. He sat down next to her. Much too close. She glanced at the door; he'd left it open.

"You live on my street," she said.

"My aunt does, and I'm staying with her

right now, have been for almost two months. Maybe you know her. Bianca Flores."

Shelley winced. Bianca Flores had planned to add a guesthouse to her B and B, kind of a honeymoon cottage. She'd hired Larry—per Shelley's recommendation—to find a contractor and laborers. After all, he had know-how and connections.

"I came to Sarasota Falls twice while I was growing up," Oscar shared. "Once for a whole summer when I was twelve."

Shelley felt her mouth open and a half laugh form. "Oscar," she said, digging for the memory.

"My brothers came, too." Oscar's words cemented what she was just now catching on to. "There are three of us boys."

"You were the one who played with me."

"That was me."

She was silent for a minute. He was the only one of the brothers who took time to play with a girl.

"You taught me how to catch air riding my bike off a curb," she said.

"And you let me use your Barbie for pellet-gun practice."

"I was eight and for the first time glad I owned a Barbie." Shelley had asked for a pellet gun the next Christmas. That hadn't gone over well with her parents. She scooted her chair back a bit, changing positions and wishing the baby wasn't dancing on her kidney again. Watching Oscar examine her way too much like a cop, she asked, "Why did you become a police officer?"

He grinned. "I'm supposed to be asking you the questions."

"You already did. I have nothing to add. I just want to take Ryan and go home."

"Back to the garage apartment?" he queried. "What happened to the Victorian your parents owned?"

"You've read my file," she countered. "You know what happened to the Victorian."

"You sold it to pay for your mother's funeral and put your father in the care center."

She waited. Most people said platitudes like "Sorry to hear...," "Bad luck..." and "Had to hurt getting rid of such a stunning piece of property." A few less subtle people had ventured a "Well, you didn't need such a big, rambling place for just one person. The upkeep must have been brutal."

Oscar looked interested. "I thought your house the coolest ever, next to my aunt's."

"I thought the same." She curled her fingernails into the soft skin of her palms and dug in. If only she hadn't acted so rashly. Her parents had money set aside, but between the funeral, the medical bills and soon the care center, it seemed to be flowing only one way. Out of the bank account, not in. "That was why I had to sell it, unfortunately."

She'd sat in this very room a good six months ago and given the details to Riley. Maybe he hadn't put everything in her file. After taking a breath, Shelley added, "I was thinking about selling it. The day I visited the care center to see about finding a spot for my dad, Cara, the woman at the front desk, was sympathetic. She listened to my story and then handed me an advertisement about a home liquidator."

Shelley gave a little laugh. Larry's business had been called Wagner's Ways: Ten Ways We Can Help You Get Rid of Possessions in a Timely Manner. It hadn't been original or even catchy, but there'd been whole paragraphs, testimonials from previous clients who extolled Larry's virtues. One woman claimed Larry had sold her home and belongings—mostly antiques—for more than she'd expected, and now she was living in a retirement community in Florida a full year before she'd planned.

"She was completely fictional, which I

didn't know until later," Shelley explained after telling Oscar the story. "But to me, it was an answer to a prayer. I should have realized the real estate value and the worth of what was inside that house. But I was still reeling from my mother one day sitting beside me, laughing, and the next being gone."

"Riley did tell me that your mother had an aggressive form of cancer."

Two weeks was all she'd had with her mother between *"I've got a headache"* to *"I've been diagnosed"* to *"Goodbye, honey. I couldn't ask for a better daughter than you."*

No, no, no, Shelley would not cry in front of this cop, no matter how comfortable he made her feel. She blinked instead until the tears withdrew.

"Larry came along after your mother's passing, right?" Oscar asked.

Good—he didn't notice her reaction. She didn't want his sympathy. She only wanted him to believe she was innocent and should be left alone, never brought to this station again. If she hadn't gone to the care center that day, if she hadn't shared so much with the woman at the front desk, if she'd been more mature and just handled everything herself...

Of course, then she wouldn't have Ryan or Isabelle.

"I was handed the advertisement two days after we buried my mother. I was still in shock. But I was quickly figuring out that I couldn't care for my dad like my mother had been doing. He was quickly getting worse. Now I'd know to do more research, but Larry seemed so nice."

"How long did you date him before getting married?"

Shelley was almost embarrassed to admit, "Just three months." It made her decide to change the subject, even though it meant going back to another topic she didn't care to discuss. "And thanks to Larry, I know all about the Sarasota Falls Police Department and what 'interrogation' means. You've established rapport. What are you supposed to ask me?"

At least she had the satisfaction of knowing she'd surprised him. He recovered quickly. "I'm supposed to see if you'd encountered any of our other neighbors during your walk. I know I didn't see anybody."

"You don't usually walk that early in the morning or I'd have run into you before."

"I'm the new man on the rotation. I primarily work graveyard, so I get off at eight. I try to take Peeve to the dog park and let him run a bit, and then I come home and go to bed."

"But something changed yesterday?"

"Just that I had some follow-ups to do on a few cases, so I got home later than usual."

"And home is with your aunt?"

He hesitated, just enough that she knew there was something he didn't want to tell her. "It is, for now."

"Why did you come to town?"

"My family was worried about Bianca. I had the time."

She nodded, but he didn't add anything else, so she said, "Often, when Ryan and I go for a walk, we see Mrs. Dupont. She walks her dog, too. Also, Abigail Simms is often working in her yard, but she doesn't stray from her house unless one of her kids comes to get her, although I think her son is living with her now."

"Yes," Oscar agreed. "I've met both of them."

But he didn't know their histories, Shelley thought. Not like she did. And it said something about her that the man had lived a block away from her for two weeks and she hadn't noticed him.

She stood, checking her watch and thinking surely it was evening. It wasn't. Instead, her watch read three o'clock. She walked to the door, insisting, "I need to get Ryan some supper. A meal of ice cream isn't good enough. And I didn't have the opportunity to feed him lunch."

"If you'll wait a minute," Oscar said, "I'm sure Chief Riley will be right back. I know he has a few more questions."

"I—"

Her cell phone rang and she answered the call immediately, noting it was from the care center.

"This is Shelley," she said.

It was Cara. "We can't find your father, Shelley. We've looked everywhere, and it appears he's not on the premises. He didn't say goodbye like he always does."

Shelley almost dropped her phone.

Normally such news wouldn't cause her this much concern. Her father tended to wander and liked to go to the Sarasota Falls Corner Drugstore. He'd buy a pack of cigarettes, perhaps remembering something from his youth. The proprietor called the care center, pretended to put the transaction through and handed her dad an empty carton. Cara or whoever was at the front desk watched for his return.

There'd been discussion about stopping the practice, but Sarasota Falls was a small town, and her father enjoyed it so. Thus it was allowed.

Not after today, though.

Today, she knew that Larry Wagner had recently been in the vicinity, knew that he wouldn't hesitate to hurt her father.

To hurt her.

CHAPTER EIGHT

"I'LL DRIVE." OSCAR guided her from the interrogation room even as she was stuffing her phone back into her purse.

Riley came around the corner. "We're not done with you," he began.

Quickly Oscar filled him in.

"This isn't the first time it's happened," Riley said, looking at Shelley. "I know I've driven him back to the care center a time or two. We'll head to the drugstore."

"It's different this time. I just know it. Where's Ryan?"

"In the break room, watching a kids' show. Last time I looked, he was falling asleep."

Shelley was already out the door, lifting her son from Leann's arms and making a beeline for Riley's cop car. She got in the back, lowered the window and tapped her fingers on the side of the door.

Riley gave Oscar a look that clearly said *Something more is going on here.*

Oscar could only nod as he hopped in the passenger side.

Once they pulled out of the parking lot, Oscar knew why Riley had given her such a long look. She was beyond scared.

Riley used his siren and was at the care center in under ten minutes. He parked right in front behind a transport van. Even before Shelley could crawl from the back, a nurse was hurrying out, shouting, "We found him. We found him."

Shelley started to exit the car, but the nurse said, "No, no. You need to go get him. He's a few blocks away."

"What happened?" Shelley queried, one foot out of Riley's car and one foot still in.

"He must have just walked out the front door and no one saw him leave," Cara said. "What gets me is he didn't say goodbye. He always says goodbye."

"Where is he? What's the address?"

"Jedidiah Carraby just called us to come get him," the nurse said. "He said that he and your dad were friends."

"We'll take care of it," Riley said.

"I know right where to go." Shelley returned to the backseat. Ryan, fully awake, banged on the mesh cage separating the front seat and back.

"We're so sorry," the nurse said. "We'll watch him more closely in future."

Oscar could tell Shelley wanted to bolt. Now he knew why she'd packed her bags to leave but changed her mind. His mother was the matriarch of the family. He couldn't imagine turning his back on her, no matter the need to escape.

Jedidiah Carraby lived in a small house three blocks from the care center.

"I knew about Carson's condition," Jedidiah said, beckoning them in. "Kept meaning to stop by and visit him but never got the time. Looks like he made the time to visit me instead."

"Dad!" Shelley, Ryan with her, was in the living room before Oscar and Chief Riley finished shaking Jedidiah's hand.

"I don't think I know you," Jedidiah said to Oscar.

"I'm new on the force."

"Bianca's nephew," Riley supplied.

"Oh, I love it when Bianca cooks her enchiladas verdes for the church suppers."

"Everyone knows my aunt Bianca."

"Dad, what are you doing in here?" Shelley's

voice came, and Oscar hurried down a hall and into a small bedroom.

Shelley's father stood on a chair with a screwdriver, staring up at a ceiling fan.

Jedidiah followed after a moment. "He said it was making a noise. While I was calling you, he found a screwdriver, and now he's fixed it. Don't know how he fixed it with his hands shaking so. But it must have had a noise because it sounds much better now."

"Did you see anybody with him?" Shelley asked Jedidiah. "The care center said he walked here. Was he alone?"

"I'm not sure. I just answered a knock on the door and there he was. I offered him a glass of water. He didn't seem to want it. I left him alone for a moment while I looked up the phone number for the care center and made the call. When I came back, he was in my bedroom. You showed up about ten minutes after that."

"Thank you. Oh, thank you for calling the care center so quickly. We were worried."

Oscar came forward and carefully helped the man from the chair, lifting him when it seemed Mr. Brubaker didn't know how to step down. She nodded her thanks as she led her father from the room, taking the screw-

driver from his hand and giving it to Mr.
Carraby as she passed by. Oscar followed,
listening as she spoke to her father in sooth-
ing tones. "It's a beautiful day, Dad. It makes
sense that you took a walk. It's hard to stay
inside all the time. You did a great job on the
ceiling fan." Carefully she helped her father
into the backseat of Riley's vehicle.

Riley stayed behind, speaking with Mr.
Carraby. Oscar hesitated. He wanted to hear
anything Shelley might have to say, but what
was happening at Carraby's front door was
interesting, as well. Riley bent down, picked
up something and showed it to Jedidiah, who
looked at it and shrugged. Riley then took a
notebook out of his shirt pocket, jotted something, then hurried toward Oscar and said,
"I'm starting to agree with Shelley. Something doesn't feel right."

Behind Riley, Carraby shut the door.

"She asked Mr. Carraby twice if her dad
arrived alone," Oscar reported.

"What is she thinking? Do you know?"
Riley asked.

"No. But something has her scared," Oscar
said. "And I want to know why she isn't telling us."

"I found this on the front step just now."

Riley handed it over. It was a three-by-five notecard with Jedidiah Carraby's address on it.

"Jedidiah says he didn't write it and he hasn't had any visitors in a few days. He doesn't know where it came from."

"So maybe Shelley's father wrote it so he—"

"I don't think so. Not this handwriting. Not the way his hands shake."

"We could ask—" Oscar began, but Riley held up his hand.

"We'll do it back at the station," Riley said.

At the care center, Ryan, now completely awake, ran ahead, leading the way to Shelley's dad's room. The nurses fussed and followed, too. Oscar stayed in the background, Ryan at his side, as Shelley guided her dad to the bathroom in his room and washed his hands for him, all the while telling him what a good job he'd done and how lucky the neighborhood was to have him for a handyman.

Her father nodded and then followed her to the community room, where he sat in a chair to stare at a television. Ryan climbed in his lap. A nurse immediately walked over to sit by him.

Oscar and Shelley stood in the doorway.

"You see why I came back to Sarasota Falls?" she asked softly. "I can't leave. We're all he has."

"You going back to the garage apartment, then?" he queried.

"If the landlord will let me. I still have five months on my lease. Unfortunately, I'm sure he knows not only that I actually considered skipping out on him but also why."

"I'll go with you to talk to him, do a little bit of explaining. You're right. By now he probably knows everything."

"And he might think I'm involved," Shelley added.

Oscar stopped himself before he said what he was thinking: *You* are *involved.*

Riley drove them back to the station and let Shelley and Ryan out, going so far as to run around, open the door for her and help her from the car.

It was clear to Oscar that Shelley was beat. He looked to Riley, wondering what the man was up to.

"I've just got one more question." Riley held out the three-by-five card and asked, "Do you recognize the handwriting?"

She took it from him and studied it, her expression carefully masked.

"No," she said.

"What?" He couldn't help it. He pressed. "Shelley, you need—"

"I need to get my son home and sort out some things. I'm not sure where you got that or why you're showing it to me."

Riley took the card back, although it looked like Shelley wasn't going to let it go.

"Oscar, follow her home," Riley ordered.

"I can get myself home just fine."

"Make sure everything's okay before she enters her apartment."

Shelley's mouth opened and closed. After a moment, she nodded and said, "I appreciate it."

It wasn't long before Oscar trailed Shelley up the stairs to her garage apartment.

"I'll go in first," Oscar said. "With the kind of day we've had, it pays to be careful."

"Thank you." Shelley held Ryan's hand. The three-year-old clearly had had enough. He fussed all the way up the stairs.

"I tired. I hungry. I want Pooh and a dog."

Not once did Shelley lose her temper. She stayed calm, saying, "We'll put you to bed," and "SpaghettiOs sound pretty good, huh? Your favorite," and ending with "Maybe we can watch Scooby-Doo tonight."

The garage was white clapboard, weathered and clearly had seen better days. Tidy, but plain.

Oscar unlocked the door, keeping Shelley and Ryan behind him, and stepped inside. He was pleasantly surprised. The paint was cheery and not faded. The windows were big and looked out on the street. Hmm, Shelley did have a good view of the Livingston house. Even if she didn't know them personally, she might have understood their habits. She'd probably even looked out to see Oscar in their backyard, knocking back a beverage and barbecuing hamburgers.

She didn't have much in the way of furniture, and based on how generic it was, either Robert, her landlord, had furnished the apartment with the most inexpensive but durable decor he could find or Shelley had done it herself by utilizing garage-sale finds. Ryan didn't appear to be underentertained. He had toys everywhere: oversize Legos, a corner of the room draped with blankets to make a fort and balls of every size.

Ryan paid no attention but dived beside the couch and came up clutching a stuffed Winnie-the-Pooh. He smiled and then dragged Pooh over to the fort.

On a TV tray, a paperback book lay open, only a few pages read.

Yesterday morning, she'd been able to walk away from all this. Nothing in this room was sentimental. Nothing couldn't be replaced.

Oscar watched her walk to the back of the apartment to a tiny kitchen. After taking a can of SpaghettiOs from a cabinet, she hesitated. He knew from the way she bowed her head that she must have been exhausted. She'd had a heck of a couple of days and had been carrying another human for the entire venture.

"Do you need anything?" he asked.

"No, I'm fine." He was sure she was lying.

It was what Oscar's mother used to say after his father took off.

"I'm fine."

He'd known better. And before his father left, she'd always said, *"Oscar, you're a lot like your dad. A leader. You could save the world if you wanted to."*

He didn't think his dad had gone to save the world. Because even at twelve, he'd known that there were more important things like making sure the woman who'd had your children was taken care of.

Oscar had paid attention to what was happening to his family, his brothers not so much.

His uncles had stepped in and repaired anything that broke, was damaged or wouldn't
move, not to mention they'd trimmed whatever was overgrown *and* opened their doors
to the Guzman kids.

He'd never appreciated his family enough.
Shelley needed a support system like he'd
had.

"What I mean to say," Oscar continued,
"is I know you have a tired kid and probably
have a dozen things to do. Let me check all
the windows and the ceiling."

She hesitated. "Ceiling?"

"You'd be surprised at the ways people access homes."

She went rigid, still holding the can of
SpaghettiOs. He moved toward her, removed
it from her hand and placed it on the counter.
"I don't think you have anything to worry
about. Your landlord pays attention, and I'm
right down the street."

She didn't look relieved.

He moved to the refrigerator, where a small
dry-erase board held a few notes. With the
black marker, he wrote his name and cell
phone number. "You can call me anytime.
I promise I'll be here in thirty seconds, and
I'll bring Peeve."

She made a wry face. "I like the idea of a dog."

"Me, too!" Ryan shouted from his fort.

The urge to pull her to him came again. This time stronger than before, probably because she was just inches from him. He could smell a hint of some orangey fragrance, not overpowering at all. Sweet. Like he imagined a kiss from her would be.

Sweet.

Until he turned it into something more.

"Check away," she said.

"What?"

"You said you were going to check the ceiling."

"Oh, right. Then I'll be on my way," he added.

She looked relieved, and for some reason he hoped the look had more to do with him checking the ceiling and windows than him leaving.

He really didn't want to leave.

CHAPTER NINE

PEEVE GREETED OSCAR warmly at the door of Aunt Bianca's bed-and-breakfast.

Oscar merely ordered, "Back."

Peeve obeyed, his tail whipping with happiness. Crouching, Oscar let his hands smooth the dog's sides before going to Peeve's ears. "I'm sorry you didn't get a walk today. I'll—"

"I walked him." Aunt Bianca joined them at the door. Aunt Bianca was a lot like his mother, except where his mother was lean, Bianca was solid. Both were imposing; both took care of their own.

"Thanks."

With a hand signal, Bianca motioned for Peeve to step to the side. "Lots of dog walking going on. I passed at least a dozen neighbors all hoping for the same thing I was. News about Candace."

"Right now there is no news. We haven't even located her husband yet."

"Not like Cody to disappear."

"I agree," Oscar said, coming the rest of the way into the room, Peeve glued to his side, looking up adoringly.

He walked over to the couch and took off his shoes, setting them side by side, ready to be put away. His aunt followed him. Knowing Candace was dead, her house a mere half block away, made him want to stay with his aunt Bianca for a little while. Maybe it made Aunt Bianca feel the same way.

"You need to get some sleep." Glancing at the grandfather clock, Bianca added, "You're due back on shift in four hours. Have you eaten?"

"No."

"I have meat loaf in the oven. By the way, Candace's dad has already called. He's booked a room and will be arriving tomorrow. Not sure if that wife of his is coming or not. Your sister's called me twice today. She's heartbroken, and you're not returning her calls."

Taking out his cell phone, Oscar scrolled through the thirty text messages. Then he glanced at the list of missed calls. He'd even stood up a witness on another case. Never a good thing. And yes, his little sister, Anna, had texted a dozen times. What was he going to say to her when they finally connected?

He reached down to give Peeve one last pat as the shepherd settled under the table. "Shelley Brubaker knows something she's not telling, and I need to find out what it is. Riley's not handling her with kid gloves. I will, and I think I can get the information from her."

"Riley has never owned a pair of kid gloves."

"He's a good cop."

"That he is," Bianca agreed. "I felt sorry for him when this all hit the fan. He wound up being the one having to tell half the town they'd been conned out of money. It didn't make him a popular man."

"I didn't realize that. Wouldn't the bank have had—"

"The bank's president called every customer who'd been a victim of fraud to the bank. Riley was there to meet with them afterward to find out details. I can tell you my meeting wasn't fun. The bank president cried more than I did. Riley's sort of hounded Shelley ever since. I think he believes she knows something she's not telling."

"Which might be why she's hesitating to

help us with a completely unrelated case," Oscar mused.

Even as he said the words, he considered that he was assuming—much like Riley— that Shelley was keeping secrets.

"Her window looks right out over Candace's house," Aunt Bianca said thoughtfully.

"I know."

"She's renting the garage apartment from Robert Tellmaster. He does my website, never goes outside. He wouldn't notice if a plane crashed in his yard."

It was the first time all day that Oscar smiled. Some of the tension ebbed away.

"Here." Aunt Bianca placed healthy helpings of meat loaf, mashed potatoes, green beans and rolls in front of him.

"Shelley's a lot like Anna," Oscar shared. "She does this half-smile thing. I always knew when my little sister lied or was displeased. Everyone else just thought she was sweetly smiling. Ha, nothing sweet about it."

Anna had gotten out of trouble way too often because of that smile.

"Okay," Aunt Bianca said. "I believe you. So, what are you doing to help Shelley? That girl was as innocent as all get-out. Her parents sheltered her so. When Larry Wagner came along, she didn't have a chance."

"He sucked you in, too," Oscar reminded her, digging into the meat loaf. "That's how I wound up here."

"No, it's not. You're here to keep an eye on Shelley. I'm not sure who you're working for, and I'm amazed Riley hasn't figured out that you're not a wet-behind-the-ears rookie, but you'll get the job done. As for me hiring Shelley's husband, if he hadn't also been working for Jedidiah Carraby, I'd never have—"

"Larry Wagner worked for Jedidiah Carraby?"

"Larry did work for a lot of people in town! I wasn't the only one suckered in, and at least he didn't steal anything from me that had sentimental value. I'm more than annoyed about the loss of money, but Jedidiah Carraby lost a Victorian brooch that had been in his family for years. He'd promised it to his daughter and had it out because she was coming for a visit. Larry took it for appraisal. Gosh, did Jed raise a stink."

Oscar nodded as he finished the last of the green beans. From the moment Bianca had called the family to tell her story, she'd said that she was annoyed more than anything and that at most it meant an extra year before she could retire. Luckily, she loved her job.

As if to prove the point, she interrupted his chewing and said, "You knew I was fine the minute you walked in the door, and I love having you here."

"I like being here." It was the truth. He was liking it more and more. Dreams changed; goals were redefined. He could breathe in Sarasota Falls. Not look for cover when a loud noise sounded or a helicopter flew overhead. Once he'd even walked up to a traffic stop and hadn't worried he'd be shot. There'd been a time when he'd worried he'd never adjust to civilian life. A four-year stint in the army, two tours overseas, had jaded him. Jaded most of those he'd served with. Four years in college afterward had done some good, but he'd never fit in. Plus, the only one who'd needed saving while he was getting his degree was himself.

As if sensing Oscar's sudden drift to the past, Aunt Bianca said, "I think you needed me as much as I needed you. No one appreciates my meat loaf like you do. Shelley, though, she's not fine. She no sooner found out that her husband was a thief and a liar than she wound up raising his son, alone, and then discovered she was pregnant her-self. That she hasn't broken under the strain shows you how strong she is."

"How far into their marriage did she wind up with Ryan?"

"They'd been married maybe two months, and he got a phone call from an ex-wife turning the little boy over to him. That girl stepped up to the plate. Had to have been hard. From what I heard, Shelley didn't even know there'd been an ex-wife."

Oscar needed to pay more attention to Ryan's part in this whole production. Some-where there was an ex-wife. But she wouldn't be easy to find.

"So, what are you going to do?" Aunt Bi-anca asked again.

In Oscar's mind, Shelley was no longer a woman he needed to meet so he could try to locate her ex-husband. Instead she was a woman he thought about way too often—and not because she was an assignment but be-cause she was the type of woman who stayed strong even when the world around her was crumbling.

Ryan was lucky to have her for a mom.

If Oscar had his way, Larry Wagner would be in prison forever.

"Ahem." Aunt Bianca had never been the patient relative.

Oscar took one last bite of his mashed potatoes, put down his fork and said, "I'm going to suggest to her landlord that he invest, and soon, in a Medeco lock. The one she has now would take an experienced burglar all of forty-five seconds to open. I'm going to redo all the locks here, too."

"Pretty much a waste of time since I leave the door unlocked so guests can come and go."

"You lock the doors at night," Oscar pointed out. "You know not to make yourself an easy target."

Aunt Bianca nodded. "True, and of course, I have Peeve. I think a dog's better than a lock. Maybe you should tell Shelley to get a dog or at least an alarm system."

Oscar shook his head. He already knew their timeline for getting a dog: ten years. An alarm system, however, wasn't such a bad idea.

"On the other hand, a dog is not something you should get on the spur of the moment. They're a lot of work." Aunt Bianca started clearing the table. "I think I trusted locks more before I met Larry Wagner. Shelley probably feels the same. A true criminal like Larry Wagner has more experience with locks than any locksmith I know."

"Do you know any locksmiths?" Oscar asked.

"No, but now that I think about it, Larry didn't need to break into any of the houses he stole from." She closed her eyes and took a long, deep breath. "Also, we're pretty trusting in this town. People gave him their keys, he made copies without their knowing and then he easily took what he wanted before he skipped town."

Oscar followed his aunt to the sink, carrying his empty glass and plate. "Maybe you should be the police officer instead of me. Do you know if Larry did any work for Candace and her husband?"

"No, I don't believe so. They were so new to town. I doubt they even met him or Shelley."

Oscar did know that, but his aunt had said something else that made a lot of sense. "Who else do you think had a key to Candace's house?"

"I do," his aunt said.

"You have a key?"

"Sure. She locked herself out one day and

asked me if I'd keep one here. I'm always home."

"Let me see it."

Aunt Bianca set the dishes aside for rinsing and went in the pantry. Oscar followed. Aunt Bianca's pantry was good-size, big enough for both of them not only to walk in but also to do a few dance steps should they so desire. They didn't. Plus, Peeve would want to join in. Opening a small drawer, Bianca took out a plastic box lined with small compartments, all labeled with the names of Bianca's friends and neighbors. She even had a key to the church! Oscar could see the compartment under Shelley's name. "Wow," he noted. "You have keys for every house on the block."

Aunt Bianca pointed to a compartment labeled Robert. "That one has both his house key and one to the apartment." She opened it, pulled out two keys, showed Oscar and then returned them.

"The apartment one has been changed," Oscar reminded her. "He did it today after he thought Shelley skipped out."

"I'll return this one to Robert, then—" Bianca looked determined "—and give him a little nudge about getting better locks."

Oscar laughed before checking Candace's

key and heading up the stairs, Peeve at his heels. Bianca had given Oscar one of her better rooms. It was more than a bedroom, with an alcove that usually served as a TV room but that he was using as a study.

Settling at the desk, he turned on his computer and went to the files he had on Larry Wagner. Townley via the FBI had been thorough. They were the big guns and they had all the bells and whistles, top-of-the-line technology that little Sarasota Falls, New Mexico, didn't have.

Quickly Oscar figured out the date that Ryan would have joined Shelley and Larry and then sent off an email asking Townley to start looking into the court system about that time.

That Larry Wagner's crimes spread from California, to Arizona, to Utah, to here, and under at least four aliases, meant the crimes he'd committed, at least according to the hotshots from the state police, were bigger than the little Sarasota Falls police force could handle.

Yeah, right.

Why did Larry Wagner do it? Was it money? Fun? A sickness?

He opened a file with transcripts taken a

few days after Larry Wagner's crimes were first discovered and he'd presumably left the Sarasota Falls area. The interview of Shelley Lynn Wagner was forty pages long. Lots of it redundant. Oscar took out a notebook. After meeting Shelley, he wanted to understand her more: her role, her feelings, her testimony.

He found the transcript he wanted and read Shelley's statement:

Everyone who's called me, asking me to pay back money Larry has taken from them, has mentioned how elusive my ex-husband is. Apparently I'm wife number two that we know about.

When this deposition was taken, Shelley'd known that there was an earlier wife, Ryan's mother. Only, according to Riley's investigation, the woman couldn't be found.

Shelley's statement continued.

He definitely is already living under a new name. And he's working some angle. I just wonder what it could be. Surely he doesn't do the same thing over and over. He'd be easy to catch then, wouldn't he?

Oscar noted how the interviewer didn't answer the question but instead assured her,

We'll find him.

The transcript recorded every detail, that was for sure, because Shelley's next words were recorded, sarcasm practically jumping off the page.

Tell me who the "we" is in that "we'll"?

The authorities.

Oscar was part of "the authorities," and they were no closer now than they had been then of finding Larry Wagner.

By all accounts, he defrauded his first victim in 1999. If the age he gave me is real, he would have been eighteen.

Oscar did the math. If the man was a teenager in 1999, he'd be in his late thirties now, possibly thirty-five or -six when he married Shelley. She'd have been, what? Twenty-two or twenty-three? He jotted down a note, because Shelley had said "If the age he gave me is real." Oscar turned to the next page, wondering now, six months later, if Shelley had figured out that, even with all the technology the cops had at their fingertips, con men still played the con over and over and almost always got away with it.

Peeve ambled to his feet, sounding a low bark before heading for the door.

"What is it, boy?"

"Oscar!" Aunt Bianca called. Her voice sounded strained.

"Be right there." Oscar locked everything away in the desk drawer before hustling down the stairs.

Cody Livingston stood next to the check-in desk, haggard, eyes bloodshot, and looking like he'd go to his knees if a breeze so much as drifted through the room. "Where's Candace? Where's my wife? What happened?"

"Did you just get home?" Oscar went to his friend and put a firm hand under his elbow, leading him to the living room couch. Bianca disappeared into the kitchen. "Call Riley," Oscar told her.

In response, via his aunt, he was given strict orders to wait for Riley before questioning Cody. Because Oscar was friends with the suspect. They not only were neighbors in

Sarasota Falls but also came from the same hometown of Runyan, Riley didn't want any chance of the case being compromised.

Meaning Riley didn't trust Oscar when it came to taking down a close friend.

"Why call Riley?" Cody roared. "You tell me. I just drove by my house. There's yellow tape all around it. I stopped in the middle of the street. I had one foot out the door when the mailman hollered, 'Sorry to hear about your wife.' My wife? What happened to my wife? You tell me. Is she here? Because she's not home. There's a sign on my front door saying I could be prosecuted if I enter. My own house! Did she come here because something happened at our house?"

Peeve whimpered and Oscar asked, "Have you checked your phone?"

"I was in meetings all day. It ran out of juice, and I got busy and forgot to charge it."

"Where were you last night?"

"Last night? Something happened last night? What happened? Tell me!"

Aunt Bianca came back in the room, setting a glass of water on the front desk near Cody and mouthing to Oscar, *Riley's here*.

Oscar calmly nodded, noting Riley at the

front door. "Where were you last night, Cody? Why didn't you sleep in your hotel room?"

"How do you know that? I had a job interview. I didn't want Candace to know. She's so happy here, and she thinks I'm happy working for her father. I'm not. Managing a grocery store isn't what I set out to do. I figured if I could find a job making the same amount of pay or more, then her dad couldn't protest too much when I quit. I drove all night Sunday from Albuquerque to Flagstaff for an early morning Monday interview. I haven't slept in forty-eight hours."

The tears started then. Tears Oscar had seen before, in ditches, in hospital rooms and even courtrooms from those who knew their lives were over.

Not a chance Cody killed his wife.

Riley stepped into the foyer. He glanced at Oscar and Bianca before heading to Cody.

"We have a few questions," he started.

"First tell me where my wife is!" Cody screamed. He actually took a step in Riley's direction, but Oscar touched his shoulder.

Cody turned, almost swinging, and stopped.

Riley came to stand beside Cody and said, "Mr. Livingston, I'm sorry to have to inform you that your wife's dead. Someone broke into your home and—"

Cody Livingston retched, his whole body convulsing.

His life over.

CHAPTER TEN

SHELLEY HAD A love/hate relationship with the media. She hadn't even watched the news before she'd made the news. This morning she sat glued to the television screen, watching as Candace's death was the focus of the morning airwaves.

Candace wasn't well-known, but she was liked by those who did know her. She was the same age as Shelley.

Candace, however, had completed college, married her sweetheart and had been living her fairy tale.

Shelley had completed college, too, although it wasn't doing a lot for her at the moment.

She thought about the young woman she'd seen dancing across her backyard, sometimes with her husband, sometimes not.

She was dead. Larry had been standing over her.

Shelley changed the channel, partly to

squelch the direction her thoughts were going and partly to see if every station was covering the story. They all were. Photos splashed across the screen. Candace with her parents at Disneyland. Candace graduating from high school. Candace getting married. Candace with her kindergarten class. The two reporters spoke politely and mentioned how fortunate it was that school wasn't in session and how the kids would have been adversely affected.

Jack Little was on his way back from vacation, mourning his only child.

One photo was of Candace and her best friend. Shelley leaned forward, studying Anna Guzman. She looked a lot like her big brother, Oscar: same black hair, same strong chin and dark eyebrows. The female reporter went on to mention that one of the officers investigating Candace's death had a connection to the family.

Speaking of photos... Oscar Guzman had caught her off guard yesterday, reminding her that they'd met when she was eight and he was twelve. Leaving the couch, she went for the one closet in the apartment and bent to pull out a suitcase. She kept thinking this one-room apartment was temporary, so why unpack? Considering her flight the other day—albeit aborted—she might have been right. There were five photograph albums. She went for the one from her school days. Because she was an only child, her parents had taken a lot of pictures.

She found the one with Oscar halfway through. It was faded, but she could tell the black-haired boy grinning jauntily at her was Oscar. His hair was shaggy and touched his shoulders. His eyes were black and looking right at her. His shoulders were broad for a kid's.

He'd been fun with a capital *F*, and not afraid of anything.

In contrast, at age eight, she hadn't even had a skinned knee.

Sighing, she went back to the television, changing the channel to the third major station. They, too, were preoccupied with the murder.

She wondered if Oscar was watching the news. Probably. She got up and went to the window, staring over at the roof of Bianca's Bed-and-Breakfast. She couldn't see if his motorcycle was in the parking area.

She went back to the couch, weaving a soft

blanket around her and wondering if she'd ever feel safe again.

The current station had an update. Cody Livingston was in the hospital. He'd collapsed after returning to town from a business trip. The hospital hadn't released any information why. The station showed some photos of him, too, same as Candace. Cody with his parents and three brothers at a beach. Cody graduating from high school. Cody and Candace getting married. Cody helping a customer at Little's Supermarket. "Up and coming," the newscaster claimed.

He continued with his report, stating, "According to private sources, Candace Livingston's body was first discovered by Shelley Wagner, wife of Larry Wagner, who…"

"Brubaker," Shelley whispered, white-hot anger causing her to clench her fingers, dig her nails into the soft skin of her palm. "I've gone back to my maiden name."

Then Shelley went cold. What if Larry was watching this broadcast? Would he think she was cooperating with the authorities? He'd threatened to make her disappear. He *could* make her disappear, too. What was stopping him?

Shelley slumped, the television remote falling from her hand.

The doorbell sounded. Shelley, pushing away dread, went to the side window to peek out.

Oscar Guzman waited at her door.

She didn't want to answer, but he'd ring again and wake Ryan.

She allowed the door to open maybe an inch. "Yes?"

"You okay?"

"No."

"I've been sent to bring you to the station. Riley has a few more questions."

"Sure he does. My responses will be the same as yesterday. Nothing's changed except now the media knows I'm the one who found the body."

"That didn't come from us."

"Mommy." Ryan joined her at the door, pushing it open and looking up at Oscar before saying, "Doggy."

"Peeve is home with my aunt. Would you like to go visit him?"

"No," Shelley said.

"Look." Oscar lowered his voice, sounding kind, intimate. "I know this is an imposition. But we've got Cody Livingston in the hospital, and it looks like he has a solid alibi. He was in Flagstaff, Arizona, the morning his wife died."

A white sedan drove slowly down Vine Street. Larry had driven a white sedan. He liked white. He'd claimed that white cars were so commonplace that it helped him fit in. More like disappear into a crowd, she thought.

He shouldn't have been in this neighborhood, not after what he'd done, what she'd seen. No, couldn't be him. He wasn't stupid. But still, the sight of that white car sent a feeling of helplessness through her so debilitating that it took all her willpower and strength to remain standing.

"What's wrong?" Oscar stepped back, turned around and scanned the street. The tail end of the white car disappeared around the corner, and Shelley knew Oscar hadn't seen it.

"Nothing. Nothing is wrong. How is Cody?"

"Extreme fatigue compounded by shock."

"Of finding out his wife was murdered?"

"He loved his wife," Oscar said simply, making Shelley almost ashamed of how defensive she was. She needed to remind herself that Oscar Guzman had been Candace's friend, and this was more than a case for him.

"I'd never personally met them," she shared. "Nothing more than a wave as Ryan and I walked by. I just knew he worked at Little's."

"I believe you," Oscar said.

Powerful words when the person saying them actually meant them. Shelley acknowledged Oscar did. That made him even more dangerous, because she might start trusting him.

That would be a mistake.

"Mommy, eat."

"I'll fix you pancakes, Ryan. Then I need to talk to Officer Guzman for a few minutes."

"'Kay."

She opened the door the rest of the way, letting Oscar in. He sat at her table, entertaining Ryan by moving a plastic train and making *choo-choo* noises while she cooked breakfast. Once Ryan was in front of the television with a Thomas the Train DVD to entertain him, she joined Oscar at the table.

"I'm on your side. I want you to know that. Here's what we have," he said. "We have a female victim with no known enemies. We have a husband with a solid alibi. We have you calling in a possible homicide and then fleeing the scene. If you'd just called without fleeing, I don't think there'd be an issue—"

"Ha! So you say."

Shelley stared hard at Oscar, knew when she'd been bested. "Let me feed and dress Ryan. Then I'll head to the station with you."

"Great. My aunt Bianca offered to watch Ryan if you don't want to take him with you."

"No. Ryan goes where I go."

An hour later, Shelley and Ryan followed Oscar into the police station and down the hall to the same room as the day before. Ryan, clutching Pooh Bear and holding a toy train for Officer Leann Bailey to admire, went to the break room while Shelley went with Oscar.

Officer Guzman, she corrected herself, shaking away the sound of his words: *"I believe you."*

Riley didn't so much as glance up from the table where he sat looking at some papers.

"We just want to catch the killer," Oscar said as she sat down.

Riley nodded his agreement.

Oscar sat at a chair away from the table and against the wall.

Riley fired the first question. "What time

do you and Ryan usually take your morning walk?"

For the fourth time, Shelley carefully went over the time Ryan woke up, how they'd started out for preschool, met up with Oscar and wound up by Candace's window.

Riley prodded and Shelley shared what she knew, and she did know the habits of those on her street. She knew what times her neighbors left for work: the car salesman and the plumber left before true daylight. She knew who was retired and who didn't work. She confessed that she knew what time Candace left to jog in the morning and that Candace went to the grocery store often.

Now that Shelley knew Candace's maiden name was Little, that made sense. Jack Little owned thirty stores across the small towns of northern New Mexico. Shelley had met him just once, back when she was in junior high. She'd known he had a daughter but not the daughter's name.

She wasn't so sure of Cody's schedule. He didn't seem to have a set one and was often gone overnight, but then, she'd been in the garage apartment only a couple of weeks.

"Could Candace have gone for an early morning run on Monday?" Riley asked.

"She could have, but I didn't see her that morning."

"Did you look for her?"

"No, not really. I was late and wasn't paying attention to what was happening outside my window."

"Besides the neighbors, what else have you seen early in the morning?"

"The garbage truck, but it comes on Thursday." She turned and pointed to Oscar. "I would see him drive home a little after eight. I didn't know who he was or that he was a cop. I knew he lived at Bianca's place, and I figured he worked a graveyard shift somewhere since his motorcycle rarely left during normal work hours. I figured he was new to town and would soon be looking for a permanent place to live."

"You're pretty observant," Riley noted, his tone a bit accusatory.

Shelley didn't care. "Yes, you can thank yourself and Larry Wagner for that. I don't ever intend to be a victim again…" Her voice caught.

"And?" Riley prodded.

"Doesn't matter what I want," Shelley said. "Here I am, in trouble again."

"Then don't be," Oscar said. "Tell us everything you saw."

"I have. I had Ryan next to me, asking if that woman was asleep. I'm pretty sure I told him yes and that we needed to get going."

"What made you so sure she was dead?" Riley asked. "If she'd been alive, even barely, you calling right away might have made a difference."

"Her eyes were open. I froze for a minute. I was so amazed that Ryan thought she was asleep when she was so lifeless. I had to remind myself later that he's barely three and that to him, she was just lying still. If I'd thought for a moment she was alive, I'd have broken down the door."

Even with Larry standing there, she thought to herself.

"She hadn't been dead long," Riley said.

"How did she die? Did someone hit her?" It was a mere forty-eight hours since Shelley had stumbled across the murder scene, and over and over she tried to focus on what her husband held in his hands. She figured it was the murder weapon. But in truth, it had looked more like a piece of paper, perhaps an envelope.

"A blow to the head. We thought at first

she'd been hit over the head, but now it looks like she caught her right temple on the edge of a coffee table on the way down. We'll know more when we get the autopsy report."

"So possibly it wasn't murder?" Shelley, for the first time, felt a glimmer of hope. Maybe Larry hadn't killed that poor woman.

Then why the threatening text, and why had he been in Candace's home?

"It was murder," Oscar said, "but maybe not premeditated. There were signs of a struggle."

Slowly Riley took a pair of latex gloves out of his pocket and put them on. Then he opened his folder and pulled out a black piece of paper. It was shiny, glossy and oversize.

Shelley looked back at Oscar. His expression told her nothing except that she was in trouble. "What's that?"

"Preinked vellum paper," Riley responded. "I'd like to get the impressions of both your hands, palms down, fingers splayed."

"Why?"

"Because Candace was pushed, and the person who pushed her had small hands."

Riley's gaze went to Shelley's hands. "Like yours."

CHAPTER ELEVEN

HER CELL PHONE SOUNDED, beating out the words to "It's a Small World (After All)" because Ryan loved the song. Not that he'd been to Disneyland. She wasn't sure where he'd heard the song. She just knew he loved it, so she'd chosen it as her ringtone.

It made him happy.

Sleepily, she turned over and reached for the bedside table. She checked the phone's screen. A local number but not one she recognized. She'd made a mistake a few days ago and answered without checking. This time she hit Ignore, rolled over and went back to sleep.

"Mommy, outside?" Ryan patted her arm. She opened one eye. Lately the only thing she wanted to do was sleep, and she wasn't sure if the fatigue was due to the pregnancy or the chaos of her life.

Ryan wasn't having the same sleep issues. He went down easily and usually slept until she nudged him out of bed. It was unusual for him to wake up without her prodding.

She glanced at the clock and groaned. She should have been up forty-five minutes ago! Ryan must have known that because he'd tried to help out and had dressed himself: a blue pair of shorts, no shirt and one shoe.

His favorite outfit. Unfortunately, the shorts were from the dirty clothes hamper and had milk stains on them, and the shoe was hers.

"No, Mommy has a doctor's appointment." Shelley twisted. Getting out of bed when pregnant took skill. "I need to drop you off at preschool, and then I'll be going into town." She didn't mention that running late was becoming a habit and that she hated to rush.

"Good. I want candy." With that, Ryan tottered away, probably in search of her other shoe.

Shelley exhaled, almost calm. Ryan had a way of doing that for her, reminding her why she had to put one foot in front of the other, keep moving, stay sane. For the last three nights, since she'd seen Candace's body, she hadn't slept well, relaxed or felt safe. Every time she closed her eyes, she got an instant replay of walking unsuspectingly up to that window, looking in and seeing that poor woman lying there with Larry standing a few steps away.

The man she'd been married to. Her baby's father.

A killer who still knew everything about her.

"Mommy looks mad." Ryan returned.

Shelley smiled. "No, Mommy's not mad, just waking up and needing to hurry." She rolled awkwardly from the bed and promised herself she'd visit the bank today, talk to the manager who was already investigating her case.

"I'll bring you shoes?" Ryan asked.

"Let me have the one you're wearing, and I'll go look for my other. Get the blue tennis shoes for yourself."

"Blue." He nodded and smiled but didn't move.

She pointed to her feet and said, "Blue shoes."

This time he toddled off.

It wasn't good for Ryan to see how tense this whole thing was making her. It was all she could do not to curl up in a ball and hide in the closet. Never, never, had she considered Larry a killer.

But now she knew different, and the cops knew she was hiding something.

For the next twenty minutes, they quickly completed their morning routine. Ryan happily let her dress him in his favorite Handy Manny outfit, only without the tools.

Finally she opened the door, and she and Ryan stepped outside. She stood, drinking in the fresh air and surveying a neighborhood that looked normal but wasn't.

"Mommy, ready?" Ryan nudged her.

Taking a deep breath, one that caused the baby to adjust and poke a toe or finger or something into Shelley's rib, she locked the door behind her.

Never had she thought she'd feel unsafe in her town.

Ryan held on to her hand as they descended the stairs. Once they reached the bottom, she pulled him into her arms. She was tired, too, but this little guy was the perfect prescription for feeling better.

"We're going to have a great day," she predicted.

"'Cause you buy me candy."

"I'll buy you candy," she promised as she hurried around to the driver's seat.

After positioning herself, no longer easy

with such a big belly, she turned the ignition key. The car sputtered, zoomed for a moment and died. She tried twice more. Then waited a moment because she didn't want to flood the engine. In the backseat, Ryan sang a silly song about crayons. In the front, Shelley tried not to worry about what the car was not doing: starting.

In the quiet, she heard the distant hum of a motorcycle. Oscar must be close. He seemed always to be around when she needed him. Didn't mean she wanted him to be around.

Or did she?

Want?

Need?

No, it was too early in the morning for an in-depth look at the only single male who'd walked through her front door, filling it and making her feel secure just for a moment; who'd sat at her kitchen table, playing a nonsense game with Ryan and acting like he enjoyed it; and who'd looked at her with something akin to longing in his eyes.

Yeah, right, longing. He longed to know where her ex-husband was. What else? She wasn't sure.

She turned the key again. This time the sputter sounded worse. Okay, she could pop the hood and look, but she wouldn't know what she was looking at.

Opening the door, she got out, telling Ryan, "Stay still. I'm just seeing if I can get the car moving."

"I help," Ryan offered, attempting to undo the belt. He couldn't yet, but soon she'd need to talk to him about his escape attempts and growing abilities.

"If I need help, I'll come get you." She walked toward the front of her aged green Impala, started to open the hood and stopped. A white minivan had pulled up in front of Candace's house. It was not Larry's favorite kind of vehicle, but it was one he'd willingly use. You could get a lot of stuff in a minivan. An older man exited, his silver hair blowing in the breeze. He stared at the house, his face stoic. Shelley recognized him even from a distance. The passenger side opened and a blonde woman, much younger, stepped out. She circled the vehicle and put her hand on his arm. Shelley didn't recognize her.

Jack Little didn't so much as move.

Shelley studied the older man. She'd grown up seeing historical photos of the Little Supermarkets coming into popularity. Jack Little and his brother had been in many of them.

There'd been plenty of photos from the seventies and eighties. He'd posed with employees, with politicians and other business leaders, even a few nationally known. None depicted the expression he wore today. It wasn't stoic; it was grief-stricken. Finally he took a step, slowly followed by another, as if both feet were weighed down.

Oscar pulled up behind the minivan on his motorcycle and removed his helmet. Not that she needed him to. She knew his body type, how he moved, by heart. Maybe her heart responded a bit too much, judging by the flutter.

No, the baby must be moving. That had to be it.

Oscar walked to the couple and said a few words. Then he put his arms around the older gentleman, holding him close, until the man collapsed against Oscar, sobbing.

Tears trickled down her cheeks.

"Mommy, why are you crying?" Ryan had been watching.

"I'm crying because I'm sad." She didn't need Ryan to know the real reason.

He nodded and said, "Dumb car."

If only it were that simple. Unless she missed her guess, she was witnessing Candace's dad and stepmother as they entered his daughter's home for the first time without her being there.

Shelley remembered coming home after her mother died: how quiet the house had been, how empty, how wrong.

Oscar stood respectfully outside. The woman stopped when she reached him and put a hand on his arm. Oscar stepped aside, and even from a distance, Shelley knew the woman was laughing. Some people dealt with sorrow by laughing.

Then, as if Oscar felt her watching, he turned to her.

Busted.

She met his gaze, color going to her cheeks as Oscar said something to the couple before heading her way. The older man stared at her for a long time.

Oscar had a five o'clock shadow and circles under his eyes. She knew he worked the graveyard shift, which had ended hours ago. He should have been at Bianca's and in bed.

"You all right?" he asked after crossing the street and finally reaching her side.

"Yes. Shouldn't I be?"

"You're not answering your phone."

"I answer only when I recognize the number," she said.

"I put my number on your fridge." He raised an eyebrow. "I'd think with all that is going on, you'd be curious."

"Not me." As if to prove her point, her cell phone sounded and played the beginning line of "It's a Small World (After All)."

Oscar winced. "That ride always spooked me." He looked over at Candace's house. "That's Jack Little of Little Supermarkets. Spend Little, Shop Big."

"I recognize him," Shelley said.

"The woman is Tiffany Little, wife number three. They've been married only a little over a year."

Shelley couldn't help it; she shuddered. She'd been referred to by the cops and by the press as wife number two that they knew about.

Oscar shared, "Candace's mother died right after Candace was born. She was mostly raised by Jack's second wife. Tiffany's maybe a few years older than Candace was."

"You like him?"

"I do," Oscar acknowledged.

"I saw him here last week. And I think I've seen his wife at least twice."

"Really?"

"From my big picture window, remember?"

Yet she didn't tell him about the white car on Vine yesterday. There were plenty of white cars in Sarasota Falls. She didn't need to fixate on the possibility that it belonged to Larry. Rubbing her hands against her jeans, she tried to squelch the jitters.

"What are you up to?" He looked from her to the hood of her car.

"Nothing, just getting ready to take Ryan to preschool. Then I happened to glance over and saw…saw you and the Littles." She walked back to the driver's side. She had things to do, and the only way she'd get them done, and stay safe, was by removing herself from both her ex-husband and the cops.

But the only time she felt safe was when this man, a cop, was around.

Please start, car.

She opened her car door, saying, "I need to go. I have a doctor's appointment."

"You need some help?"

"Everything's fine. The doctor only has to check a few things, like my weight, my blood pressure and the baby's heartbeat."

"Do you know what you're having?"

"A girl."

"Mommy!" Ryan protested. "Not s'pose to tell."

Shelley laughed. "I did say that. I'm sorry. But if a policeman asks, you're supposed to tell…"

Her words tapered off.

She'd believed the words once upon a time. But then, she'd also believed in the tooth fairy.

CHAPTER TWELVE

"COPS ARE THE good guys," Oscar reminded her. Knowing that Shelley didn't believe in the badge, didn't believe in him, hurt.

She gave him a tight-lipped look that wasn't a frown but definitely wasn't a smile, either.

"And," he reminded her gently, "if you'd trust me, I'm sure I can help. Just answer my questions."

"What question haven't I answered?" She carefully, as only a pregnant woman could, maneuvered her way behind the steering wheel.

"It's not what you've answered. It's more what you haven't shared."

"I've told the truth." With that, she reached out and started to close her door. He finished for her, giving it a push and stepping back.

She turned the key. The engine rolled over once and sputtered. She tried three more times before he commanded, "Pop the hood."

She closed her eyes, and he knew she

wished it were anyone but him, a dreaded cop, helping her. Still, she reached down, and he heard the ping of the hood's lock disengaging.

He checked for the easy fixes, but everything appeared connected and in working order.

"What time is your appointment?"

She looked at her watch. "Ryan's preschool started five minutes ago, and my appointment is in twenty minutes."

"I'll take you."

"You have a motorcycle!" Her cheeks turned a faint pink that looked good on her, except that it matched the faint red of her eyes. There were no tears, and he knew she'd deny them if he asked.

"You get the car seat while I borrow my aunt Bianca's SUV."

Five minutes later, they were on their way. Ryan thought it great fun to have a new person around and be in a different vehicle. After giving directions, Shelley picked at the hem of her red shirt.

"Nervous?" he asked.

"I've never liked going to the doctor."

"I meant about being in the car with me."

She stopped fidgeting. "You mean being with a cop?"

"Yup."

"I'll tell you what," Shelley said. "If you don't ask me any questions that I've already answered, I'll try not to act like I'm stuck with you."

He couldn't help it. He laughed. "Okay, but only because I've always heard that you should let pregnant women have their way or they get really cranky."

"It's true. I've been cranky for the last eight months."

"You've had good reason to be cranky," Oscar observed.

The preschool came into view. Shelley showed him where to park, told him to wait, quickly unbuckled Ryan and hurried him inside a double set of doors. When she finally returned, she changed the subject. "So, what do you think is wrong with my car? It worked fine yesterday."

"I don't know. I gave it only a cursory look. I'll tinker with it more when we get back."

"You know cars?"

"One of my uncles owns an auto repair shop. I worked there while I was in high school."

"I worked with my mother."

Oscar let out a whistle. "I remember your mother. She used to bring desserts over to Bianca every morning. I thought her chocolate muffins were the best things I'd ever eaten."

Shelley nodded, her pursed lips relaxing a bit. "I remember you sometimes convinced me to snatch them, especially right out of the oven."

"Never," Oscar protested. "I'm an officer of the law. I'd never encourage stealing."

"You were twelve."

"I'm glad you remember."

They drove through one residential street and down another, passing parks and a grade school. Downtown Sarasota Falls came into view, and Oscar felt a moment's disappointment. For the last few miles, they'd dropped the cop/suspect personas and had actually had a conversation.

Perfect timing. Just as they hit the street, the ten o'clock train approached, the lights started blinking and the post went down. From their left came a long, low whistle.

"I'm really late," Shelley muttered.

"I'm glad we're stopped by the train. It gives us more time to talk." He ignored the face she made. "I promise, nothing about your ex-husband or Candace. Did I tell you when I was young, I thought the Sarasota Falls City Hall was haunted?"

"Really? Why?" Her fingers tapped on the door handle.

He knew she was just itching to get out. "Because of the gargoyles."

She laughed, and it surprised him so much his foot almost slid off the brake. This was the second time she'd laughed today. The first time, she'd laughed with her son, but now she was laughing at him.

With him.

"Hey," he protested. "The gargoyles scared me."

"I love those gargoyles, especially after a rainstorm when the water pours from their spouts. You know that's what they're for."

He didn't know, but he liked that she did.

"They're a type of drain. When it rains, they allow the water from the roof to pour down without having to touch the side of the building."

The train finally arrived, going slow because it was traveling through a town. Shelley took her fingers off the door handle and looked at him. "I know the history of Sarasota Falls. During Sarasota Falls' Founder Days, I not only rode in the parade but also I participated in some of the reenactments. There were about fifteen of us schoolkids. I usually played the town's schoolteacher. But—" she gave him a look "—I did not go about slapping any knuckles with my ruler."

"I wasn't going to say a word."

"Cops always have something to say." She gave him a look. Then she turned her attention to the train and muttered, "It's going to be a long one."

Oscar noted he couldn't see the end of the train. "I've always liked trains."

"Have you been to the Station Diner? It used to be a depot and has a bunch of original railroad stuff. During reenactments, the owner, Jimmy Walker, even makes boarding passes that he hands out with the names of famous Sarasota Falls citizens on them."

"Really? Who from Sarasota Falls is famous?"

"Billy the Kid came through town."

"Okay, now I'm impressed. Does someone dress like him?"

"Of course, but everyone fights to be him, so the role doesn't belong to just one person.

Once Tom Riley played the part, but that was before…"

Oscar silently added the words she didn't say. *Before his partner died and his wife left him.*

"Tom used to be a lot of fun," Shelley said. Then she quickly changed the subject. "Sometimes your aunt Bianca's home is on the tour. You should ask her."

"Really?"

"Sure. You know its history, right?"

"I know only that it was built to house the main officer who ran the munitions depot."

Visibly she relaxed. This might be a tactic he'd want to use later. Get her talking about her town. It was a great way to have her open up about people. Maybe she'd accidentally share something.

"You do know," she asked, "the name of the area of town you live in?"

"Claradan."

"The munitions depot's head officer was Daniel. His wife was Clara."

"Clara and Dan. Claradan," Oscar figured out. "But Sarasota Falls is older than the munitions depot. Aunt Bianca has some of the old photos on display in the living room. Her guests like to see them."

"You're right. At the turn of the century, the twentieth century, Sarasota Falls was called Dead Bull's Corner."

Oscar looked at her. "You're kidding."

"Nope. No one knows why, but I'm guessing some cowboys sitting around a campfire had great fun coming up with the name."

"Could have been worse," Oscar considered.

"The town first changed its name when the school for the deaf was built. Guess the more genteel people in town didn't think Dead Bull's Corner would inspire people to send their children here."

"How did a school for the deaf wind up here?"

"A wealthy cattle rancher built the school, recruited a doctor and teachers and then advertised."

"One man?" Oscar queried.

"It's amazing what one person can do, both good and bad, especially one with a daughter who's deaf."

Oscar got the idea she wasn't thinking about the town's history anymore. Because he didn't like the tenseness already forming around her lips. He asked, "Why wasn't the town renamed for him?"

"Because his name was Cornelius Pigg, and he didn't think the town's reputation would improve much by the changing of Dead Bull's Corner, New Mexico, to Pigg, New Mexico."

Oscar suddenly appreciated the name Guzman a whole lot more.

The last train car rambled by, but the post didn't immediately rise.

"The school was called the Academy for the Deaf of New Mexico. Soon the town voted to change its name to Academy."

"Academy, New Mexico." Oscar didn't think it rolled off the tongue well.

"Yup, Academy increased the size of the town's dot on the map tremendously. For a few decades, the cattle farmers and the school coexisted, and the town had something for everyone. When the school closed, though, the population decreased by half and the town stagnated.

"Some say that for ten years, the town existed with only a post office and a train station. Hard to imagine."

The warning arm finally rose, and Oscar followed her directions to the parking lot of the doctor's building, the same one he'd been to at age twelve when an attack of vertigo hit during a tree-climbing contest. Funny how some of those long-ago memories came back.

He parked, and for a moment they sat. Sensing her discomfort and knowing she needed a ride back home, he said, "I want to get a few things at the store. Why don't I do that? Call me when you're done, and I'll come back."

She hesitated, then seemed to realize she had little choice. She knew, after all, that he had her number. Now she just had to accept his.

"Perfect." Her tone implied anything but. She opened the door and hurried toward the entrance without a backward glance. She was a woman on a mission and intent on doing her battling alone. He'd admired that, but he also saw the look in her eyes and the slump of her shoulders.

He really didn't need anything, so he parked down the road and called Townley, the man responsible for Oscar's assignment to get close to Shelley Wagner and delve into her secrets.

Oscar was delving a bit too deep, because he was starting to care more about her than her secrets.

This could be a problem.

CHAPTER THIRTEEN

ANY DAY NOW. That was what the doctor said.

She stepped out into the sunshine, part of her wanting to dance and the other part of her wanting to hide. She'd be holding a tiny being soon, in charge of shaping a life. Unfortunately, at what should have been the greatest moments of her life, she had to be on the lookout for a man who'd taken almost everything from her.

Patting her stomach, she reminded herself that he hadn't taken what was important. No, he'd left what was most valuable behind: Ryan and little Isabelle.

She watched as Oscar brought his aunt's SUV slowly to the curb. Before she could open the door, he'd jumped out, rounded the vehicle and opened the door for her.

A gentleman.

She put the seat belt on, adjusting it for comfort, looking out the window to see if there were any cars slowing down or pedestrians acting strange. The streets of downtown Sarasota Falls looked quaint and sleepy. She sat back and let herself breathe as the baby moved sharply.

"Ohhhh."

Oscar got behind the steering wheel. "You okay?"

"Absolutely," she answered honestly. He was, after all, asking about the doctor's appointment and her health. Nothing else, at the moment.

He started the engine and pulled out of the parking lot. Part of her wished that the trip home would take longer. She wanted time to reflect and someone to reflect with. Being with Oscar, she was starting to feel like she wasn't alone. Plus, thanks to Oscar, she felt safe.

The feeling wouldn't, couldn't, last.

"Sure you're all right?" he asked, waiting to turn onto the street.

"Amazingly so," she answered. "Soon I'll be a mother. Oh, I'm a mother already, but this time I'll get to start from scratch."

"You'll make a go of it," he said.

She almost laughed. He was such a guy, and probably what he'd just said was high praise. "If you have a moment, I want to stop at Sell It Again Sam and buy a few things for the baby. I've held off." She'd gotten a call this morning from the bank. It would be another two weeks before her money was returned, but because she'd reported the fraud quickly, she'd been covered by Federal Reserve regulations. She'd receive all but fifty dollars back, freeing her to spend a little of the pocket money she'd earned.

"No problem." He took the next left and then a right into the parking lot. Shelley was opening the passenger door almost before he'd pulled to a complete stop.

Inside the store, Oscar stayed with her as she went to the section featuring baby resale items. Picking up a set of onesies still in their original wrapping, she said, "The nurse told me I needed onesies, socks and diapers more than anything else."

"Socks?"

"Apparently Isabelle will sleep better if her feet aren't cold." She held up a tiny dress, red, with white polka dots, and a pant that had ruffles on the seat.

"That's not a onesie or socks," Oscar observed.

"No, but look how tiny it is."

He didn't reach out a finger to touch. He

just nodded and stood at a small bin, pulling out little socks.

"You been around babies much?" she asked.

"No. My siblings and I are close in age, and I don't remember them being real babies."

"As opposed to fake babies?" she queried.

He laughed and added, "None of us are married. I'm twenty-eight, the oldest. And yes, my mother is constantly annoyed that I haven't married and given her grandchildren. I keep deferring to my two younger brothers and little sister, who aren't doing their part. See, I have an excuse. I spent eight years overseas in the Marines. Problem is, we're all single, although Victor, the youngest of my brothers, has had the same girlfriend for two years. No one in the family likes her much. Anna, my little sister, is in college, majoring in fun."

It was the most he'd shared about his personal life. It somehow made him more appealing, not that he wasn't already appealing enough.

"So, why aren't you married?"

He took a moment before answering, which surprised her. He seemed always to have an answer, almost as often as he had questions.

"I'm not sure I believe in marriage," he finally said.

"I'm not sure I do anymore, either," she shared. "I used to believe in it. My parents had an awesome marriage. I think some of my favorite memories are of sitting in the backseat of the car while we drove places. They'd laugh and talk. Sometimes they'd share what they'd done while dating."

"My parents weren't like that."

"Why not?"

"I barely remember my dad. He was in the military, too. He was gone a lot. He was discharged when I was twelve. He came home for a week, and then one morning, he walked away and never looked back."

"I'm sorry. I can't…" She'd been thinking of her parents. She couldn't imagine her dad walking away. But her husband, Larry, had walked away. She tried again. "I'm sorry. Not all dads are like that, but the ones who are…"

"My uncles are good guys, like your dad," Oscar said. "I have more than twenty cousins, and my siblings and I were always doing something fun at their houses."

"Maybe you can be more like your uncles."

He'd been somewhat animated while talking about his family. That expression went away as he said, "I joined the military like my father. I was mostly special ops, lots of danger. I saw firsthand how someone like me shouldn't be married. After my discharge, I majored in criminal justice and worked at a law firm while in college. Saw up close quite a few nasty divorce and abandonment cases. Left me with a bad feeling about marriage and why I've always tried to help others."

"Sounds lonely," she said.

He paused, seemingly a bit disconcerted, then finished with "I've mostly been around dedicated men and women in difficult, sometimes life-threatening situations that—"

Shelley nodded, understanding. "I get it. You've been busy and jaded. It makes sense." She took the socks from him, picked three pairs and then headed to the cashier with her loot.

"Three dollars and fifteen cents," the cashier said.

"I don't need the white socks." Shelley pulled them from her pile.

"Two dollars and ninety cents," the cashier said, not even blinking.

"I'll get the other pair of socks," Oscar offered.

"No, I don't need them. I picked them up by accident." Shelley put the dime in her purse.

They stood in front of Sell It Again Sam, the mood somber. Finally Shelley said, "I'm being careful with my money until I go back to work."

Oscar stared at her, his steely gaze daring her to tell the truth, open up, about everything.

"I didn't say anything, but if you need help, I'm here."

They stood a few more moments, the ebb and flow of Sarasota Falls surrounding them. Finally Oscar moved toward the SUV, asking, "How much do you know about babies? You're an only child."

Shelley chuckled and rubbed her stomach. "What I know, Ryan's taught me. I never even babysat. I didn't need to. I worked for my mother."

"She was a great cook as well as a great baker," Oscar said. His eyes lit up. "You hungry?"

"I'm now craving a chocolate muffin," she joked, trying to push away the worry about money and her ex-husband and the attention of this man who might or might not have been an ally.

"I was thinking something a bit more nu-tritious," Oscar said, "but I'd never say no to a woman in your condition."

"I need to find out what's wrong with my car."

"I can help with that. But if I don't eat first, I'll faint, and you'll have to drag me off the street. My treat."

She had food at home, but she also had, here, a man willing to look at her car. She gave him directions to the Station Diner. It was late for breakfast but early for lunch, so only a few customers occupied the red vinyl seats. Shelley figured it wouldn't appear un-usual if she just ordered soup. Buying clothes and going out for a meal were not in her bud-get.

"About time you visited me," Jimmy Walker scolded Shelley as she walked through the door. "I was beginning to think you didn't like me anymore."

"I like you just fine." She went behind the counter and gave him a hug. "How are you feeling?" He'd been on oxygen ever since she could remember, and she'd bullied him into not smoking when she was twelve.

"Can't complain."

Oscar chose a booth near the back of the

diner. She used the facilities and joined him, thinking that if she got any bigger, she'd need to sit at a table instead of a booth. It was that tight a fit.

"Need a menu?" he asked.

"No, I memorized the menu years ago. I'll have chicken strips and french fries." Not good for the baby, but excellent comfort food.

He put down the menu and said, "Me, too."

She knew then that she could really like him. He was easy to talk to when he wasn't acting like a cop, and he picked up on the little things that mattered.

"You'll need to go tell Jimmy. He doesn't keep a waitress during off-hours."

Oscar headed back to the cash stand, placed the order, said a few other things to Jimmy— making the older man laugh—and then returned to the booth.

"You come here often, then?" he asked.

"I used to. My mom actually made desserts for Jimmy. I would deliver them here. He'd always set me in a booth and give me a cup of soup while I waited for her carryall bags."

"He's a tough old bird," Oscar observed.

"He's had a few offers to buy the restaurant, but he says he'll work here until they carry him out. Some people are like that. Their job is their world. I've always felt sorry for him."

Oscar frowned. "Well, some jobs are so important that—"

"Not more important than family or health," Shelley said.

"I disagree. When I was in the military, I'd be off the radar for months. If I weren't willing to make the sacrifice, then who would?"

"I didn't say that people shouldn't sacrifice," Shelley pointed out. "What I am saying is that priorities are important and that knowing when to change a priority is important, too."

"How did we get on this subject?" Oscar still frowned.

"You said that Jimmy was a tough old bird. Well, Jimmy made this restaurant his life. Work shouldn't be your life. My mom invited him to our house for Christmas, and he didn't want to come."

"If he didn't want to come, he shouldn't have had to."

"But what's the joy in working on a day when everyone else is opening presents and catching up with family?"

"What if even one family needed a place to eat on Christmas? Like the movie where the dogs got the Christmas dinner and the family wound up having Chinese food."

"Fiction," Shelley argued.

"Not everyone is blessed with a family like you had."

"You've talked about your mom, your siblings and your uncles' families. Sounds like you had a pretty good childhood."

Oscar slowly nodded. He'd spent way too long thinking about the empty space where his father should have been.

"I did," he admitted. "And I didn't appreciate it enough. But also, I didn't appreciate my freedom to choose. In Afghanistan, I saw entire villages completely pulverized. Whole families gone. They'd never break bread again. I never thought about that, not completely."

Shelley felt something stir in her heart. Entire villages completely pulverized. That was so much worse than what her ex-husband had done to Sarasota Falls, to her. She'd been telling herself over and over how blessed she was to have Ryan and soon Isabelle in her life. But heck, she was lucky to be sitting here, across from a handsome man willing to buy her lunch, and to have a home—albeit small—to return to.

She cleared her throat, her respect for this man growing. Her desire to confide in him nudged her, making her reconsider, but she wasn't ready yet, wasn't willing to put Ryan at risk.

She had no legal hold on Ryan.

None.

"How did you wind up working as a cop here in Sarasota Falls?" Her voice was thick. "I mean, I know your aunt lives here, but…"

"Order!" Jimmy called.

Oscar fetched their soup and brought over a pitcher of water. After finishing half the bowl, he said, "I came here to check on my aunt, and the opportunity to work for the police department more or less fell in my lap. It's only temporary."

Disappointment swelled, but she pushed it away. She needed to be glad he was leaving. She'd been divorced only a little over six months, and she carried enough baggage to sink a ship.

"Hard to imagine you being pushed into anything you didn't want to do."

"Sometimes you do the job that needs to be done because you're the only one who can."

Chicken strips didn't take long to eat, and too soon, he was holding the door open for her and guiding her out of the diner and back to the SUV. He'd just settled behind the wheel when his phone rang. He answered it with "Guzman."

She listened to one side of the conversation, catching on that it was something that concerned her, concerned her very much.

When the call ended, she looked at him and asked, "So, Jedidiah Carraby found the brooch that my ex-husband stole from him?"

"Yes, and Mr. Carraby insists that it just appeared on his bedroom dresser. He says it couldn't have been there all this time. He's wondering if your dad could have had it. Maybe even gotten it from you."

"No, I didn't have the brooch, and I don't know how my dad would have come to have it."

Her ex-husband had taken the brooch. That she knew.

Most likely her ex-husband had returned the brooch. Why? To send her a message? Again, why? Having her dad go missing from the care center was message enough.

But if the brooch was worth what Jedidiah claimed, her ex would never have returned it.

"Any chance the brooch is a copy, a fake?" she asked.

"What makes you ask that?"

"Just the way my mind works."

Oscar made another phone call. After hanging up, he said, "Riley's not happy, but he's willing to check it out."

She rubbed her stomach. Any joy the day had offered had been sucked away by the thought of her ex-husband. It was only a ten-minute drive home, and Oscar parked behind her car, the neighborhood strangely empty. Unusual given the activity of the last few days. The news media had made frequent appearances, visiting Vine Street with crews from both the Albuquerque and the Santa Fe stations. They'd turned their cameras toward her apartment but hadn't said too much about her since the first few days.

Strangers, too, had taken to walking the street, gawking at Candace's house. Their vehicles drove up and down Vine Street, slowing for a look. A good number of the cars were white, blending into the universe like her ex-husband always tried to do. He was here, nearby, playing with her, and now she knew he was capable of murder.

Telling the police didn't mean they'd find him. They hadn't in the six months they'd been looking for him.

They didn't seem to be able to find him; he easily found her, and he knew how to get at her emotionally when it came to her father and son.

She wanted to stamp her feet, wanted to curse, wanted to shout to the world how unfair all of this was. She was having a baby! And the only person around who temporarily cared was a cop who'd probably been assigned to watch over her in case she decided to take flight again.

Unfair.

"Looks like Candace's dad is down at my aunt's place," Oscar remarked. "Probably checking in."

Shelley looked, and sure enough, the white minivan was in front of Bianca's Bed-and-Breakfast. "Maybe you should head home. He might have some questions for you."

"Oh, I'm sure he does," Oscar said easily. "But I have even more for him." He got out of the SUV, came around and opened her door, then walked to her car. Shelley disengaged the seat belt, rubbed her stomach and followed. She felt unwieldy but somehow right. Her doctor had been pleased with the baby's heart rate and growth and with Shelley's blood pressure.

Harmony within chaos, Shelley thought,

because her blood pressure should have been shooting through the roof. The same with her heart rate.

A door slammed behind her, and she jumped. Oscar gave Robert Tellmaster, her landlord, a wave and said, "I'm impressed with the locks. Good work."

Shelley looked between the two men. She'd wondered why Mr. Tellmaster had installed new locks. She'd ask Oscar when the opportunity arose. She forced a smile before saying, "Morning, Mr. Tellmaster."

"Something wrong with your vehicle?"

"Yes—it didn't start this morning. Have you seen anyone near it?"

"No, but I thought I heard something this morning about three. Abigail's yappy dog. Wonder if somebody was out here? Come to think of it, I heard that dog the morning Ms. Livingston was murdered. I think I mentioned that to the cops."

"What time did you hear the dog the morning of Candace's murder?" Oscar asked.

"That would have been about five. I know because I looked at the clock."

"You sure of the time?" Oscar asked.

"Five minutes after five."

"You open the window, look out or anything?"

"Nope," Robert said.

"I heard Abigail's dog that morning, too," Shelley said. "I didn't hear her this morning."

Oscar wrote something down on a tiny notebook he pulled from his shirt pocket. Then he raised her hood and slowly looked at all the components inside. Shelley stood next to him and stared at the engine, black; the battery, black; and the coolant container, white. There were plenty of hoses and belts, too. Nothing looked out of place.

"See anything?" Robert queried, edging closer.

"Not yet." Oscar apparently wanted to be thorough. He not only touched everything but also touched it twice and jiggled it.

"I saw you two take off this morning in Bianca's SUV. I wondered what was going on."

Shelley rolled her eyes. This was the most conversation she'd gotten from Robert. "Nothing's going on. I had a doctor's appointment, and Officer Guzman happened to be across the street—"

"I saw Jack Little across the street." Robert looked impressed.

"—and Officer Guzman," Shelley continued, determined to have her say, "offered me a ride when he saw my car wasn't starting."

"Everything okay?" Robert looked at her stomach, and to Shelley's surprise, he appeared concerned.

"Yes."

Oscar went down to his knees and peered under the car. "Nothing leaking."

"Well," Robert said gruffly, "if you need a ride to the doctor and Officer Guzman isn't around, just let me know. I'll take you."

Shelley looked at the man. He neither smiled nor appeared enthusiastic about the offer he'd just made, but he was wringing his hands and chewing on his upper lip.

"Thank you," she managed.

As if afraid he might say something else nice, he turned and walked stiffly back to his front door. She watched him go, an old man just as alone as she was.

Oscar was too busy walking the length of the car to have paid attention to the exchange. "I don't know what's wrong. We'll need to get it to the shop. I can—"

"No, really, you've helped enough. I can get it to the shop. Thanks for driving me today."

"I can—"

"No, you can't. This is something I have to deal with myself."

He stared at her, a look she was familiar with. He'd stopped being her friend and had returned to being the cop investigating her. One who was dancing too close to the truth by asking questions like, *"Do you think whoever killed Candace might have something to do with your car?"*

She didn't know how to respond. She'd been looking over her shoulder, expecting the worst, for four days now, ever since seeing Candace Livingston's body. She'd managed to keep her fears from Ryan. Maybe keeping them from Oscar Guzman, a cop who wouldn't go away, was a mistake. Inside her, the terror festered.

Larry could be somewhere nearby, watching her, wondering why she was spending so much time with a cop. In truth, if Larry had the ability to get this close to her car and money—heck, to her father and Jedidiah Carraby—he could get close to her.

Oscar returned his cell phone to his back pocket. The New Mexico sun shone behind him. His eyebrows weren't nearly as bushy as she'd made them out to be. His hair was longer than that first impression, and the tousled look might be something he should attempt more often.

Maybe, though, she didn't need to tell him the truth. Possibly he'd figure it out himself.

He paused, and she knew he was hoping for a response from her. No matter how good-looking, no matter how polite and caring, he was still a cop. Definitely so, because his next sentence was "Maybe it was the murderer, but maybe it was your ex-husband."

Right on both counts.

CHAPTER FOURTEEN

THE LOOK SHE gave him proved one thing. Her ex-husband scared her more than the thought of a murderer in the neighborhood.

And maybe she should be scared. He'd just found a GPS tracking device on her gas tank. Oscar assumed it was Larry Wagner taking an interest in his ex-wife's whereabouts. But why? Wouldn't Larry have left this town and all his victims behind?

"So, could your ex-husband have done this?" He asked the question, searching her face, trying to decide if he wanted to tell her about the GPS tracking device. One thing for sure—he didn't want to scare her into premature labor. She had enough on her plate. He just kept adding more.

She looked at Oscar as if expecting help.

"Why would he want to disable my car?" Shelley asked, her voice soft and raspy.

"You tell me," Oscar suggested.

"I don't know."

"That it was him who did it, or you don't know why he'd want to scare you?" Oscar asked.

"I don't want to talk about my ex-husband."

"You're going to have to. This is no longer a simple car breakdown but vandalism. The brooch turning up is also a big concern. If your ex-husband is back in the area, we might have an opportunity to catch him. We'll need your help."

"I gave my help last time you went after my husband. It did no good and made me a nervous wreck. I can't afford the mental anguish." She looked from him to her stomach and back to him. "I can't offer my help."

"You might not have a choice," he advised.

"There's always a choice." She turned and headed for the stairs to her apartment, leaving Oscar watching her retreat.

"I just wish," Oscar muttered under his breath, taking one step in her direction. Her apartment door slammed, a clear message that she didn't want anyone to follow.

Oscar opted to drive the SUV back to his aunt and handed her the keys. She took them and said, "Jack's in the living room."

"Did he book a room?"

"Yes."

"And Tiffany?"

"She's here right now, but I don't see her staying long. We don't offer the kind of room accommodations she's used to."

Oscar paused in the doorway, taking out his cell phone and sending a quick text to Townley letting him know about the GPS tracker. Then, stepping into the living room, Oscar walked over to Jack and sat beside the man. Jack was staring at his hands and didn't look up. Peeve trotted in and sat to the left of Oscar, politely waiting for attention. Oscar knew how important a moment of silence could be, and he knew this man, knew how much he'd loved his daughter.

There'd been a time after he'd joined the service when Oscar felt detached from the people he worked with, worked for. Then, in Afghanistan, away from all he knew and loved, when Oscar'd had to follow orders, trust those in his company and get close to them—closer than he'd gotten to friends in the civilian world—he'd felt a shift in the way he looked at life.

In some ways, the military had saved him.

He'd never thought about why he'd been so gung ho to join. Maybe he'd been looking for his father, trying to find the man he re-

membered from childhood. The type of man
who wouldn't walk away from his wife and
children.

And along the way, Oscar'd gotten a taste
of how important it was to serve and protect.

It was too late for Candace but not too late
for Shelley.

Where had that thought come from? He
was getting too attached to Shelley, and the
sooner he admitted it, the sooner he could
maybe deal with it.

"Jack," Oscar finally said, "we're doing everything we can to find out who committed
this awful crime, and when we do…"

Jack looked up, eyes red-rimmed, cheeks
splotchy.

"I'd ask you how you're holding up." Oscar
cleared his throat. "But I already know the
answer."

"What's happening with the case?" Jack's
voice was thready. The man was battling for
composure. "What do you know besides what
the news has been reporting? I want the truth.
All of it."

"We're calling it a home invasion," Oscar
said. "We're looking for a male, probably a
small male."

"What did he take?"

"As soon as Cody is out of the hospital, he'll go through the house. It was torn up, although we're not sure what the person was looking for. Nothing seemed missing from her purse. Her wallet was there with fifteen dollars, her credit cards and driver's license. There's plenty of jewelry in her top dresser drawer."

Jack's hands balled into tight fists. "That's where she always kept it."

"We've sent her personal computer to a lab. The television and cell phone were untouched."

"So, no fingerprints?"

"Not on the furniture. We've taken an impression from the nylon shirt she was wearing, but not a solid print. We've been able to ascertain only hand size. That's how we know the assailant was small."

"Could it be a woman?" Jack asked.

"Possibly," Oscar said. "We also believe that if something was taken, the culprit either knew where it was…or she might have been forced to tell him where it was," Oscar admitted, not liking the word *forced* but knowing Jack wouldn't want him to sugarcoat.

"Is—" Jack stumbled "—is Cody a suspect?

Has he been one hundred percent cleared? Is there any doubt? I—I don't believe he did this."

"He's given us his itinerary and everything checks out. Plus his hand size isn't a match."

"Why wasn't he home with her?" Jack burst out.

Slowly and carefully, Oscar shared what they knew about Cody's activities, including his desire to make more money and move Candace away from Sarasota Falls.

"I told them," Jack said. "I told them I'd help. I'd have purchased them a house just down from me, us, and Cody could have worked for me at the office. But no, they wanted to make it on their own."

Oscar's aunt came in with a tray. "Here's hot tea," she said, "and you both need to lie down and get some rest. You won't be any good at all if you don't take care of yourselves."

"I can't sleep." Jack accepted the tea.

Oscar stood, accepted a cup and said, "I'll take this to my room. I work graveyard shift again tonight, and you're right. I want to be ready both physically and mentally."

He and Peeve left them, with Bianca sitting next to Jack, patting his hand and telling him how awesome his daughter had been.

OSCAR WOKE ON his own, an hour before the alarm, and dressed for work. Thursday nights were sometimes busier, and since Candace's murder, there'd been an increase in crime. Burglaries had doubled. There'd been four reports yesterday. Oscar had also arrested three drunk drivers this past week.

Tonight he had more on his schedule than usual, and most of it had to do with Candace. Funny, he'd come here to get close to Shelley, and he finally was. Just not how he'd planned.

When he closed the door behind him, his watch read straight-up seven. The sun still shone and the quietness that had overtaken the neighborhood continued. It was a waiting kind of quiet and one he knew well. All he could do was put one foot in front of the other and hope he made the right decisions. He started by going to the Duponts' house. They were neighbors of Candace and Shelley. The Duponts had a twelve-year-old son who was in a wheelchair. The mother often took the boy for walks at odd hours.

"Tom was already here." Gerald Dupont was a slight man, pale, with soft hands. He led Oscar into an old-fashioned living room. "Not sure what else we can add. Told him everything."

Tom? Oscar had never heard Chief Riley referred to by his first name, not at the station or in town. When Oscar and Riley went anywhere together, everyone called him Riley.

Oscar sat on an olive green couch that had seen better days. Almost immediately Gerald's wife came in, handed Gerald a beer and asked Oscar if he wanted something to drink.

"No, thank you." Oscar took out the small notebook he kept in his shirt pocket. "I'm on duty, but please sit down. I have a couple of questions to ask you."

She glanced at her husband and hesitantly perched on the end of a flowered chair.

Oscar noted the exchange and was curious.

"I know that Chief Riley was here and asked questions. But I'm hoping to come at it from a different approach. You had met Candace and her husband, right?"

"Yes," Gerald said impatiently. "You know that. One time you participated in a conversation we had in front of her house while I was out walking with Timothy. You had your dog with you."

Oscar remembered. Gerald Dupont hadn't liked his conversation with Candace interrupted, and Peeve hadn't been impressed with the man. "Right," Oscar said. "Besides then, did you talk to her?"

"No."

"How about you?" Oscar asked Mrs. Dupont, feeling even more strongly there was a story here and one that focused on her husband.

"Nothing more than a wave as Timothy and I explored the neighborhood together. When we found out the extent of Timothy's prognosis, I quit work. Gerald's busy earning a living, and I take care of Timothy."

Except for the one time Gerald did it two weeks ago. Oscar hadn't thought much of it, but now he wondered why Gerald had been taking Timothy on a walk.

Maybe Gerald had wanted to meet Candace and had seen her in the front yard, gardening.

"Did you and Timothy go for a walk on Sunday evening or Monday morning?" Oscar pushed away a lock of hair tickling his forehead. He could feel the first faint traces of sweat starting to form.

"Both," Mrs. Dupont answered. "I try to take him outside three times a day."

"Did you see anything out of the ordinary?"

"No, not really," Mrs. Dupont admitted. "Do you think something happened Sunday night? It was really late when I took Timothy that night. Gerald wasn't feeling good, so I stuck around until he fell asleep. Then Timothy was cranky. It took me a while to get him in his chair. It was midnight by the time we took a look around the neighborhood."

Oscar had read the report. Almost word for word, Mrs. Dupont was sharing the information she'd shared with Riley.

"And Candace's light was on at midnight?"

"Yes, when we started out, but when we returned, it was off, and it couldn't have been more than a half hour. When it's that late, I don't stay out long. You never know what might happen."

Oscar decided not to mention that Mrs. Dupont had been safer outdoors than Candace had been indoors.

"Chief Riley seemed to focus his questions on Monday morning," Mrs. Dupont said. "I figured it was because the light had been turned off. There wouldn't be enough light for the killer to see. I told him that Timothy and I had gone our usual time then, just after seven. I try to get back by eight because

Timothy and I go into the city on Mondays for his therapy."

"Can't get any home health care here," Gerald said. "No one to do it."

Oscar knew that if someone wanted something bad enough, it could be arranged. He figured Gerald to be the kind of man who felt his wife should do everything. He also thought about Shelley and her adherence to schedules.

Carefully he recorded the times in his notebook. "Do you ever see Shelley Wagner when you're out on your walks?"

"No, Oscar, we don't," Gerald said. "We don't have the kind of money her husband seemed to be attracted to, and we're careful. I've told Julie to avoid the woman. We don't want trouble."

Ironically, it seemed to Oscar that this guy was trouble. He also wasn't much impressed that Gerald Dupont called him Oscar. It tended to make them peers, and Oscar didn't want to be this man's peer.

"I appreciate your time." Oscar stood, the room suddenly feeling cold even though the late evening held the remnant of the May sunshine. He'd get nothing from Mrs. Dupont while Mr. Dupont was in the room. Luckily he now knew that Julie Dupont walked Timothy at seven in the morning. Oscar was usually at work, but one day this week, he'd get off early and walk Peeve. They'd just happen to run into Mrs. Dupont, and Oscar could get his questions answered then.

After Gerald Dupont walked him to the door and firmly shut it behind him, Oscar took a deep breath. He'd started to feel claustrophobic. It had been a few months since the feeling of confinement had sent him onto the seat of his motorcycle and riding for hours until he chased away the demons that had followed him home from his last tour.

Abigail Simms, who lived across the street from Aunt Bianca, was next on the list. She welcomed him in, and his feelings of claustrophobia went away as she gave him bottled water, sat him in a flowery armchair and gave him a pleasing look when her poodle, Buttercup, jumped in his lap.

"Chief Riley's already spoken to me," she said. "Candace would come down here and ask me gardening questions. I actually went to the store with her and we picked out some perennials. Did you know she'd never worked in the dirt before?" Abigail Simms didn't wait for an answer. "Course, now that I know her father owns the Little Supermarket chain, I understand. They probably had a lawn service come in once a week to do everything. What's the fun in that?"

Oscar didn't have an answer. Growing up, he'd pulled weeds and dug holes. He hadn't enjoyed it at all.

"I told Chief Riley that I didn't notice anything out of the ordinary Monday morning, but at about five in the morning, Buttercup here started barking."

After saying goodbye to Abigail, Oscar took Peeve for a walk. The dog pulled at the leash, happy to be outside. Oscar was just as happy. When he got back to his aunt's, he grabbed one of her homemade brownies and sat at the kitchen table, adding details to his notebook. Once he got to work, he'd type them into the timeline he'd created on his computer.

His cell sounded before he finished. "Where you at?" Riley queried.

"I've been working. I've spoken with both the Duponts and Abigail Simms."

"I already did that," Riley protested.

"Since they're neighbors, I thought they might remember a few details once prompted."

"Either of them confess?"

Oscar snorted. "Abigail's mourning the loss of a fellow gardener, and as for the Duponts…"

"He's a piece of work."

"I wondered if you knew them well. He kept calling you by your first name. Then he did it to me."

"They've been in Sarasota Falls only ten years."

"What does he do? I don't remember."

"He's an insurance agent and has an office downtown. He also owns the laundry and dry-cleaning store right next to it."

"I can't see him working in a dry-cleaning store."

Riley laughed. "He has three employees working for him, and I doubt he's paying them what they're worth."

"I hear you. Have you checked him for priors?" Oscar asked.

Riley returned, "You telling me my job?"

"No," Oscar said slowly, wishing he were on equal footing with Riley. It would make things so much easier.

"Good. Of course I ran him. He's got a few speeding tickets and one disorderly conduct."

"For what?"

Riley chuckled. "Public urination."

Oscar shook his head. "There's nothing on his record mentioning his wife?"

"You picked up on that, too? No, nothing."

Over the phone, Oscar could hear someone talking to Riley, and the other officer gave a few curt orders. Then he got back on the line. "Two things. One, the brooch is a fake. How did you know?"

"Shelley told me to check it out," Oscar replied. "She said it was just the way her mind worked."

"What do *you* think?" Riley queried.

"I think we know Shelley is afraid of something. Only problem is, why would Larry Wagner return a useless brooch? Why put himself in danger of getting caught?"

"Larry is very capable of and enjoys playing mind games."

"This worries me," Oscar said. "He's trying to scare Shelley, and it's working. She's eight months pregnant."

Riley snorted. "Don't tell me what I already know. Look, you've been spending time with her, earning her trust. Find out what's going on, and do it quickly before something happens. In the meantime, we have an accident out on the 285. No injuries, but a truck hauling baby pigs—of all things—tipped over, and we've got about two thousand pigs to catch."

"Can you call an animal control—"

"Small town," Riley reminded him. "We *are* animal control. I'm heading out there now."

"I can go."

"No, I need you to concentrate on this case. Every hour that goes by means Candace's killer is walking free."

Oscar agreed and ended the call. As soon as Shelley finally did open up to Oscar, he'd find and shut down Larry Wagner, and then Sarasota Falls would become a memory, pigs and all.

And because Shelley was part of Sarasota Falls, it would be a memory Oscar wouldn't be able to forget.

CHAPTER FIFTEEN

FRIDAY MORNING, Shelley walked Ryan to school and then sat on a bench outside and stared at her phone. She felt safe here as parents were in and out, dropping off their children. A few gave tentative waves, but no one came to sit by her.

"I wish I could get rid of this phone," she muttered. There were six messages waiting for her: one from Chief Riley and five from Oscar. She hadn't answered any of them, including the one from last night.

Deputy Guzman, she corrected herself.

The man who'd said, *"Maybe it was the murderer, but maybe it was your ex-husband."*

He was figuring things out without her help. No way, though, would Larry believe that. Fear settled in the pit of her stomach. It was getting to the point that she no longer knew what it was like not to be afraid. She'd been trying so hard to hope and pretend that nothing was wrong. Then it wouldn't be wrong. But she knew two terrible but true things. One, odds were her father hadn't wandered away from the care center on his own accord last Tuesday. Two, Larry had wiped out her bank account on the same day. According to the bank president, her old boss, the withdrawal had happened online in a bank transfer. Already the account it had transferred to had been closed. Her old boss doubted it had been a data breach. It wasn't phishing; it was outright fraud.

He hadn't come out and said that her ex-husband had relieved her of the money, but she'd worked at the bank and knew had she been in his position, she'd be thinking it.

She made a note to have her cell phone number changed yet again, but it was a Band-Aid, not a fix. It wouldn't keep Larry from finding her. Heck, he could get to her bank account even after she'd changed the name on it. He already knew where she was, was even using her dad as collateral.

What she should have done was turn the phone over to the police the minute she'd received his first text. They might have been able to trace his call and arrest him. Something they hadn't managed to do six months ago.

Eight months ago, though, her ex-husband

hadn't threatened her. And since Larry had walked away from Ryan, Shelley understood that to Larry's way of thinking, the boy was inconsequential.

She felt like her feet were in wet cement. If she stepped from the mixture, she'd only drag her problems with her. Sure, she could cover up her transgressions, but they would always be with her.

If she stayed, nothing changed.

Nothing changed.

Except she'd have to live with herself.

"Shelley?"

Looking up, Shelley saw Rick Vaniper. He'd been a few years ahead of her in school and had attended her church, but she knew him better now. His grandfather was in the same care facility as her dad, and he'd been ripped off by her ex-husband.

"Rick, how are you doing?"

"Not too good." He sat next to her.

Shelley shifted uncomfortably. The last hundred times people she knew said those words to her, they were followed by a story about what her ex-husband had done to them.

"You know my brother."

"Yes." Rick's brother was the last person Larry could con. Rick's younger brother, who might be all of twenty, owned nothing but a drug problem.

"He showed up at the care center last night. Looking for cash and whatever else he could get his hands on."

"I'm sorry. I know he's done that a few times."

"Officer Guzman caught up to him pretty fast. I guess my brother took a swing at the policeman, and now he's in jail."

"Maybe your brother will get the help he needs," Shelley offered.

"I hope. Dad couldn't make it down to check on Grandpa last night, so I went. I got there right when they were leading my brother out. He made quite a mess. Your dad got in the middle of it."

"What?"

"Oh, your dad's not hurt. He was in the piano room when my brother arrived. My brother was so hyped up, he didn't realize that your dad wasn't Grandpa."

"They don't look anything alike."

"No, they don't. What I wanted to tell you, though, is your dad said something that really struck me. See, my brother kept trying to get to him. It scared your dad a bit. But Officer Guzman stood in the way."

Officer Guzman, whose call she hadn't returned because her fear of Larry was keeping her from getting important calls that might pertain to her father. Officer Guzman, who seemed always to be where she needed him to be and willing to help.

"After my brother was handcuffed," Rick continued, "your dad followed Officer Guzman out the door and said to my brother, 'I forgive you.'"

"Dad never was one to hold a grudge."

"It made me think about how of all people at the care center for my brother to mess with, it had to be your dad. You've gone through enough."

He didn't know the half of it.

"Anyway, I just wanted to tell you that my wife and I were talking, and if you need anything, a babysitter or just a friend, come on by. One thing my brother has taught us is you can't always control what the people you love do and that you shouldn't judge."

"Thanks."

He stood, pushing himself off the bench and rubbing his forehead. "Last night was a mess. I had to check on Grandpa, fill out forms and then call my dad and tell him the bad news. Dad's not bailing my brother out this time. Our son's turning four tomorrow. I'm supposed to be ordering a cake, but it's the last thing I feel like doing, and I'm late for work."

"My mom used to make cakes."

"I remember. Your mom made the best chocolate muffins. Sometimes my mom used to stop by your house on the way home from work to buy a couple to surprise me, and…"

Looked like she wasn't the only one who stumbled when talking about family members who messed up.

"You know," she said, "my mother taught me everything she knew. I can make the cake. I'll give you a fair price."

"You'd do that?"

"I need the money," she admitted.

He pulled out his wallet, peeled off two twenties, handed them to her and asked, "When can you have it done?"

"What time do you get off work?"

"About six," he said.

"What kind of design were you hoping for?" she asked.

"Legos."

"Done. Pick it up after six." Shelley stood, too, using the bench as a crutch. She was feeling more and more pregnant, and moving wasn't as easy. Baking, though, she could handle.

It felt a little like betrayal to use the grocery store close to the preschool instead of Little's. It was smaller and a bit more expensive. But she was without a vehicle and crunched for time. Funny, perusing the baking aisle brought back memories of being with her mom, when everyone was healthy and happy. She'd sold most of her mom's cooking utensils. Luckily, a Lego cake was fairly simple.

She'd no more stepped out of the store than a squad car pulled in front of her and Oscar lowered the window. He accused her, "You're still not answering my calls."

"Sorry. I just met Rick Vaniper. He told me what happened last night."

"I was heading to your place to tell you in person. I let the care center know I'd notify you. Your dad's fine."

"I hear you stepped in front of him."

Oscar laughed. "There really wasn't much of a need. Rick's brother took a swing at me and immediately toppled over and fell. I think it was the most entertainment the care center's had in months."

"Since the last time he was there." She remembered one of the nurses telling her that Rick's brother had stolen Mr. Vaniper's Purple Heart medal. The staff had taken the theft harder than Mr. Vaniper, who'd thought the crowd around him wanted to hear him play the piano, so he had.

"Hop in. I'll give you a ride home."

She hesitated only a moment. She had quite a few items in her grocery bag, and time was flying by. The ride was an answer to an unasked prayer.

"I liked Rick Vaniper," Oscar said. "He seemed to have his head on his shoulders. What happened to his brother? Do you know?"

"No, no one does. Up until he was sixteen, he was fine. He just hopped on the party train and never got off."

"I've known a few people like that."

For the first time, Shelley didn't feel uncomfortable in the squad car. Maybe because for the first time, she was in the front seat. It wasn't cramped, but no way could she spread out, either. Some sort of monitor was mounted on a steel lever. Every once in a while Oscar glanced at it, but nothing seemed to need his attention. Beneath the dashboard was a radio. Unlike on television, it wasn't sputtering out the need for Oscar to respond to a crime scene, nor did it report the whereabouts of other officers.

"Are you off duty?" she asked.

"Pretty much. I'm coming in from near the county line. A truck carrying baby pigs overturned last night. Riley got most of them, but a few were still loose this morning, so he and I engaged in a little pig rodeoing."

"You had to catch pigs?"

"Yes, ma'am. You're looking at Sarasota Falls' number one champion pig catcher." He used an old-fashioned Western accent and winked, making her smile.

He wasn't like any cop she knew. Any man, either. He had a seriousness about him that made him seem mature, although she knew only four years separated them. Yet he could be funny, right when she needed him to be.

"Yes. Life is never boring in a small town."

He pulled up in front of Robert Tellmaster's house. Quickly he was out the door, opening hers and then carrying her grocery bag up the apartment stairs.

"I found out something interesting yesterday," he said while waiting for her to unlock the door.

"What?"

He stepped over a brown stuffed animal and a stack of Legos in order to put the bag on her kitchen table. "Jedidiah Carraby's brooch is fake. Just like you thought. Want to share what gave you the idea?"

"If it were real, he'd have kept better track of it," she said.

He changed the subject. "Oh, and remember, you told me that you heard a dog barking at five in the morning on the day Candace was killed. Abigail Simms says her dog started barking at the same time."

"You think that has something to do with the murder?" Shelley reached in the bag and started unloading items.

He pulled out a chair and sat down before answering. "It could mean that there was suspicious activity going on. Someone coming or going."

"Interesting. You learn anything else?"

"No."

She knew doubt when she heard it. Still, this whole conversation was about Candace, not about her, and she wanted him to catch the killer. Really wanted him to catch the killer. Only without her help.

"How much do you know about the Duponts?" he asked.

"They moved here right before I started junior high, I think." The last of the items out of the bag, she folded it and stuck it under the sink, then sat across from him, glad to be off her feet, before continuing. "My mom took them a cake. The husband opened the door, and Mom handed him the cake. He didn't invite her in. She said she didn't feel very welcome."

Oscar nodded but said, "What about since you moved to this location? Have you spoken to either of them?"

"The woman walks her son three times a day. Morning, noonish and late evening. I've nodded at her, but she tends to move fast. I've seen the man do it only twice. He always seemed to have an agenda."

"What do you mean?"

"One time he stopped me as Ryan and I were getting into the car. He said he was sorry about all that happened to me and if I needed anything, he'd be glad to help."

"And that made you feel like he had an agenda?"

Shelley thought back to the incident. "No, it made me feel like he was coming on to me in a sleazy way."

Oscar raised an eyebrow. "He was hitting on you?"

"It's been known to happen a time or two," Shelley protested and laughed. "Married men do hit on women who aren't their wives."

"Yes, but…" Oscar looked at her stomach.

"Okay," she admitted, "now you see why it felt so sleazy."

"Did he threaten you?"

"No. I told him that I was busy and would be busy for the next eighteen years."

"Harsh."

Shelley liked the look that accompanied the word. It was approving. Still, she hesitated before saying more. She was, after all, confiding in a cop, and yes, anything she said could and would be used against her in a court of law. But what exactly was she sharing, and could it help?

"I learned the hard way," she admitted, "that being nice just makes the inevitable long and drawn out. I didn't want that man anywhere near me. But in his defense, he merely nodded and walked away. He hasn't bothered me since."

Shelley peered at the huge window overlooking the street. "I can see quite a bit. Mr. Dupont left his house, came to talk to me and then went right back home. Not much of an outing for his son. The only other time I saw him walking the boy, he went over to your friend Candace's place. She was outside gardening. He left his son in the wheelchair on the sidewalk and came to crouch down by her. After a moment, she shook a shovel at him, and he went back to his son and high-tailed it home."

"You think he pulled the same thing on Candace as he did you?"

"Sure looked that way."

"You think she felt threatened?"

"Not really. I watched her, and she handled it much better than I did."

"What do you mean?"

"After he walked away, she just laughed it off. She thought whatever he'd said was funny."

Oscar leaned forward. "That could have stuck with him."

"I never saw him bother her again."

"But you haven't been in this apartment very long. There could have been other encounters you don't know about."

The baby moved, sliding a foot across her abdomen in what felt like a gentle caress.

Something Candace Livingston would never get to experience.

"You and Candace were friends," Shelley said. "If she felt threatened by Mr. Dupont, she'd have told you, wouldn't she? Before that, she would have told her husband."

Oscar took his notebook out of his shirt pocket. She watched him write in tiny block letters. While he concentrated on his job, she started organizing her purchases. Funny, his presence should have been making her nervous, but it wasn't. When he finally finished writing, he yawned—looking suddenly younger—and watched her for a while before asking, "What are you going to make?"

"A birthday cake for Rick Vaniper's son."

"Cool. That's nice of you."

"Not so nice. I charged him."

Oscar didn't look surprised. Instead, he merely nodded.

"I think I might even try to revive my mother's career. I still have most of her recipes, and I remember what she charged. I need to earn a living, and I can do this at home."

She looked at the tiny kitchen. Sure, she could make a birthday cake, but she had a two-burner stove and an oven that made a child's Easy-Bake look upscale.

"Make me some chocolate muffins. A dozen. Charge me the going rate." He scooted back, the chair legs dragging against the floor as he stood, yawning again before offering, "Should I tell my aunt what you're doing? I know she'll be interested."

"That would be great." She followed him to the door and held it open as he exited. He paused before going down the first step.

Maybe he felt like she did.

She didn't want him to leave. She, in just this short time, had started to like having him around.

But he was a cop, and she was keeping a potential murderer's secret.

"Candace's memorial is next Friday. Come with me."

"Oh, no. I really didn't know her."

"I realize that. But you might see somebody in the audience who'd visited the house. Please. We'd appreciate your help. Candace…"

It was the look on his face that had her nodding. She wished there was someone in her life who cared that much, felt that much.

She stood at the door until he'd gotten in his squad car and driven down the street and out of sight. Slowly, from the opposite direc-

tion, came a white SUV with tinted windows.
It paused in front of her apartment and then
continued on, picking up speed.

CHAPTER SIXTEEN

OSCAR WORKED THE whole weekend, both Friday night and Saturday. Ten-hour shifts turned into twelve, then fourteen, and he had to satisfy himself with driving by Shelley's apartment. Oh, he'd called twice, but no surprise, she didn't answer his calls. He wondered what it would take.

Once he caught a glimpse of her and Ryan at the park. They were off to the side, away from the other moms and kids. Why? She'd grown up in the town. He'd slowed, looking for a place to park, but then she'd seen him and instead of smiling a welcome, she'd turned away.

He figured that she didn't want to be seen with a cop. He didn't blame her. With all she'd gone through, him in the squad car and in uniform would mean questions she didn't want to answer.

Still, it bothered him how she separated

herself. When would the townspeople realize they were punishing the wrong person?

Her loser of an ex-husband was the real
culprit.

He spent the next few hours wishing he
hadn't signed on with the police department
so that his only job would be watching over
Shelley Brubaker. Then he felt guilty because
working for the police department meant he
had a part in solving Candace's murder.

It also meant he had hours alone to think.

He came to the decision he didn't really
like being alone.

Monday morning he arrived home just
after ten.

"About time you're here," his aunt called.
"I'll cook you breakfast."

"Just toast. I want to shower and get to
bed."

Apparently his aunt agreed. "Shower first.
Then breakfast."

He almost fell asleep standing under the
relaxing, hot jets of water.

He was toweling his hair dry when he
joined his aunt. "Jack still here?" he asked
after acknowledging Peeve, who was looking for some attention.

"I've never heard a dog talk like yours,"

Aunt Bianca said. "Jack's over at Cody's. The medical examiner released the body. The two men are finishing up burial arrangements."

"I heard," Oscar said. "They're aiming for Friday. You want to drive up with me. Shelley's coming along, too."

"Well, well," his aunt said. Oscar didn't like the sound of it. Probably because she was picking up on a truth he couldn't accept.

"She's coming as a witness," Oscar protested. "She's supposed to see if she recognizes anyone who might have visited the Livingstons."

"Yeah, right."

"I've been meaning to tell you," he said after finishing his second piece of toast. "Shelley's planning on resurrecting her mother's home bakery business. I told her you might be interested in placing an order."

"Shelley, first name, huh?"

"I'm watching over her as part of my job. Two syllables are a lot easier to say than five."

"Sure," Aunt Bianca said. "I suppose you want me to order more chocolate muffins?"

"More?"

"She delivered twelve Saturday afternoon. The bill is on the kitchen counter. I ordered some cookies and bread. We won't have a full house for the next month or two. I'll order more when business picks up."

"Go ahead and order more now. I'll pay for it."

"It's not the money," Aunt Bianca said. "They would go bad."

"Not the chocolate muffins," Oscar predicted.

Upstairs, something thudded to the ground. Aunt Bianca looked up, rolled her eyes and said, "Tiffany is packing."

"So Jack's leaving once the service is over?"

"I'm not sure. Especially since Cody says he can't leave until the investigation is closed."

"How's he feeling?"

"I imagine pretty wretched. He slept here Friday night and didn't get up until Saturday afternoon."

"You're kidding. How did I miss that?"

"Too many hours, not enough sleep," his aunt said simply.

"You ever have an encounter with Gerald Dupont?" he asked.

"No. I don't see him much. I do know he doesn't help his wife much with Timmy."

"You ever talk to her?"

"No. I took food over when they first moved in and invited them here for a meal. I found my casserole dish on the front porch two days later. Once I saw her at the grocery store and tried to invite her again. They're not interested in socializing."

"Can you guess why?"

"No." Aunt Bianca leaned close. "You going to tell me?"

"I wish I knew the answer. I spoke to the Duponts and to Abigail Simms. The only information I came away with—and you may not share this—was that Abigail's dog barked at five in the morning. There's some chance it was due to something unusual going on."

"I didn't hear anything, but then, I slept through the explosion two years ago."

Oscar knew she was talking about Abigail Simms's water heater exploding at two in the morning and rocketing through the roof. Aunt Bianca hadn't awakened in spite of her living room window shattering or the sirens that shrieked through the neighborhood shortly after. Not good for a bed-and-breakfast proprietor.

"You know, Aunt Bianca, I don't care that you sleep like the dead. I'm just glad you're out and about during the day. I've got a job for you."

She leaned forward, eager. "What?"

"I want you to keep an eye on the neighborhood. Don't let anyone know. Get a notebook or use a computer spreadsheet. I don't care. I want to know the comings and goings of the people on this street, especially the Duponts and Simms."

"Abigail Simms? Really?"

"More her dog and absent son," Oscar cautioned, wondering if he'd made a mistake.

"Her son's too lazy to commit murder," Aunt Bianca scoffed. Then she stood, fetched a spiral notebook and went to the front window. She was already taking too much pleasure in her new task than he was comfortable with. The last thing he wanted was his aunt winding up in some kind of danger.

"How fun," she said.

"Not fun—serious," he reminded her, feeling a bit of role reversal. He'd never imagined he'd be telling his aunt what to do and feeling a bit like reprimanding her for being too free-spirited.

"Anything to help Candace."

"And you can't let Jack Little know what you're doing," Oscar cautioned.

"I should ask him to help. The man's more wound up than you, and that's saying something. His wife checking out isn't helping."

"You're not a marriage counselor," Oscar reminded her.

"Maybe the woman's bored," Aunt Bianca reasoned.

Oscar reminded himself that he wasn't a marriage counselor, either, and that he, too, often compared Tiffany with Jack's second wife, Candace's mother. Stepmother, really, but only in words, not actions. Valerie legally adopted Candace, but that was only paperwork. Her heart had sealed the deal. She'd died just over a year ago: car accident.

Adjectives he'd heard to describe wife number three were *self-possessed*, *vain*, *uncaring* and *selfish*. Tiffany thought that gorgeous made up for her shortcomings. Not in Oscar's book. Not in Candace's, either. One reason why she and Cody had moved to Sarasota Falls.

For the next few days, Cody and Jack planned a memorial, Aunt Bianca patrolled the neighborhood, often with Peeve by her side, and Oscar kept his eyes on Shelley.

Every once in a while, his hands were on her, too. Never inappropriately. But he liked helping her up the stairs because he needed to make sure no one had access to her apartment. He liked brushing a bit of chocolate off her cheek after she'd baked something. A few times Oscar had really let loose with Ryan: running through the apartment, swinging the boy in the air—tossing him and catching him—and then both of them falling to the ground laughing. Watching Ryan and him roughhouse seemed the best way to get her to relax. He could tell.

It didn't inspire her to let him stay long. She always seemed to be looking out the window, the expression on her face indicating she expected a storm.

A bad one.

Which didn't explain why she routinely hustled him out of her apartment after only a few minutes.

Friday morning, Oscar grabbed a muffin from the kitchen and headed out the door. It was ten in the morning, the neighborhood was empty, and daytime gave Oscar even more opportunities to figure out what had happened to Candace. Her funeral was tonight. He dreaded it.

He climbed on his motorcycle and headed for work. He slowed the Harley down when he got to Shelley's apartment. He wanted nothing more than to run up the stairs and see what she was doing. One of these days he'd like to do something fun with her, like take her to a movie or dinner or even to play putt-putt golf. Right now, the mixed feelings he had kept him from asking for what felt like a date. Didn't keep him from spending time with her, though.

Ordinary concerns in an extraordinary time.

He sped up and went to the station. Riley was in his office, talking on the phone and fingering a file that he closed when Oscar came in the room. After hanging up, Riley got right to the point. "The prints on the back of Candace's nylon shirt don't belong to Shelley. They were slightly bigger." Riley sounded resigned.

Oscar hadn't for a moment thought there would be a match. Still, he studied the film hanging on the whiteboard in Riley's office. It was a bit like an X-ray but greener. A ruler had been affixed to the paper. In black ink, it said "7.2 inches."

"An average-size man has a hand measuring 7.4 inches," Riley said.

"That might eliminate Abigail Simms's

son. He's a big guy," Oscar reasoned. "But what about Gerald Dupont?"

"I didn't know they were suspects," Riley said. "Where is that written down? Not in any of your reports you've turned in to me."

"Nothing definite to report," Oscar said easily. "I was investigating. Still am investigating. And I'm also thinking about who could be a suspect."

"You might have a hard time with Abigail's son. He spent the night in jail, which makes quite an alibi."

Oscar said, "I'll add that information to my notes."

"Do that. And most likely, Dupont didn't kill Candace," Riley said.

"How—"

"Gerald Dupont has heart disease." Riley took a notebook out of his pocket. Oscar had never noticed the chief utilize it before. Now Riley read, "'Atrial fibrillation. A type of arrhythmia.'" Looking at Oscar, Riley said, "If Gerald Dupont exerted himself, he'd be asking for a heart attack."

"Is that why he seldom walks his son?"

"Yes. And it's why he has employees to do all the heavy lifting for him. He's mostly the man pushing papers at the desk."

"But he hit on—"

"Should we arrest him for that?"

"No, but—"

"You're indignant because Candace was a close friend and because you're getting too close to Shelley Wagner. And why exactly are you getting so close to Shelley? It's become an obsession. It has nothing to do with the Livingston case, does it?"

"It has everything to do with Candace's case. Shelley not only found the body but also sees what's going on in the neighborhood."

"If she sees everything, why didn't she see who killed Candace?"

"We'll find that out tonight. I'm taking her to Candace's memorial."

Riley shook his head. "You're either brilliant for a rookie, or you're not a rookie."

"I don't know what I am anymore," Oscar said. "I just know I have to solve this case before I lose track of who I am and what I want."

Riley looked like he wanted to ask something else, but the phone rang, and the moment was lost.

Good thing, because Oscar wouldn't have been able to answer another question without lying. No, he wasn't a rookie. And yes, he was obsessed with Shelley.

She was chipping away at defenses he'd put in place long ago, making him believe that he was a hero not because he was watching over her but because he cared.

Really cared.

For her.

CHAPTER SEVENTEEN

RUNYAN, NEW MEXICO, was twice the size of Sarasota Falls. Shelley had never visited it before. No need. Tonight, in a dark blue dress and sensible shoes, she held Ryan's hand and followed Oscar into a pretty church with a white steeple and a huge parking lot.

"You're not getting by me without a hug." The words came from a woman about four-foot-eight, who weighed maybe eighty pounds and who sported shock white hair.

"And I never want to." Oscar grinned, lifting the woman in a hug that had her feet dangling.

For all that, he was amazingly gentle, because the woman had to be in her eighties or nineties. Shelley almost scolded Oscar. This was a funeral! But when he set the woman down, she said, "I've organized the meal. It will happen about two hours after the burial. I can't believe Candy is gone."

No one, in Shelley's presence, had called the dead woman Candy.

"When I think about how Candy and that sister of yours would come over to my house and learn to sew and eat supper with me, well, what's happened to her makes me ill."

Before Oscar could introduce Shelley, another older woman stepped up for the same kind of hug, and soon Oscar and Shelley stopped every three or four steps, greeting people, him introducing Shelley and accepting handshakes, hugs and always condolences. It was a side of him she'd not yet seen. Hometown boy. It was easy to tell he was well liked.

Oscar's aunt Bianca was getting plenty of hugs, too, before she slipped off to find Oscar's mother. Shelley accepted a few, but most people recognized that when she stepped back, it was a sign she didn't want hugs. Ryan held out his hand for a shake. Didn't matter age or gender.

The church she and her family once went to was small, maybe two hundred people. Walking into the foyer, signing her name in the guest register and feeling Oscar's hand on her back, she realized she'd missed attending services, missed hearing the snippets of conversation about who was on vacation, who was seeing who and how everyone was feeling.

Another thing Larry had taken from her. She'd complained that the townspeople of Sarasota Falls hadn't forgiven her, but she hadn't forgiven herself.

"I'm not sure I should be here," she whispered to Oscar. "I really didn't know Candace. And I'm not walking by the casket."

"You don't have to. You're supposed to view living people," Oscar reminded her. "Tell me if you see anyone who visited the Livingstons or that you saw in the neighborhood."

Shelley nodded, holding Ryan's hand and heading for a pew in the back. Oscar nodded in return, figuring it would be easier to spot people if they were in front of her.

"I should go sit with my family," Oscar explained.

He hesitated, looking beyond her at the foyer still full of people and then at the church already crowded. He gave the church a scan, his eyes pausing at a point near her.

She looked, too, but didn't see anything. Just people either whispering to each other or sitting silently. Another family with children shared her pew. At the end was a lone man.

She'd never seen any of them before. Oscar sat down beside her. Before he could settle in, someone called his name, and after a moment she watched him set up folding chairs. She'd forgotten how well-known Candace's family was. They just might need a bigger church.

She handed Ryan her phone, knowing he liked to watch cartoons on it and didn't mind if there was no volume. She'd take it back when the service started. Even at this young age, Ryan should be learning respect. Looking around, she saw lots of respect. People had their heads down, praying. Others held their heads high with a few tears wet on their cheeks.

A hush seemed to sweep the room. Shelley watched as Cody walked down the aisle flanked by a couple who must be his mom and dad. Judging by how pale he was, it was good he had their support. Three young men who looked a lot like him followed. She scanned the memorial card she'd picked up when she'd signed the guest book. It not only proclaimed Cody a loving husband but also mentioned his family, brothers. It proclaimed that Candace was an only child like Shelley was. Both Candace and Cody were born and raised in Runyan.

At the front of the church, Cody was talking with Jack Little and his wife, Tiffany. Both men were openly crying. From the last time Shelley had spoken with Candace's father to now, the man seemed to have aged twenty years. Wife number three, Tiffany, looked like she belonged standing next to Cody instead of Jack Little. Shelley glanced at her simple one-piece dress, nylons and flats.

Black was no longer the only color of mourning. The congregation wore muted colors, lots of grays and dark blues. Tiffany Little, however, wore a glossy emerald green with some sort of sequins at her shoulders. She leaned toward her husband, patted him on the shoulder and giggled.

Giggled?

"Even at a funeral, she has to stand out." The words weren't bitter, more amazed. Shelley looked up at a short black-haired woman with red-rimmed eyes and thick eyebrows who was taking Oscar's place. "I'm Anna Guzman, Oscar's sister."

"I'd have recognized you anywhere," Shelley said, scooting over.

Anna had paper towels in her hand and was using them for tissues. "And me, you. Oscar talks about you. First time he's ever shared details about somebody in a case he's working on." Anna blew her nose. "At first I thought it had to do with Candace's murder, but then I realized it was more."

Shelley didn't know how to respond. She was more than eight months pregnant, tired and scared, and knew it was the absolute worst timing for falling in love.

So she wasn't going to.

"The news said—" Anna started and then began again. "The news said…said…that you found… Candace's body."

Shelley nodded.

"Just tell me—she was my best friend and I loved her—did she suffer?"

Shelley closed her eyes. She'd been asked this more than a dozen times at her mother's funeral. Yes, her mother had suffered, not pain-wise but in knowing she wouldn't get to see her only daughter married, grandchildren, grow old next to her husband. "I don't think so," Shelley said. "I didn't see much, but if I had to guess, I'd say everything happened quickly."

"A cop from Sarasota Falls came down and spoke to those of us who were close to Candace. Really, she didn't have an enemy. She was from the wealthiest family in town, maybe in the state, but she was down-to-earth, caring and fun."

"I could tell that."

"She and Cody were together from the time we were in high school."

Shelley nodded.

"I was her maid of honor."

"I'm so sorry."

"She would have been mine, too."

"Oscar told me how close you were."

"She thought she was pregnant and hadn't even told Cody. Just me. She said she was tired all the time and feeling a little off in the mornings."

Pregnant?

If that were true, then Larry really was a monster.

"AUNT BIANCA'S STAYING with my mother tonight," Oscar said, situating a sleeping Ryan in his car seat.

"How will she get home?"

"Someone will bring her, or I'll fetch her."

Shelley nodded. It had been a long evening. After the viewing, there'd been a meal. Shelley'd met every member of his family and then some. Ryan had played and played and played until he came and crawled in Shelley's lap. He didn't fit, so he crawled in Oscar's and fell asleep. Oscar'd been carrying him ever since.

It appeared to Shelley that Ryan had found a pillar to lean on.

The moon was full, and there were plenty of cars on the highway.

"Most of these are people heading home," Oscar observed. "There were visitors from all the way in Arizona."

"Candace was well liked," Shelley noted. "I'll miss her."

Silence followed. After a few minutes, Shelley said, "Your sister mentioned that Candace might be pregnant."

Oscar's foot pressed down on the gas pedal before he could recover. "No, she wasn't. The medical examiner would have noted it."

"Phew. I was worried."

"Why? Why would that make you worry?" Oscar passed a car driving too slow. His headlights swept an empty field. Next to it, a house stood. The inside lights were on, and Oscar could see a family gathered around a table. He glanced over at Shelley. She'd noticed, too.

Then she took a deep breath, and the words

seemed to burst out of her. "I thought maybe Candace was pregnant. And if that was true, I couldn't live with myself knowing I'd done nothing about seeing him there."

"Who? Who did you see?"

"When I looked in the window that morning I saw my ex-husband standing over Candace's body."

Oscar slammed on the brakes.

What!

Words he shouldn't say in front of Ryan simmered below the surface. He looked in the rearview mirror, checking how close the car behind him was. Nowhere close. Quickly Oscar pulled to the side of the road. "Larry Wagner was there? Your ex-husband? You saw him?"

Even in the darkness, he saw Shelley nod. He also saw the haunted expression in her eyes, the set of her lips, the way she clasped her hands in her lap. He reined in his anger. "Why didn't you tell us, tell the police?"

She fished her cell from her purse, punched in a code, waited and then handed him the phone with a text message showing. It took him about three seconds to fill in the missing pieces.

"Did you block his number after this?"

"Yes, but he seemed to find other phones to use and—"

It took him less than a second to pull her into his arms and tell her that no way was Larry Wagner getting close to her or making anyone that Oscar loved disappear.

Loved?

Well, sure he loved her. She reminded him of his sister.

Right?

CHAPTER EIGHTEEN

SHE SPENT MOST of Saturday at the police station, answering questions. Riley wasn't happy that she hadn't shared Larry's appearance. Sunday she met with the state police as well as the FBI.

If Larry was watching, there was no turning back.

Monday, Oscar Guzman slowed his motorcycle down right beside her after she dropped Ryan off at preschool.

"Hey, there." He wasn't in uniform, and she realized how used she had become to seeing him in dark blue, with a badge. Today he wore a white T-shirt and jeans, reminding her of the morning she'd met him—right before she'd seen Candace Livingston lying dead on her living room floor.

With Larry Wagner standing over her.

"Hey, yourself. What are you doing here? Shouldn't you be sleeping?"

"First day off in almost two weeks. And

my hours changed. I'm on days now. As you know, Riley agrees that right now my main job is watching over you."

The look in his eyes invited her to believe him. *Trust me*, it seemed to say. Yeah, she'd seen that look before. A little over a year ago, Larry Wagner, pretending to be a nice guy. Maybe Oscar was pretending, too.

"Actually," he said, "I came here purposely to see you."

"Why?"

"I could tell you it's because I'm worried and that I noticed you now sleep with every light in your apartment on. Or I could tell you that I'm here on behalf of my aunt, who wants to order chocolate muffins."

"I'll make the muffins."

"Shelley, it's not just your baking I'm here to talk about."

For the life of her, she couldn't figure out if she was his inspiration or if what she knew was his inspiration.

Either way, she lost.

"I stare at my phone," she said. "Terrified I'm going to get a text."

"We want a text. Then we can try to trace it." The cops had verified that Larry used a different phone every time he texted. The texts he'd already sent were no longer traceable.

"My baking is the only thing I'm willing to talk about. I can't talk about Larry anymore. I'm talked out."

"Okay, I can understand that. You want me to give you a ride back to your apartment and we can talk, or—"

"No, nowhere near my apartment." This morning, Sarasota Falls was enjoying a beautiful May morning. The sun shone and the world seemed especially bright. Yet Shelley couldn't enjoy the view. Her ex could be hiding behind a tree or a car or even pretending to be one of the parents standing by the four- and five-year-old preschool room.

He was a master at blending in.

"How about coffee at the Bean Stop?"

Shelley shook her head. "Here is fine. Let's just sit on the bench."

He easily swung his leg over his bike and in a few steps was beside her.

After she sat down, he joined her. "Look." He pulled a piece of paper from his back pocket. "Aunt Bianca found a blank order form of your mother's and filled it out. I've even got a check to pass on to you."

Why did Bianca of Bianca's Bed-and-

Breakfast have to be Oscar's aunt? Shelley needed the money; she couldn't turn the woman down. After delivery of the child's birthday cake, she'd recorded a whopping ten-dollar profit.

Her mother always said, *"Whatever you sell should be double the cost it took to make it."* But Shelley'd had to buy eggs, milk, flour, baking soda, pretty much everything except the cake pan. She'd kept a few of her mother's essentials.

This morning when she'd dropped Ryan off at preschool, she'd been stopped by two moms wanting to order cakes fairly identical to the one she'd just made.

Too bad she'd need more ingredients, because one mom wanted a lemon cake and the other marble. Both wanted the Lego design.

She looked at Oscar. She'd regretted telling him about seeing Larry the minute the words were out of her mouth. This past weekend, she'd known she'd made a mistake.

Larry always kept his promises.

These past few weeks, her ex had known her every move, it seemed. How could Oscar compete?

Rubbing her stomach, she thought about how good it had been to bake. Stirring the batter, she'd remembered almost twenty years ago and her mother's hand on hers counting the beats: more than a hundred in just over a minute. Shelley'd learned to put in dry ingredients last. That long-ago kitchen had been huge, while the one she had today was small. Didn't matter the size, though, because when Ryan crawled up in the chair beside her and she'd handed him a spoon and started counting, she'd felt a connection to her mother that brought tears to her eyes.

She'd have told her mother about what Larry had done.

She'd have trusted her mother.

"I am excited," she told Oscar, hoping he couldn't hear the break in her voice. "I'll think about it. I need to work, and part-time baking would allow me to be home with Ryan and get some things for Isabelle." Shelley hesitated. "It's just there are a few logistics I need to work out."

"I can understand that." He stood, stretched and jutted his chin toward his bike. "Come on. I'll take you to my aunt's. She can talk to you about what she wants and when. I know you need the money."

Her eyes swept the landscape. Surely Larry

couldn't be everywhere. And the preschool wouldn't release Ryan to anyone but her.

"Have you ever been on the back of a Hog?"

"Yes."

"When?" He sounded doubtful.

"In college, but I wasn't pregnant."

The sun went behind a cloud, and although it was a warm day, she shivered. The places where she imagined Larry hiding now seemed cast in shadows, and the words *Better the enemy you know than the enemy you don't* sprang to mind.

The real saying used the word *devil*, but she couldn't think of Oscar that way.

She felt like walking again and stood. She wanted to talk to Bianca, and she figured if Larry Wagner was nearby, right now she'd rather face him with Oscar by her side.

"I'll leave the Hog here and walk with you. But you have to promise me that someday, soon, after the baby is born, you'll let me take you for a spin."

They started off and had taken only a few steps when Oscar slipped an arm around her shoulders.

Now she wished he had more on than a white T-shirt. She could feel his skin through the material. He walked slowly, as if she were something precious, and she almost lost her breath before they got to the stoplight.

At the one intersection they had to cross, she found herself chuckling. The light turned green and she struggled. Just his arm around her felt too intimate. She didn't mind, though. She'd needed this because it got her mind off her problems for all of seven minutes.

To her delight, he steered her to her old neighborhood, only two blocks and a lifetime away from where she lived now. Together they perused her once-upon-a-time home.

"I remember it as being bigger," he said.

"I would never have painted it this color." It was now orange with green trim instead of blue with white trim. The fence around it needed fixing. That was nothing new. The yard hadn't been tended in a while.

"It looks a little empty," Oscar observed.

It did. Shelley moved up the walk and went through the gate. "My mother never wanted a new home," she said. "She wanted something that had history. I think that's why I always did the reenactments. They meant so much to her."

"Which do you prefer," Oscar asked, "the newer adobe homes that are being built on the west side, or do you like this side with all the older stuff."

She didn't hesitate. "Definitely the older stuff. It's got character." She nodded toward the Folk Victorian. "It was built in 1887 and made to last."

Oscar laughed. "I grew up in a house built in the fifties. It was made of blocks and had these strange pocket doors. Mom used to close the one in the kitchen so we couldn't sneak food when she was cooking."

"So it wasn't just you making me sneak food from my mother," Shelley teased. "You did it to your own mother."

"No, I didn't," Oscar protested. "Remember, I was the oldest. I made my little brothers do it."

"There's a word for that."

He smiled, and her heart fluttered. He followed her up the walkway and to the front porch that stretched from one end of the house to the other.

"We had three rocking chairs up here," she shared. "One for each of us." She bent, peeked in a window and felt a slight catch in her throat. "It's completely empty. There's no furniture. Not one piece."

"When did you sell it? And to who?" Oscar laughed.

"Larry sold it. He said to a family with five kids."

Oscar looked around. "I don't think they'd tear this house down to put in a business. It's not zoned for business."

Shelley thought a moment, then walked around to the back. He followed. "I'd forgotten," he said. "I'd forgotten your backyard."

"A full acre and then some. Big enough for four houses. You don't think…?" Her words tapered off.

"I do think," Oscar said.

"This is just one more of the mistakes I've made." She walked to the front, peeking in the windows again, noting the windows that stretched from ceiling to floor, noting the ornate wooden edgings and the hardwood floor.

"The kitchen was the only room my mom modernized," she told Oscar, "since that's where she worked. We had an extra stove because one wasn't enough. They were across from each other, and Mom would stand in the middle sometimes, multitasking."

Oscar was staring at her, and she knew he didn't know what to say. "Come on," she told him. "We need to get going."

The rest of the walk lost some of its joy. Finally they approached the bed-and-breakfast.

"That was fun," she said. She stumbled a bit, and he caught her elbow. First she'd enjoyed his fingers on her cheeks, the arm around her shoulders, and now she liked his hand on her elbow. Must be the pregnancy hormones, because no way was she feeling attraction for the man who was keeping tabs on her because it was his job.

"I'll just go in and talk to your aunt." Anything to avoid being alone in the apartment. Anything to get away from him.

He didn't seem to understand that he made her nervous.

Before she could move, three serious barks sounded. "Peeve thinks we should just come in and stop wasting our time when we could be petting him," Oscar remarked.

"I didn't know dogs could talk or that you were well versed in their language."

"You'd be surprised," he told her, "what I'm well versed in." He led the way through the back door and into a kitchen to die for.

"Oh," she breathed.

Peeve sat somewhat patiently on the smooth floor, his body shaking with joy, his tail sweeping back and forth, and the expression on his face saying *Notice me.*

"Why do you have a motorcycle if you have such a big dog?" Shelley asked.

"I have a detachable sidecar. He loves riding in it."

Shelley wanted to see that. Even more, she wanted Ryan to see it.

"You haven't been in Aunt Bianca's kitchen?"

"Not in a long time."

"Aunt Bianca serves a full breakfast every morning and supper on Fridays and Saturdays. She's even had a few people show up to her table just for the meal."

"My mom said Bianca made the best meatballs."

"Nope, she makes the best fried chicken." Oscar sat in a hard chair and patted his knees, and Peeve hurried over to lay his head on Oscar's hands. Shelley knew a look of contentment when she saw it.

Bianca came through the door then, smiling at Shelley and saying, "I thought I heard Peeve and then voices. I take it Oscar's told you I want to place an order? I've got a full house coming up in about two weeks. Hunters."

"He's even given me the check." It didn't escape her notice that these last few days, Oscar had been the glue holding her together.

She very much doubted anyone else could have inspired her to trust.

But for some reason, she trusted Oscar.

Next thing Shelley knew, she was sitting at the kitchen table with a glass of milk in front of her, Peeve sitting at her side and a rough draft of the kind of ordering Bianca would do for the next month. "Unless you have the baby," she said. "Then we'll make do until you're back in the kitchen. When are you due?"

"Could be any day. The doctor says I'm right on schedule."

"And you'll have the baby here?" Oscar looked doubtful.

"Just because the hospital is small doesn't mean it's inadequate," Shelley said. "Twenty-three years ago, I was born in it."

"It was even smaller then," Bianca added.

Before anything else could be said, Oscar's phone pinged. He stood, excusing himself, and exited out the back door. Shelley focused on the giant bulletin board that took up almost one whole wall. There were a few photos as well as a calendar with names written on almost every day. Near the top left was a blueprint. Shelley wished she hadn't noticed because she knew what it was.

Bianca had hired Larry Wagner to build her a guesthouse in the backyard. She'd made a substantial down payment and hadn't received so much as a nail in return. No, wait—Larry had provided the blueprint. Stolen, probably.

Shelley put a hand on the table. She needed to get home, make a supply list and figure out how to open a checking account her ex-husband couldn't hack, because it was time to earn a living, take care of both her children. What little she'd made off baking these last few days had gone toward essentials: milk, eggs, a new pair of shoes for Ryan.

Before she could push herself up, someone entered the room and cleared his throat. Jack Little stared at Shelley, his eyes hungry. She knew what he was hoping for. He wanted information that would lead to his daughter's killer.

CHAPTER NINETEEN

By the time Oscar got off the phone, Shelley was gone. Bianca sat at the table frowning at Jack, and Jack looked angry.

"What did you do? Say?" Oscar accused him.

"I just told her I wanted all of the truth and that I wasn't sure she was providing it. I don't know that you can trust her. I've read about her ex-husband. How can you be married to a criminal and not know it?"

Peeve whined a bit, and Oscar refrained from bringing up the absent Tiffany. His wife might not be a criminal, but what she was doing seemed criminal. Oscar knew better, but the difference in character between Jack's second wife, Valerie, and Tiffany rankled him. His sister had mentioned time and time again how Tiffany seemed to think spending money was a social skill.

"I fell for Larry Wagner's spiel," Aunt Bianca said. "I believed every word. Can you trust *me*?"

Jack let out a low growl. "What a mess, and I don't know who to trust or believe." He looked at Oscar. "Tell me what you've learned since the last time we spoke."

The police weren't ready to go public with what Shelley had shared about Larry Wagner's part in Candace's death. Not until they were sure they could keep Shelley safe. Oscar shared what he could. "The medical examiner says Candace died between midnight and eight."

"And Shelley found her just after eight, so it was probably a bit earlier," Aunt Bianca put in. Oscar worried once again that giving her the job of keeping track of the neighborhood's activities was going to make her a detective wannabe.

"We know," Oscar continued, "that Cody spoke to her at ten, told her good-night and hung up."

"He should have been there. He never should have left my baby alone."

Bianca got up, poured a cup of coffee and set it in front of Jack. "Candace would have hated that. She was very independent. Cody was doing what he thought was right. Providing for her, thinking about the future. Don't you dare make that boy feel any guiltier than he already does."

Oscar decided not to mention that Jack left Tiffany on her own all the time, like right now. As far as Oscar could tell, Tiffany liked being away from Jack unless he was indulging her.

Oscar said, "One of the neighbors reported seeing her living room light was turned off a little after midnight."

"Doesn't mean she turned it off," Aunt Bianca pointed out.

"She always stayed up late when Cody was gone. Said she couldn't sleep without him," Jack mused.

Oscar was aware of the fact. What time had Larry Wagner entered Candace's home? Just thinking that Shelley was across the street and his aunt just down the street had him losing even more sleep than his duty hours could be blamed for.

"Who did this Shelley Wagner see going in and out? I investigated her, you know, called in a few favors."

Oscar wished he was surprised.

"Was she what you were expecting?" Oscar asked. She certainly hadn't been what Oscar had expected. He'd expected the eight-year-old daredevil from his childhood to have turned into an ice princess or hard-as-nails diva. She'd been taken in by Larry Wagner. By rights, she should have been bitter, broken. Instead, she was...

Perfect.

"I—" Jack hesitated. "Yes, she surprised me. From what I read, I expected someone weak, someone who not only allowed her husband to steal from the people she knew but also accepted it. She's got more spunk than I thought."

Oscar nodded, thinking about their walk home, about her being so close, sitting in the interrogation room—a room she hated—and implicating the person she feared most.

"The only one she's mentioned who doesn't live in the neighborhood is the garbageman, and collection doesn't happen on Sunday night or Monday morning. Still," Oscar said, "I went out to Sarasota Falls Public Service and spoke to the man whose route is our neighborhood. I spoke to a long-term employee. He said that the Livingstons always put their trash out and they never left things piled up in the yard. I got the idea not leaving things piled up in the yard earns the respect of our garbageman."

"Had he noticed any change in what they were leaving out? Were they leaving out more? Less?" At least now Jack Little was asking a question that pertained to the case instead of looking for blame.

"He didn't know. His truck has one of those arms that picks the bin up, dumps it and then sets it back down. He said he'd know what the trash was only if it spilled."

"And it didn't?"

"No, but he did say that he always knew when Candace's husband was out of town."

"How?"

"Apparently Candace would leave the bin on the sidewalk. Easy for him to pick up but against the rules."

"It gets in the way of pedestrians," his aunt explained.

"Yes, and in our neighborhood, we have a special-needs boy in a wheelchair who gets walked by his mother quite often. She's the one who gave us the time the living room light was turned off. If the bin is left on the sidewalk, she complains. The garbageman says he left a note twice."

"What else?" Jack asked.

"Everything we've got is pure speculation

that needs verification. Not worth reporting yet."

"Everything's worth reporting," Jack retorted.

"I'm glad you think so." Oscar rubbed Peeve behind the ears until the dog lay down, stretched out and relaxed. Oscar wished he could relax. "Did you find out anything on Shelley that I should know?"

"Oscar!" Aunt Bianca protested. "This isn't the way—"

"Yes, it is. And—" he gave her a pointed look "—the only way I can keep her safe is to know what's going on in her world. Finding your daughter's..." Oscar almost said *body*, but both Bianca and Jack seemed to pale, so Oscar backed up. "Finding your daughter has put Shelley back in the spotlight, in danger, and she's terrified."

"Then leave her alone," Aunt Bianca said.

"What did you find out?" Oscar asked Jack.

"She's broke, completely wiped out. Someone did a bank transfer, emptied her account, and when she went to the bank to question why, they figured out that whoever took the money had already closed the account where the funds had been moved to."

"Oh, dear," Aunt Bianca whispered.

Oscar knew this from Townley's updates, but Shelley'd shared this piece of information, too. It was interesting that Jack knew. Apparently, Jack didn't know the money would be returned.

"My investigator says the bank has reason to believe it was her ex-husband. There's no way to prove that she didn't provide him with the details he needed to make the transfer. So, there's no recourse for her."

"Not fair," Aunt Bianca said. "Anyone who's been watching the news knows that six months ago she turned her husband in and soon after divorced him. Wasn't easy, either. No way could that—" she frowned at Oscar and cleared her throat "—no way could that husband of hers be served. She had to do a default divorce. Cost a pretty penny for the attorney."

"Plenty of people go back to their spouses time and time again," Jack said. "Even after they pay out all kinds of legal fees."

"Shelley hasn't." Oscar knew it was the truth. She was someone who'd been dealt a bad hand and couldn't seem to step away from the poker table fast enough to escape the players. He needed to mention the default divorce and attorney to Townley. Maybe a process server had tried to find Larry Wagner.

"Here's the thing," Jack said. "It was only two thousand dollars. But if my source is correct, it was all she had."

The information silenced the table. Jack, judging by the woebegone expression on his face, was thinking about how inconsequential two thousand dollars was and that no amount of money could bring his daughter back. After a moment's hesitation, Aunt Bianca patted his hand, then got up and started cleaning the already spotless kitchen. Oscar wanted to move, do *something*, so he headed up to his room and called Townley.

His boss at the FBI wasn't in a good mood. "I'm not sure how long we can keep Larry Wagner from realizing we're onto him. I'm going to send a few more agents to Sarasota Falls. You need some help."

"If you send agents," Oscar argued, "he'll know. Either we need to put Shelley in protective custody or we have to wait."

"I don't think we can wait," Townley said. "We know he's in the area."

"He's like a top quality cat burglar," Oscar agreed. "He's here, then he's gone. No one sees him. It's as if he's invisible. You'd think,"

Oscar said, "between the three different agencies looking into his activities, and all of us knowing he's somewhere nearby, we'd be able to find some trace of him besides the destruction he leaves behind."

"You check your email lately?"

"What did you send me?"

"A video. I told you that we knew he was in the area. Well, we've got something new. Take a look."

Oscar went to his desk, set his phone to speaker and propped it against the computer. Then he logged on. It took him only a minute to find Townley's email and start the video. The bank looked like every bank he'd ever been in. However, he noticed the Runyan branch sign behind the tellers. The line at the counter wasn't that long. Maybe five people: three women, two men. It was the last man who drew Oscar's attention.

Standing about five-ten with a baseball cap, dark hair curling from its edges, and a goatee, the man took off his thick glasses and cleaned them at least three times. He wore gray overalls and looked like a blue-collar worker. His shoes were wrong. They were white tennis shoes and way too clean. He wasn't carrying it off; he looked serious.

"What time was this taken?"

"Noon, Saturday."

The day after Candace's funeral. The video still ran. The man took off his hat to scratch his head, but his face was still obscured from the camera.

"He's clean," Oscar said. "And the shoes are wrong. If he's wearing overalls, he's some kind of laborer or repairman. At noon, he should have already put in six hours. He'd be dirty, or at least rumpled. It's Larry Wagner, isn't it?"

Townley let out a snort. "Can you believe it? He was in your hometown. Two days ago, Saturday morning, he checked into the Runyan Lowland Motel. Clerk said he paid in cash under the name of John Butler. He had identification. The clerk didn't make a copy. We have footage of him in the parking lot getting out of a white Camry."

Oscar's aunt had seen a white Camry in the neighborhood a few days ago.

"What we do know is after he checked in, a few hours went by and then he went to the Commerce Bank at noon."

Oscar recognized the name. It was in the hub of downtown, and lots of local businesses used it.

"Then Saturday night, he met a woman at the October Terrace restaurant."

"I've been there," Oscar said.

"Pricey joint."

"You know who she was?"

"No, but we're sure it was him because he paid with a stolen credit card. We talked to the server and showed him a few pictures. He spotted Larry almost immediately—it was Larry's bald spot and chin. He also mentioned that his customer cleaned his glasses more than once."

"What do you know about the woman?"

"Whoever he met was probably about his age, dressed to the nines and acted like it was a first date. Waiter said she was blonde, thin and laughed a lot. The waiter got the idea she was excited about something."

"Maybe he's picked his next victim?"

"That's what I'm afraid of. But he's already gone."

Oscar said a few choice words. "He should be states away. This is not how he usually operates. I've gone over his history a hundred times. How did you figure out he was in Runyan?"

"It's worse," Townley said. "Are you sitting down?"

"What? I am sitting down. What's that got to do with anything?"

"Zoom in on the bank photo. Really look at the overalls. Do you recognize them?"

"No."

"Well, the logo just under his left shoulder says Rudy's Garage Repair and Sales. He pretended to be your uncle Rudy."

Now Oscar knew why Townley wanted him to be sitting.

"Larry Wagner pretended to be your uncle, went to your uncle's bank and cashed a counterfeit cashier's check."

More choice words.

"This morning, your uncle was notified that he needed to pay back the money the bank gave him. That's when everyone realized they'd been had. Your uncle hasn't gone to the bank in over a year. He does everything over his phone and the computer. The police were called, and I happened to recognize your uncle's name. I'm in Runyan now."

"I'm amazed my uncle hasn't called me. I—"

"Your uncle hasn't called you because we asked him not to."

"Why?"

"We believe he picked your uncle because of you."

Townley's words sent a chill down Oscar's back. "Why?"

Townley didn't respond.

Oscar tried to wrap his mind around the sudden shift, the involvement of his family besides Aunt Bianca. "You think it has to do with my relationship with Shelley."

"Not just me," Townley said, "but the Bureau. We've kept track of how close you're getting to his ex-wife. Maybe he's asking himself the same questions and doing something about it."

"That makes no sense," Oscar argued. "It's not like he wants her back. Like she'd take him."

"No, but it's becoming clear he sees her as a threat and so sees you as a threat. Which is why I want to send at least two more agents. We need to keep her safe."

"Are you pulling me off the case? Because no one will work as hard to keep her safe as I will." He swallowed, feeling the sweat form on his forehead, and realized just how much she'd come to mean to him.

"No, you're still on the case. You've gotten a response from Wagner, and he's taking risks that make no sense. At least to us. And he's stayed in an area this long only once before that we know of."

"Why did he stay this long once before?"

"He made off with millions."

"By robbing a small town?"

"No, just one person."

"Shelley doesn't have money." Oscar paused, his mind wrapping itself around the scenarios. "But Candace had money, lots of it. And there was a time when Shelley's father worked for Candace's father. Did you find a connection?"

"No, and we've looked."

"And now," Oscar said, "you have no idea where he is?"

"The motel clerk said he left early Sunday morning."

"So he could be here in Sarasota Falls?"

"Could be, and if he's not liking you being around Shelley, maybe you should hang around her more. It might inspire him to try something else. If he keeps it up, especially so close to where we are, we'll catch him."

"How much did my uncle Rudy lose?"

"Nothing, now that the bank knows it wasn't him. But the cashier's check was for two thousand dollars."

"Must be his favorite number. That's about how much he got from Shelley's account."

When the call ended, Oscar went to the front porch. Staring down the street, he considered his next move. Shelley wouldn't let him stay with her, but maybe she could take a room with Aunt Bianca. That might put Bianca in danger, though.

A light went off in Shelley's apartment, and he saw her come to the window. He waved, but she didn't wave back. She probably couldn't see him. Lately, though, he sure saw her. Even when she wasn't with him, he was thinking about her.

THE NEXT MORNING, after driving Ryan to preschool and escorting Shelley to and checking out her apartment, Oscar stepped outside and sat on the bottom step to call and update Riley concerning Wagner's whereabouts.

"You're kidding" was Riley's response. "How do you know this?"

Oscar answered honestly but not quite thoroughly. "Jack Little hired an investigator."

"I'm amazed Wagner's still in New Mexico, though sometimes it's best to hide in plain sight," Riley mused.

"He's not hiding all that well," Oscar pointed out. "We found him."

"Finding and catching are two different things."

Oscar knew that. "Keep sticking to her like glue," Riley said. "She's already starting to trust you."

Oscar checked his watch. "Shouldn't be too hard. She has baking to get done. I'm going to tell her about the Bike Fair the police are hosting at the First National Church next week. I thought I'd ask her to bake cookies or brownies for us to sell to raise money."

"Good thinking," Riley replied.

Oscar hung up and headed back up the steps. He knocked before entering and waited for her to come to the door. When she did, she sported a smudge of flour on her cheek.

"I can help," he offered.

"I work better alone."

He certainly hoped that wasn't true. "I've got more baking orders for you."

"I'll call your aunt later on today."

"The order is not from my aunt. It's from Riley." He followed Shelley through the door. The coffee table was no longer Ryan's play table. It now had baked goods cooling as well as a few condiments.

"Efficient," he commented.

"It's the best I can do and it's working." And she kept working, breaking eggs into a bowl using just one hand.

His mother had done the same.

"You've heard about the Bike Fair?" he queried.

"There are posters all over town."

"The police department's involved. We'd like you to bake some stuff for us to sell." Oscar quickly laid out how many cookies the police department needed her to bake.

She'd switched to measuring flour and baking soda into a mixture. Then she stopped, washed her hands and got out an order form. "Take this back to him, have him fill it out, and he can write me a check or pay cash."

"What kind are you going to bake?" he asked.

"Chocolate chip is a favorite. So are snickerdoodles. I'll need to go to the store."

"Your car working yet?"

"No, it's at the end of my list to fix. I need to repair my life first." She actually laughed as she said the words. It was good to hear her laugh. It lit up her whole face. Her cheekbones looked more pronounced, and the combination brought out the deep brown color of her eyes.

"I can run to the store for you. I've got time."

She shook her head, and Oscar thought that running to the store for her was what he wanted to do more than anything.

Great, thought Oscar. It was starting to look like the hardest part of this assignment was remembering that Shelley was the assignment.

CHAPTER TWENTY

A LOUD NOISE first alerted Shelley that something was happening out front. Then a clanking had her rolling from the couch. She hadn't bothered to pull out the hide-a-bed. She'd worked in the kitchen well into the night.

Ryan slept through it all.

She grabbed her robe as she hurried toward the picture window and looked outside. A tow truck with two men standing behind it stared mournfully at her car.

No, no, no. She wasn't double-parked, she'd earned no tickets, and surely if Riley had ordered cookies from her, he wouldn't be impounding her vehicle.

With a quick look at Ryan, she dived for the dresser door, snagged a pair of jeans that refused to button and threw on a shirt. Still buttoning the jeans, she stumbled out the front door. "Wait!"

She'd only skidded halfway down the stairs before she saw him.

Oscar was talking to the tow-truck drivers. No, no, no.

She tapped one of the drivers on the shoulder, getting his attention, and said, "I can't afford this right now." Then she glared at Oscar. "Did you call them?"

He'd been a pest yesterday, offering to stir a batch of cookie dough, offering to run her to the store, offering to pick up Ryan from preschool. She'd been able to convince him to leave only after yawning excessively and pleading the need for a nap. When she'd left the house to go pick up Ryan, he waited for her in his aunt's SUV.

She'd accepted the ride only because she was eight months pregnant and had lied about taking a nap.

Now here he was again, eight o'clock in the morning, and doing something she hadn't asked him to do.

"Look, Oscar, I get that you're trying to help. But I can take care of myself, and I haven't asked you for anything. Nor do I want it."

"Dude," the shorter tow-truck guy said, "did you call us out here for nothing?"

Shelley recognized the man. He'd worked as sacker at her dad's store when he was about sixteen. It hadn't been the job for him. Mostly because he often called the women customers *dude*.

"You need a vehicle." Oscar walked over to her, and it irritated her that she took a step back. Why did he seem so much bigger than everyone else, so much more capable? It wasn't that she minded people getting close. More that she minded *him* getting close. He threatened her in a way she couldn't handle. Namely emotionally. Because it wouldn't take but a nudge to have her grateful to be in his arms.

"Give me a few weeks and I'll take care of it," she said.

"They're going to tow it to their body shop. It's probably something small like a timing belt or transmission fluid."

"I get it," she growled.

"It shouldn't cost more than a hundred dollars, which I'll front you until you're back on your feet."

She looked down. "I can't even see my feet. No."

"I promised my aunt I would do this. She's worried about you and nagging me."

"I don't believe you."

"It's true. Come to my place and she'll tell you."

Shelley turned to the tow-truck drivers. "I'm sorry you came out here for nothing, and unfortunately, you can't charge me. I didn't call you."

The taller man turned to Oscar. "That will be a hundred dollars. We have a base fee. Doesn't matter if we're used or not."

"A hundred dollars!" Shelley sputtered. "But that's what you were going to charge for the whole thing."

"Yup," the man said a little too cheerfully. She didn't know him, but he looked an awful lot like the shorter guy. Father and son, maybe.

Oscar took out his wallet.

"Shelley," he reasoned. "Let me do this. The money's coming out of my pocket anyway. It might as well go for good. For Ryan."

She hesitated. Since telling Oscar the truth, her fear had escalated a thousandfold, and she didn't like how trapped she felt. Both good and evil wanted to dance with her, and she was too tired to run. In truth, she didn't know whether to be angry or relieved that Oscar acted as her bodyguard. On one hand, she wanted Larry to know she would fight to the death to save herself and Ryan. On the other hand, angering Larry more was a dangerous game. Also, fighting to the death wasn't easy when you were eight months pregnant.

"Okay," she said to Oscar. "But it's just a loan, and now we're done. I'm fine. You've accomplished your good deed for the year. If I think of anything else concerning Candace's murder, I'll contact you. I need some breathing room."

"Dude," the shorter tow-truck guy said, "I know your dad. He managed the supermarket. And you're the woman from the news. I read about you. Didn't know you were pregnant."

"Ahem." The man who was probably his father gave him a *stop it* look. Then he turned to Shelley. "If you'll just give me the keys, ma'am, we'll be on our way. Probably have it done for you tomorrow."

Both Oscar and Shelley watched the men hook up her car and take off. Then Oscar said, "I'll go get my aunt's SUV. You won't have time to walk him to preschool."

"I don't mind being late."

"It's the last week of school, isn't it?"

Shelley was well aware of the fact. Come

next Monday, Ryan no longer would attend school every morning.

Part of her was thrilled. More time to be with him. Part of her worried. She was finally making money, but now most of her cooking would happen during nap time and bedtime.

Then there was the matter of her having the baby and needing a safe place for Ryan to stay while she was in the hospital. She'd never expected to be so alone during what should have been the best time of her life.

"He's three. He'll get over it," she said.

Was that disappointment flittering across Oscar's expression? No, not a chance. He was a Dwayne Johnson wannabe without a tender side. Cops didn't have tender sides.

"I'll make a contract about the money I owe you." She turned and trudged back up the stairs, feeling older than she was.

"Let me help," he said softly.

Halfway up, she whirled but wisely took a breath before responding. "You've helped enough. I kept quiet and felt…okay. Now I've told the truth, and every time I turn around, I worry about me, about Ryan. If you're helping because you're sorry you pressed me until I finally told the truth, then I don't want your help."

"Did you get another text from your ex-husband?"

That stopped her. She hadn't, but she kept expecting one. She'd told, and so far it appeared her ex wasn't aware of that fact. When he figured it out, there'd be a price to pay. And in her grumpy, too pregnant mood, she was blaming Oscar.

Unfair, yes. Possible to change, no.

"I have to help," Oscar said.

Have to?

"No, you don't." It was the boost she needed to hurry up the rest of the way to her front door.

"Mommy." Ryan waited at the top. He'd dressed himself in a white T-shirt adorned with the Batman cape from his favorite pajamas. He wore red sweatpants and one sock.

"Time for preschool," she said brightly. "I'll hurry and get ready."

"You look ready," Ryan observed.

"You look great," Oscar agreed from the sidewalk.

Looks were deceiving.

WEDNESDAY MORNING, it all started again, and in Oscar's mind, he'd made very little headway getting close to Shelley.

Two days in a row, she'd held him at arm's length. He didn't want to push any harder because if he did, she'd totally block him from any contact.

Yesterday he'd watched from a distance as she and Ryan went to the store.

His first inclination had been to offer her a ride, but he'd known, 100 percent, that she'd turn him down. Then, watching as she pulled an old red wagon with Ryan sitting inside it clutching a Thomas the Train backpack, he'd figured out that he didn't want to give her a ride.

No, he wanted to be walking beside her, helping to pull the wagon and laughing.

Living.

For so long he'd forgotten what living life really was. For him, it was holding a warm-blooded woman while she smiled at you and your children chanted, "Dad, Dad, Dad, Dad, Dad."

Too bad he'd decided long ago that he wasn't cut out for marriage. So why was he thinking about it now? He should never have taken this assignment. Now he couldn't walk away.

What he could do later on this afternoon was return her vehicle. It was under his name at the garage, and at least he could be with her while he explained exactly what the automotive service crew had done with her faulty water pump. She'd be a captive audience. Shelley's car should be fine.

During the briefing this morning, Riley hadn't had much to add about the case but told Oscar to keep watching Shelley between calls. So far this morning, the only call had been about a dog pooping on a neighbor's lawn.

Townley hadn't had much to add this morning, either. Larry Wagner had slid back under the rock he'd come from. Oscar knew the reprieve wouldn't be long. Both Riley and Townley thought Larry Wagner was still near Sarasota Falls and that for some reason there was unfinished business between him and Shelley.

Riley thought it might be money. Townley thought it might be the baby. Oscar didn't think much of either theory. It was something that involved Candace, too. Then there was the woman Larry had met up with in Runyan: his next victim.

Oscar exited the police station. He grabbed a bottled water before getting on his motorcycle.

By his estimate, Shelley would be dropping Ryan off at preschool about now. He wished he could do the sensible thing and offer her a ride home, but no way would she say yes. He didn't blame her.

He parked a block down behind a huge tree and in front of an old Jewish cemetery that he wished he had time to explore. The preschool was at one of Sarasota Falls' biggest churches, and the parking lot was already full of people coming to pick up their little ones.

Ahead of him, Oscar watched as Shelley entered Sarasota Falls Valley Preschool. A few people stopped and exchanged words with her. That was new. She'd been alone the first weeks he'd watched her.

Ryan was skipping. Today instead of a Thomas the Train hat, he wore a Davy Crockett type, although he still carried his Thomas backpack.

Shelley wore the same red shirt from their first encounter, but this time she had on a flowing black skirt and black sandals. She didn't look comfortable. She held her back and was walking slower than she had yesterday. He hoped she was just tired.

She made it to the sidewalk and started down the street when she was sidelined.

Oscar sat up, his first thought to start his motorcycle and zoom toward her, but at second glance he recognized the man talking to her.

Candace's father, Jack Little. He was hard to miss as there was nothing little about him.

Oscar hopped off his motorcycle, wishing he wasn't wearing his full uniform. Even when approaching friends, a cop in full uniform signaled a sense of formality that Oscar didn't want right now.

They were so deep in conversation that neither Jack nor Shelley looked his way as he approached.

"I'm really sorry," Shelley was saying. "I've told the police everything I can. There's nothing to add."

Good—she was keeping to the advice they'd given her in case the press or others cornered her.

"Jack," Oscar said, stepping up.

"Oscar." Jack nodded.

Shelley merely shook her head.

"Something I can help with?" Oscar was starting to feel like that was his calling card when it came to Shelley.

"No," she said, "everything is fine. Mr. Little and I were just talking. I have some things to finish and a good walk ahead of me."

"I can offer you a ride," Jack said.

"No, I like walking."

Jack gave Oscar a dirty look, first time ever, nodded and walked to his vehicle.

Oscar was torn. He wanted to tell Jack to be patient and trust the local authorities, assure him that justice would be served. That was important. But maybe Oscar should go after Shelley, who was already briskly walking away.

He chose Shelley, a vague unease telling him that should the choice arise again, he'd choose her over and over no matter the consequences.

"Shelley, wait."

She stopped, trembling slightly but otherwise the same Shelley he was learning to respect.

"What did Jack Little want?"

"You know the answer to that. He wanted to know if I saw anything."

"Then why are you nervous?"

She gave a half laugh. "Because he offered me a reward. He said if I provided any new information leading to the arrest of his daughter's murderer, he'd give me a hundred thousand dollars. Can you believe it?"

Oscar did, and he also knew how much Shelley needed the money.

"Did you tell him anything?" Oscar had to ask.

"No, but I wanted to. I've trusted the police before. Didn't work out too well for me."

"This time I thought it might be different."

She looked him up and down. "I trusted you, and I'm worried you'll let me down."

Was this what had her holding him at arm's length the last day and a half? She'd trusted before, during a turbulent time, and her whole world changed. No wonder she worried.

"Won't happen," he promised.

"How do I know?"

That was when he made a mistake. He reached out, touching a lock of her hair and then pulling her into his arms. He'd been thinking to comfort her, but soon he knew he was comforting himself. She thought he might let her down? No way.

On the street in front of her son's preschool, Oscar kissed her, noting how she pulled away, but then she let out a sigh and sank against him.

He wouldn't let her down. The truth was

that he was so intent on not letting her down that he just might start to think about settling down.

CHAPTER TWENTY-ONE

ROBERT TELLMASTER SAT in a rocker on his porch when Oscar pulled up in front of the house. Shelley sucked in a breath. Never, not once during the pregnancy, had she felt this bad. Oscar had offered to go back to his aunt's and substitute the motorcycle for the SUV, and she'd reluctantly agreed to the ride home.

Oscar nodded at Robert and then turned to help Shelley from the vehicle.

"You okay?" he asked.

She put her hand over her mouth, and when he moved to help her, she waved him away.

"You're turning green. Should I call somebody?"

She shook her head, but immediately stopped as another wave of nausea swept over her. She'd had motion sickness a couple of times just descending the steps of the apartment. Her doctor had told her to be careful.

Robert stepped down onto the front walkway and said, "Where's your car? You getting it fixed? I've been meaning to ask."

"It should be delivered today," Oscar answered for her. She reached out and clutched at his upper arm, her fingers digging into his uniform as she dragged herself forward. She wanted inside. She wanted air-conditioning. She wanted to lie down unmoving in total darkness.

Oscar leaned toward her, and his arm went around her gently.

It wasn't fair that the guy whose face was taking over her dreams had to see her like this.

Robert peered around Oscar, trying to get a look at Shelley. "I hope she's all right?"

"She's going to be," Oscar promised, guiding his other hand under her arm. She managed to take a few steps and stay on her feet. He eyed the stairs. "I can carry you if you want."

"No," she hissed.

"Did you find out what's wrong with her car?" Robert asked.

"Someone messed with it." Oscar took one step with Shelley holding on, and then he took another. She tugged at his arm, sagged against him, until he looked at her and she begged, "Stop moving."

He visibly swallowed, and she wanted to tell him it would be all right as soon as the town of Sarasota Falls quit tilting, and her stomach left her throat and returned to the vicinity of her belly button.

"You didn't by any chance see anything?" Oscar was asking Robert. "I've been meaning to stop by and talk to you."

"My gosh, no. I'd have told you. I rented to her even though…even though…"

"Even though what?" Oscar asked patiently.

"Even though her ex-husband scares me."

"Oscar," Shelley said, "I'm going to be—"

"Your door unlocked?" Oscar asked Robert.

"Yes, but—"

Her feet barely touched the ground as he guided her up Robert's front stairs and through the door. The house was icy cold and spotless. Instead of a typical living room, it held about five computers all connected and only one chair. A huge television took up one wall.

"Here you go." Oscar helped her through

a door and to the bathroom sink. "Are these towels clean?" he hollered behind him.

"Yes." Robert had followed them.

"Just give me a minute." Shelley managed to shut the door before bending over the sink, splashing water on her face and fighting off more nausea. She gripped the edge of the sink, liking the cool feeling, liking that her feet were in one spot and if she melted, it would be onto a floor.

She'd rather it be the garage apartment bathroom, though. But quite honestly, this might have been the cleanest bathroom she'd ever seen.

The door opened. She should have locked it. Oscar held out a glass of water and a wet washrag.

"I'll be fine," she told him.

"You get like this often?"

She took the water and made herself drink, slowly. Oscar dabbed at her forehead with the washrag.

"Once or twice." The bathroom was a whole lot smaller now that he was in it. She closed the toilet lid, sat down and held the washcloth against her forehead.

"From stress?"

The room stopped swaying, and she no longer felt like she was going to throw up. She held on to the washrag a minute longer. It felt good. "You've read my file, right?"

"Ah, yes."

"Then, if you do the math, you'll figure out that I was probably several weeks pregnant the day my ex-husband disappeared."

"I didn't do that much math."

"Well," she said, "that day back in December, after a couple of phone calls and realizing that he'd packed up the few belongings he had, I threw up. I threw up for five days straight, and then I stopped. It was a month before I figured out I was pregnant. You tell me. Was it pregnancy or stress?"

"Both." He helped her up, and she liked this part of him, the part that wanted to serve and protect. Maybe she could pretend that he was doing it because he liked her, not because he was getting paid for it. He guided her from the bathroom and into the living room, where Robert stood nervously waiting.

"You okay?" Robert asked.

It occurred to her not only that she'd never been in his house but also that she'd never seen anyone else going in or out. "I am okay. Thank you for letting me use your restroom."

"No problem." He didn't sound convinced.

"Hmm, your state-of-the-art computer equipment is better than what we have at the station," Oscar observed.

"Probably," Robert agreed, looking proud. "It's amazing what a single chip of silicon can provide. I've got speech recognition, voice synthesis and my user interface…"

Robert must have noticed her eyes glaze over as she studied all the wires tangled across the floor and leading to five desktop computers. Two laptops were open. One looked like Robert had been doing something with a webpage. The other had a Simpsons screen saver.

"What do you do for a living?" Oscar asked. "Anything besides handle a few of the town's websites?"

He shrugged. "I design websites, battle viruses, help companies with security. I'm a survey taker and website tester. Things I can do from home."

"Could you locate private phone numbers?" Oscar asked.

Robert blinked. "What? Of course not. That's illegal. What made you ask that?"

"I'm not accusing, but I want to know. Do you, or could a computer guru, find private phone numbers?"

Robert slowly nodded. "They'd need only a smartphone. Hacking's easy."

"So," Oscar continued, "if Shelley kept changing cell phone numbers, how quickly could a good hacker get her new information?"

"Minutes."

Oscar heard Shelley's intake of breath. She was already on edge. He changed the subject. "What else do you do?"

Robert looked relieved at the question. "Well, I collect rent not only from Shelley but also from two other properties. I sold one of my properties last year. That really put me in the black."

Ever the cop, Oscar asked, "Where are your rentals?"

"The Duponts down the street. I'm amazed how long they've stayed, but then, I've not raised their rent since they moved in. Trying to give them a bit of a break."

It seemed to get colder in the room, but Shelley didn't complain. She just moved closer to Oscar. He was hot enough for both of them, but that might be pregnancy hormones acting up.

"That's nice of you," she said.

"I know. First I rent to them, and the husband's a real piece of work. He's actually tried paying late, making it a little later each time, until he pays a month late, on the date the next payment is due, and then pretends he's up to date."

"What did you do?" Oscar asked.

"I told his wife. She straightened it out right away."

"Who else do you rent to?"

Robert named a family on the next street. Shelley vaguely knew them.

"And you say you sold a property?" Oscar encouraged him.

"Yes, but I wish I hadn't. I sold the Livingstons their house."

Shelley shivered, and this time it wasn't from the cold.

Oscar didn't so much as pause. "Did you keep a spare key to their house?"

"Of course not," Robert sputtered.

"Do you know how to break in?"

Robert shifted uncomfortably. If he said no, he'd be lying. She just knew it. She switched her gaze to Oscar. Okay, she was getting good at reading him, too. His gaze dared Robert to lie.

Robert sighed. "About Christmastime, Cody locked himself out. He came over here asking if I had a spare key. I showed him how to get in through his garage door. He never gave back the clothes hanger."

"That easy, eh?" Oscar said.

Robert shrugged. "The chain on the back door is unusually long, too. If one of them forgot to turn the lock, it would be easy to break in."

Oscar shook his head.

"Hey," Robert said, "you won't find my fingerprints inside. I just pay attention to things."

"If you pay attention to things, why didn't you notice someone messing with Shelley's car a few days ago?"

"I avoid watching her. If I see something I shouldn't see, it could mean trouble."

"From the police?" Oscar asked.

"No. I've dealt with her ex-husband."

Surprised, Shelley asked, "When?"

"Almost a year ago, right before Thanksgiving. I drove to Albuquerque to pick up a semiconductor and was driving back when I saw your husband on the side of the road. He had a flat."

"So you helped him?"

"Yes. I can't drive by someone I know without helping."

Robert Tellmaster seemed a strange, aloof man, but piece by piece, a softer side was appearing. He rented to her even though he didn't want to—all because of her mom. He'd never raised the rent on the Duponts, even though Mr. Dupont was a jerk, and now he was talking about helping her ex-husband.

"That was before he took advantage of half the town," Robert reminded her.

Okay, she thought, Robert wasn't that soft.

"Did you tell the police?" Oscar asked.

"Nothing to tell. He didn't have a spare, and we were driving the same kind of car, so I lent him mine from my trunk. He gave it back later."

"Where were you when you saw him?"

"About twenty miles past Runyan."

Oscar straightened. "Really? Had you seen him on the road earlier, coming back from Albuquerque, or do you think he'd been in Runyan?"

"Oh, he was going to Runyan. Not leaving it."

"How do you know?"

"Well, the woman with—" Robert stopped, looking at Shelley apologetically.

"Go on," she said. "You're not telling me something I don't know."

"The woman with him said she needed to be home by eight, and if I remember, it was a quarter to."

"What did she look like?" Oscar asked.

Robert made a face. "It's been almost a year!"

"Try," Oscar pushed, his voice stern.

"She had blond hair, down to her shoulders, shimmery, so probably a dye job."

"Go on," Oscar urged.

"I'd say she was between twenty-five and thirty and had work done. She had that plastic smile. She was thin and dressed flashy. I remember that. And she giggled a lot."

"Was there anything in the car that you could see?" Oscar now had his notebook out.

Shelley took a seat in front of one of the computers. The world no longer spun, but she felt like she could sleep a week. What she didn't feel like was going up the stairs. For the next twenty minutes, Oscar pulled details from Robert, who, after a few minutes, really got into answering. Shelley thought he felt important.

"I didn't want to tell you," he said to her.

"Don't worry about it," Shelley said. Actually, except for the fact that her husband was with another woman, there wasn't much to tell. There'd been no suitcases in the back-seat, no belongings that Robert saw, just two people out together. Before he took advantage of Sarasota Falls, she'd have assumed he was with a client. Maybe he had been. Maybe there was some blonde somewhere who was thousands of dollars poorer. Maybe the blonde was one of the many female voices who'd called Shelley hoping to get reimbursement.

Or Larry might have been cheating on Shelley.

She pushed aside a keyboard and balanced her head on her hand before closing her eyes. A dull headache ebbed and flowed. She welcomed the darkness. She was just drifting off when the conversation moved back to how Robert knew to break into the Livingstons' house.

"If I didn't have a key to the Duponts', I could still get into their place. They've got a window on the second floor that doesn't latch. The tree might be tricky at my age, but I could do it, especially with a ladder."

Oscar advised against it.

"And," Robert continued, "the garage apartment Shelley's renting isn't that tricky, either. There's a trapdoor going into the closet. If you can get the garage door open, then all you have to do is climb."

Shelley sat up, glaring at Robert. Oscar didn't look too happy, either.

"Don't worry," Robert said. "No one knows about the trapdoor but me. And I'd never break in."

"I'm feeling better." Shelley stood, afraid to stick around because in her mood, she might just throttle Robert. "I need to do some things upstairs."

To her relief, Oscar came over and helped her up. Together they left Robert's and headed to her apartment in the back. "You learn a lot?" she asked Oscar.

"I'm not surprised that he knows how to break into your place, the Duponts' or Livingstons'. Like he said, he pays attention."

Shelley held tight to the banister and started pulling herself up. Her back protested, but she didn't care. Twelve steps were between her and the couch.

Oscar came up behind her, his body cushioning her. Gently he guided her up the stairs. Before they got to the door, she turned to look at him. He had a dimple. How had she missed that? And one of his eyebrows had a tiny scar running through it. She reached out without thinking and traced it with her finger.

"How did this happen?"

"Airport in Afghanistan. Angry mob. They weren't angry at me."

"I can't imagine anyone being angry at you." She smiled at him, letting him know she was teasing.

He smoothed her hair away from her forehead. "If you get angry at me, I'd enjoy the making-up part."

Warmth spread across her cheeks. Yes, making up would be fun. She thought about the kiss earlier, how she'd felt in his arms, how she wanted to feel that way again.

As if sensing her thoughts, he leaned in and kissed her. It was even better than the one in front of the preschool.

She could get used to this.

CHAPTER TWENTY-TWO

THURSDAY, OSCAR REPORTED to work, ready, willing and able, but Riley wasn't there yet. Lucas Stillwater sipped coffee at the front desk and yawned. He wasn't thrilled about having his hours changed to graveyard, but the guy actually was doing a pretty good job.

"You've got only the one pending call," Lucas said. "All are pretty routine. Oh, and I drove by your girlfriend's place three or four times. Seemed quiet, no lights on or anything. I noticed the Dupont woman walking her son."

"Appreciate that." Oscar didn't bother to correct Lucas referring to Shelley as Oscar's girlfriend. Most of the townspeople had noticed how much attention he paid to her. Small-town tongues were wagging. Luckily they were now more interested in Shelley having found Candace's body than they were in Shelley's ex-husband.

"Leann's going to be a few minutes late,"

Lucas reported. "Something about waiting for a plumber."

"I'll be okay on my own. Riley will be here any minute." Oscar checked the squad car, making sure everything was in working order and double-checking that one of Stillwater's collars—there'd been two, both public intoxication—hadn't left contraband in the backseat.

Funny how quickly he'd settled into a routine with the Sarasota Falls police.

Then he drove by Shelley's, slowing to watch her walk with Ryan. He really wanted to pull up and open the passenger door, give them a ride. But he was on duty, and yesterday he'd overstepped.

Twice.

It might have only been a kiss—okay, two—but she'd sighed and leaned into him. It had taken all his willpower to not kiss her more.

He'd stopped seeing her as an assignment, and that put her in danger because his number one job, besides finding Larry Wagner, was keeping her safe. Wanting to kiss her kept distracting him. So he watched as she and Ryan made their way down the sidewalk.

She made him think seriously about what

it would be like to be a police officer in Sarasota Falls, with a wife and family to come home to. There wouldn't be the adventure, not like when he'd been in the military or the last few years working for the FBI.

But the fringe benefit? He'd take one of her kisses over a high-stakes collar any day.

Worry gnawed at him, a sense of doubt that he often pushed away.

If he settled down, would there come a day when he walked away from it all?

Was he capable of turning his back on family like his dad had done?

Better not to risk it.

Instead, he'd always chosen to concentrate on the job.

His only call had to do with the alarm going off at the Sarasota Falls Medical Center. He'd been there not long ago with Shelley when she found out she was due any day now.

Any day now?

He pulled out his phone, texted her a How are you doing? and headed for his destination, arriving to a waiting room filled with people, mostly pregnant women, and an annoyed receptionist who didn't like the ceiling panels hanging down as if they would fall.

"It's not like they could get any medicine," she told Oscar. "It's locked up."

"Anything missing?"

The doctor on call had met Lucas last night. According to the report, tired and angry, he'd walked through the premises, but once the drug cabinet proved to be intact, he put off the report until morning.

"At first," the receptionist said, "I didn't think anything had been disturbed, but my computer is acting funny, so I went to the event log, and sure enough, about one this morning, someone logged on to my computer."

"Actually signed on?"

"As a guest, but that wouldn't allow them to access anything important."

"What else?"

"I went into the search engine and tried to track their activity. I found only one patient referenced."

"Who was the patient?" Oscar figured he already knew.

"Shelley Brubaker."

Not surprised, Oscar asked, "What kind of information could they learn?"

"I'm not sure they found out anything. We've got password protection. But the file they attempted to hijack had the medication she's on, her blood-pressure readings, the sex of her baby, the estimated delivery date and the type of birth."

"Type of birth?"

"Whether she's having a C-section or a vaginal birth."

"Which is it?"

"Can't tell you," the receptionist said. "That's patient-doctor privilege."

Oscar's phone pinged, and he checked his text messages. Shelley'd sent back an I'm good.

"I suppose you've already touched everything around your desk?" Oscar queried.

She looked guilty. "I put everything back in order, like my keyboard and the tilt of my screen. But, in my defense, I didn't even know there'd been a break-in until the doctor showed up, ten minutes late."

"Is there an alternate computer you can use until I can get some prints?"

"Sure, I'll use the doctor's. It's his fault for not telling me."

Oscar spoke to the doctor, mostly about how long it had taken him to get to the clinic and if he'd noticed anything unusual once there. Nothing looked out of place or missing.

This was Larry Wagner or someone he

knew. What it meant, Oscar wasn't sure. Except that for some reason, Larry wanted details concerning his and Shelley's baby.

Shelley's baby, who Oscar intended to keep safe.

If Larry Wagner showed his face, he'd be arrested on the spot. So maybe the man wanted something he could use to blackmail Shelley.

The man was scum.

The morning continued with Oscar finishing the report and emailing it to Riley.

Within a second, he had a return text:

Meet me at the diner for lunch in five minutes.

For the month he'd been working with Riley, this was the only meal he'd been invited to share, and Oscar got the idea this wasn't a casual kind of meeting.

Oscar radioed Leann that he was taking a code seven and drove the squad car to the diner. The Station Diner, housed in what used to be the railroad station, definitely had ambience, from the animal heads fastened to its walls to the leftover railroad paraphernalia that took up all the other decorative space.

Jimmy Walker, the owner Oscar met when

he'd shared a meal with Shelley, used to be a conductor. Once a day, when the train traveled through, he blew a special whistle he'd designed and hung by the cashier stand. People loved him but hated the whistle, which sounded around ten in the morning some days and eight at night on others—depending on whether the train was coming or going. Jimmy didn't get paid for blowing the whistle. His real job now was sitting behind a cash register with oxygen resting on one side of him and an order pad on the other.

It felt good to be off night shift and eating meals when they were supposed to be eaten.

"Oscar," Riley greeted him as he entered the diner and joined Oscar at the cash stand.

"Don't hold up the line, Tom." Jimmy Walker easily addressed Riley by his first name and ignored the fact that there wasn't a line. "You know you're going to have the chicken-fried steak, green beans and mashed potatoes. Why bother coming over?"

"Just to see your ugly face," Riley returned before asking, "You've met Oscar, right?"

"Once," Jimmy said, "but then, I'm competing with Bianca's cooking. I can't say I blame him."

"I'll have a hamburger, medium, and fries,

thanks," Oscar ordered. "Not something Bianca cooks often."

"Gotcha," Jimmy said.

The two men settled at a booth against the back wall. Riley took the position from which he could see the door. Oscar, not liking it much, sat across from him with his back to the door.

"Thought you'd like to know I just got word that a fingerprint found in the Livingston home belongs to Larry Wagner."

"Good," Oscar said. "Then Shelley's not the only proof. We're getting closer."

"I agree."

Outside, a white car sped by. Riley sat up, no doubt annoyed that somebody would speed in his town. Oscar squinted, not liking that it was white, and that Wagner preferred white.

"You liking Sarasota Falls?" Riley asked.

"I like it just fine." Unbidden came the thought of Shelley. Oscar pushed it away. "I've always been close to my aunt. She needed family now."

"And that's really why you moved here?"

"Yes. You probably know that she lost some money, thanks to Larry Wagner, along with most people in town." Always stick as close to the truth as possible. Oscar continued, "My family worried about Aunt Bianca, and I had the time."

The bell over the Station's door sounded and a customer came in. Oscar didn't recognize her and Riley kept talking.

"Yes, I took Bianca's report. She was angry, mostly at herself. I've always thought she was pretty self-sufficient. You being here really hasn't changed anything for her."

"Self-sufficient she is," Oscar agreed, aware that Riley was fishing. "But there are a few other reasons for my being here."

"Like?"

"I'd been serving my country for quite a few years. Taking a civilian job could have been therapeutic."

Could have been were the key words. From Oscar's first day in town, he'd been working for Townley, watching over Shelley. It hadn't been dull. He wished he were watching her now.

"I'm glad you offered me the job," Oscar said. "I'm finding that I enjoy being a small-town cop." It was true, but Shelley Brubaker had a lot to do with the feeling. He couldn't push the thought away this time.

"You're not cut out for a small town." Riley didn't mince words. "How did you wind up working for me? You're not a typical transfer."

"It was convenient. I needed something to do."

"I'm not sure I buy that. Want to tell me why and who you really work for?"

Oscar hadn't been prepared for the question.

"I can't," he said simply.

Behind them, Jimmy Walker bellowed to another customer that her salad was ready.

"What?" she asked, the woman's voice sounding Southern.

"It's off-hours," Jimmy called out to the lady. "The waitress won't be back until eleven."

The woman, on the short side, pretty with straight brown hair, stood and retrieved her salad from the pass-through. As she headed back to the table, Oscar got a good look at her face.

"You know her?" he asked Riley, turning to see that she'd chosen a table nearby.

"Got into town late last night. She's staying at the Claradan motel and drives a ten-year-old minivan."

"So, you do know her?"

"No, I happened to run into her last evening. Her name's Maureen Peterson and she paid for only one night."

Oscar resisted the urge to turn around and study her. He just sensed she'd be looking right at him.

"Jimmy, our food about ready?" Riley yelled.

"Few more minutes."

"I figure a few more minutes gives you plenty of time to tell me who you're working for besides me," Riley said.

Oscar'd understood the meaning of *Don't blow your cover* since he'd been an adolescent playing war games in the front yard with his brothers.

"Why are you asking me now?"

"Because you identified the tracking device on her car and got it right. Then there was that piece of jewelry, which you brought forward and also got right. And, oh, yeah, two FBI guys showed up at the station this morning and asked a few questions about Larry Wagner. I get the idea they were wanting to ask you the questions instead of me. Want to tell me why?"

"I am FBI," Oscar admitted.

"Order!" shouted Jimmy Walker.

Riley didn't move, just sat looking irritated.

Oscar assumed he was on server duty. The waiting plates sat in the window.

The waitress hadn't been there the last time Oscar ate at the Station Diner, either. Sometimes he wondered if she really existed. Oscar took the plates, nodding at the brown-haired woman who'd finished her salad and now was looking through photos from a folder. Oscar set the plates on the table and snatched a ketchup bottle from a nearby booth.

Jimmy tilted his head back and let out a long breath. "Must be something important, for them to blow your cover like that."

After a few bites, Oscar said, "I had ties to the community, already knew Shelley from when we were kids, and I did a few years in military intelligence. I was the best man for the job."

"Not a cop."

"I was military police, too. I know how to do my job."

"Then do your job. I don't care that you're FBI. I do care about this situation and that we get Larry Wagner behind bars and see if we can't return some of the money that was stolen. Yes, pipe dream, I know." Riley leaned forward. "I'm surprised at how close you are to Shelley and her situation. I've known that girl since she was a baby. Your personal feelings will get in the way, you'll let your guard down, and you'll get hurt or worse. You have the makings of a fine officer, and I don't want you to die under my watch."

"I'm fine," Oscar started to protest.

His mother used to say that after his father left.

"Die under my watch..." Townley had said much the same thing that long-ago day in Afghanistan. Oscar knew firsthand how it felt to lose those you worked with, those closest to you, brothers in everything but blood. His appetite waned. "I know what I'm doing."

"No, you don't," Riley said. "You're supposed to watch Shelley, not help her carry groceries, drive her and her kid back and forth to the doctor or help with getting the kid to and from preschool, and—"

"You told me the day I was hired that in a small town I was required to do all that," Oscar reminded him. "You called it community policing."

"Yes," Riley said evenly, "but when it's a person under surveillance, a lawyer's gonna turn around those good deeds and call them harassment at best, entrapment at worst."

"Shelley wouldn't do that."

"I guarantee you, Shelley's number one goal in life right now is survival, namely keeping herself, her unborn baby and Ryan safe. If she starts relying on you and you betray her, she'll turn on you faster than you can blink. When you're a cop, the job comes first."

"You're thinking about your ex-wife, aren't you?" Oscar hated to bring it up, but he was seeing a side of Riley he'd not seen before, the crack in the mortar. It had been the downfall of many a soldier. Sarasota Falls didn't need their chief to be divided because of a past he'd had no control over and couldn't fix.

Riley jabbed at his chicken-fried steak with his fork. Oscar could only imagine what the man wished he was stabbing. After a few bites, Riley sputtered, "What made you think that?"

"Putting the job first," Oscar said simply. "It doesn't always pay, does it?"

Riley took a drink of water before heaving a long sigh. "A good cop is never off the clock. I am driven. Maybe a bit much. But I had a partner die. It's not something you get over."

"No, it's not," Oscar agreed.

Riley wasn't listening. "One day, a little

over five months after my partner's death, a vase of flowers was delivered to the station. My wife had sent them as an anniversary present. I barely acknowledged them. And I certainly hadn't thought to get her anything. Lucas tried to tell me that I needed to do something with my wife, stay home more, but I didn't listen."

Oscar was patient.

"Before then, I thought Lucas half a cop. He isn't driven, and after he leaves work, he's annoyed when I have to call him back. Working graveyard is driving him nuts. He doesn't want to be gone in the evening. That's when he sits and watches television with his wife."

This was the heart of a chief of police, one who knew his town and knew his officers.

"He doesn't want his wife to go to bed every night without him there."

Oscar felt a heat start at the base of his neck. If he had a woman like Shelley at home, as his wife, he wouldn't want to be gone all the time.

"Lucas came into my office one Wednesday and said, 'Chief Riley, you need to stay home this weekend. Do something with your wife.' I thought he was being funny."

"I take it," Oscar said, "that you didn't stay home with the wife."

"No. There'd been some drug activity in the next town over. The police there contacted me, saying they wanted me to see the operation and talk to one of the men arrested because he claimed to have been here. Cathy and I were supposed to go to dinner and a movie, but I canceled. I put her last. Work came first, and she got what was left over."

"And as a police officer, there's not much left over," Oscar observed.

Both men continued eating, Riley with gusto and Oscar more slowly. Riley was halfway through his chicken-fried steak when Oscar casually remarked, "So, you didn't listen to Lucas, and your wife left you."

Riley stared at his plate and then put his fork down. "It didn't happen right away. Maybe a week after. I figured out that I'd worked twelve days straight. We were short because one of the guys had major surgery. Funny to think now, but I was happy to work all those hours. I was saving the world."

"Oscar, you're a lot like your dad. A leader. You could save the world if you wanted to." Oscar could hear his mother's words. Did he still want to? He knew people who'd made

the military their life. He'd never considered whether they were happy or not, whether they were making the right choices or not. He'd just thought they were doing what they had to do.

"I came home late on a Friday night, about eleven. I went in the bedroom to see if she was okay, and her things were gone."

When Oscar's dad left, he hadn't taken anything, not even his clothes. Oscar's mother had later given them to the Goodwill. "He's not coming back," she'd told Oscar.

She'd kept his dad's tools, though, saying she'd need them for repairs and such. Oscar could still see her standing on the roof one July when their air conditioner had stopped working. *"The fan's stuck,"* she shouted down to her two oldest boys.

She'd wanted Oscar to help her, but he'd climbed three rungs on the ladder and froze. Heights bothered him, then and now.

For a minute, both Oscar and Riley sat deep in thought. Finally Riley continued. "My wife had signed up to be a teacher overseas. I found the advertisement in the kitchen, right on the counter. She hadn't hidden her actions. If I'd been around, paid attention, I'd have seen what she was doing. But I was so involved in work that my home was just a place to sleep. My wife was just a person who kept the home clean and had food in the fridge."

"What did you do?"

"It took only about five minutes of going through the mail to figure out what time her plane left. I'd missed it by five hours. She was gone. I called her cell phone, but she'd disconnected it. Come to find out, she'd purchased another phone and had another number for months."

"I'm sor—"

"Officers, do you have a minute?" The brown-haired woman stood at the edge of their table. She held a manila folder.

"Certainly," Riley said. Any trace of the sorrow his ex-wife had caused disappeared, and Oscar saw the actions of a man who was married to the law.

Did Oscar really want that?

She opened the folder and drew out a page. Setting it on the table, she asked, "Have you seen this boy?"

She spread more photographs on the table: a little boy in a child's swing, a little boy with a messy face eating something orange, a little boy by the woman's side going through the It's a Small World ride at Disneyland.

Oscar thought about Shelley's ringtone that Ryan loved.

The little boy was Ryan.

CHAPTER TWENTY-THREE

DESPITE HER CAR being fixed, Shelley had half expected Oscar to be outside waiting when it was time to go pick up Ryan. But he wasn't out there in his squad car with a smile on his face, and she wasn't sure how she felt about that.

For once, she didn't check the gas gauge when she started her car. Thanks to the money she was making as Bianca's baker, she'd filled the tank and had a little cash left over in case of an emergency. She put her foot on the pedal, adjusted how she was sitting when a sharp pain hit her side, and started to drive, catching sight of Robert waving good-bye to her from the front porch. What a difference a few weeks could make. She'd gone from lonely to loved. She pushed away the notion that it couldn't last.

She turned the car's radio to rock and roll and sang as the blocks rolled by. The parking lot was full, and Shelley had to opt for a space a good distance from the preschool. Walking was good for her, the doctor said, but lately she'd not been enjoying it. Today, at least, she didn't feel so clunky, and the pain in her lower back had moved to her side. The pain she'd experienced earlier returned but went away quickly.

She joined the throng of mothers, a few dads, too, as they headed toward rooms for pickup. She liked Ryan's teachers. They'd gone to school with her, and even when her ex-husband had been the major headline in Sarasota Falls, they acted like nothing was wrong. They hadn't embraced her, no, but they'd not pushed her away, either.

They'd fallen under the category of friends who were now wary.

Today they were definitely wary.

"Ryan's in the director's office," one of the teachers said, helping a small girl zip up a backpack. "You're supposed to go there."

"Why? What happened? Is Ryan hurt? Did he do something?"

"Ryan's fine," the teacher rushed to assure her. "He's not hurt, and he didn't do anything. Quite honestly, we don't know anything. He was called to the office about fifteen minutes ago. We were told to send you there when you arrived."

Dread put a choke hold on Shelley's heart. "Ryan is in the director's office," she whispered over and over to herself as she hurried in that direction. "Larry hasn't taken him."

The director's door was closed, and while Shelley wanted to yank it open, she knocked.

"Come in" was the immediate response.

Ryan stood in front of a fish tank. "Look, Mom, pink fish." There were some greens and reds, too.

"They're beautiful," Shelley said, falling to her knees next to him, engulfing him in a hug that he squirmed out of.

"I still want dog," Ryan announced.

"Count how many fish are in the tank," Shelley suggested and then asked the director, "What's going on?"

"Someone is on the way to escort you and Ryan to the police station. I don't know why." The director spoke kindly, but her eyes were worried.

Shelley wanted to scream. If the cops were going to play this game, there had better be a good reason. "What exactly did they say on the phone?"

"Chief Riley said someone would be by

to escort you. I was to request that you stay. That's all."

"Why can't I drive myself?"

The director stood and came around her desk. She drew Shelley into a hug and said, "I don't know, but with all you've been going through, it has got to be about the Livingston girl or your ex-husband."

Shelley stepped away from the hug. She didn't want it now; it wasn't reassuring. She wanted Oscar, but he hadn't said anything new about Candace other than that Cody was going to sell the house and move. "That doesn't explain why I can't drive myself."

"No, it doesn't," the director agreed. "But the police have procedures to follow, and that's probably what they're doing."

"It's exactly what we're doing," Oscar said from the doorway.

Shelley turned, her first impulse to run to him. A hug from him would have made a difference, but one look at his face and she knew that nothing was right. Everything was wrong. Standing in front of her wasn't the Oscar who had rubbed her back yesterday, who had kissed her as they walked up the stairs to her apartment. This wasn't the man who'd tossed Ryan in the air and caught him again as the boy giggled with laughter.

Oscar said, "Riley asked me to accompany you to the station. There's a matter we need to look into."

"What matter?"

"I'm not at liberty to share."

The words were like a bucket of cold water for Shelley. Not so for Ryan, who left the fish and ran over to Oscar. The stoic cop stance faded for a moment as he bent and picked the boy up, and Ryan immediately nestled in.

Shelley noted the look on the director's face. It wasn't hard to add two and two together.

"Thanks for your help," Shelley said, gathering her purse and taking her son from Oscar's arms. His left foot accidentally bumped against her side, and the pain came, but the weight of carrying a three-year-old didn't bother Shelley at all. She needed her son's touch. She just made sure to carry him on the side that didn't hurt.

Walking out the door and down the hallway, Shelley nodded at a few parents. They were getting used to seeing Oscar, but most seemed to sense that something was different, and they moved out of the way.

"Why can't you tell me what's going on?" Shelley hissed once they were away from prying ears.

"Riley's orders."

"But—"

"Please don't ask me." His voice cracked. "This is the hardest thing I've ever done."

Shelley stopped. She absolutely did not want to take another step. "Oscar, tell me."

"The only thing I will tell you is that whatever you need, I will be there. Just please come to the station, and even if I have to quit my job, I will be there for you."

"Oscar," she whispered, but he simply shook his head.

Anger roared, deep, heavy and hurting. She hustled Ryan to the car and had him in the backseat and buckled in under a minute. Oscar drove up in the squad car. He looked angry, too. Well, that made two of them.

When they finally got to the station, Lucas Stillwater was at the desk. "They're waiting in back," he said.

"Who? Who's here?" Shelley asked.

"Three state troopers as well as…as well as representatives from other government agencies," Lucas said, his eyes sliding to Oscar.

"State troopers? Other government agencies? Does this have something to do with Larry?"

Lucas moved aside, and Shelley, carrying Ryan, entered a hallway she knew too well and grew to hate more every time she walked it. Voices echoed down the corridor.

"Ma'am." A man wearing a gray suit and red tie stepped from the interrogation room she'd been in most often. "You must be Shelley Wagner?"

"It's Brubaker. I've gone back to my maiden name."

"I did, too," came a voice from inside the room. "I did the same thing the minute Henry left. I wanted everything to do with him gone except for Billy."

The man in the gray suit held out his hand. "My name is Warren Trimble. I work for the Office of Children's Issues in the Department of State's Bureau of Consular Affairs."

"You work for who? And who's Billy?"

The man didn't so much as smile. "I work for the Office of Children's Issues, meaning I work for a government agency that deals with child abduction or wrongful retention."

"Okay, but what does that have to do with me?"

Leann Bailey knocked on the door. Everyone quieted. She gave Shelley a sympathetic look and said, "I'm so sorry. I'm here to watch over Ryan. I…" Her words tapered off and tears formed.

"No," Shelley said, but she wasn't really talking to Leann. She was coming to a horrible, horrible realization.

"It's best for Ryan," Oscar said in a low voice. "Leann's driven here on her day off because she wanted to help."

"Help with what?"

"Shelley, if you'll come in here, we can get to the bottom of this quicker." For the first time, Shelley felt relief at hearing Riley's voice. He wasn't on her side, but he, at least, spoke so she understood him.

Oscar was still beside her, so close she could feel the scratchiness of his uniform. "Come on, Shelley. Let's figure this out."

"Figure out what?" Panic peppered her voice.

"Ma'am." A second man, this one in a black suit and matching tie, stood up. "I'm Karl Culpepper, with the Federal Bureau of Investigation. Please sit down."

Shelley's eyes landed on the other female in the room. A woman with straight brown hair and pale skin.

"When can I see Billy?" she asked Culpepper.

"Who's Billy?" Shelley asked, not sitting down and not liking this one bit.

"I've some pictures and paperwork to show you," Culpepper said. "But first a few questions." The brown-haired woman looked vaguely familiar, something about her eyes, how they were spaced, and the shape of the eyebrows.

"Do I know you?" Shelley asked.

"No," the woman replied. Tears streaked her cheeks.

"Shelley, sit down." For once, Riley's words were soft, kind, and that scared Shelley even more. Oscar moved up next to her, taking her elbow, and guided her to her seat.

Sucking in a breath, Shelley asked, "Do I need a lawyer?"

Oscar answered, "You're not under arrest."

Culpepper and Mr. Trimble took seats across from her, next to the brown-haired woman. Shelley felt outnumbered. Only Oscar sitting next to her seemed even remotely on her side.

And he'd brought her here.

The man she trusted most had brought her here.

"We're here because the child you've been raising for the last year is Billy Williams."

"I don't know any Billy Williams." Shelley stood, partly because she wanted to get out of there and partly because the pain in her side had kicked in, literally. Every instinct she owned was telling her to get out of there. Grab Ryan, run. But she had a cop on both sides of her—one she was half in love with—and two other men—both in suits, not good—crowding the small room. Shelley glanced at the brown-haired woman and realized she looked like Shelley felt: shell-shocked and ready to throw up.

"Ma'am," said Culpepper, "we need to hear the story of how you came to have Billy."

"Ryan. My son's name is Ryan. Larry had custody papers. I can show them to you."

Oscar ever so gently guided her back to a sitting position.

She asked, "Does Larry taking custody of his son from an unfit mother and bringing him home to me have to do with his crimes and disappearance or with Candace's murder?"

Culpepper opened his mouth to answer, but Oscar stopped him and spoke instead. "It appears we have a new crime to add to Larry's rap sheet."

The pain in Shelley's side moved to her back. She straightened, resisting the urge to scream. But the pain wasn't only physical, and Oscar's next words didn't surprise her. "If what the state troopers say is correct, then Larry's a kidnapper."

"He kidnapped my son," the brown-haired woman said softly. "I never stopped looking for Billy. And I was never an unfit mother. If you only knew… If you only knew."

Shelley wanted to say how sorry she was, but deep down she recognized the truth and knew she'd be even sorrier. Oscar's arm went around her. She saw Riley shake his head no.

Oscar didn't remove his arm and said, "Shelley, this is Maureen—"

Culpepper interrupted, "You've gotten in way over your head, Guzman, way too involved. Let me take charge. See how it's done."

Oscar took his badge off and set it on the table. "I know how it's done. I've handled delicate situations in environments that make your biggest nightmare look like a kindergarten romp. The badge represents my promise to serve and protect. You might remember that."

Culpepper nodded. He turned to Shelley. "Ryan's real name is Billy Williams. He went missing on September twelfth."

"We know that Larry Wagner took him," Oscar said.

"Henry Williams," the brown-haired woman said. "My ex-husband Henry took him. Right from his preschool." She glared at Shelley. "Didn't you see the Amber Alert or the news? Don't you know how worried I've been?"

Her dad had been sick, and Shelley had been busy caring for him. She'd also been helping Larry inventory goods from an estate sale, the profits of which he pocketed. Shelley still remembered roaming the internet and looking for comparison prices. If she'd seen a missing-child photo of Billy, she'd have done something.

She never would have let some other mother feel the heartbreak she was feeling now.

"Why would Larry steal a child?" Shelley asked Oscar. "He has no interest in being a father."

His jaw went tense. "We're not one hundred percent sure. Anything I said would be speculation."

"Did he take Ryan to hurt you?" Shelley asked the broken woman sitting across from her.

Ryan's mother nodded, and Oscar tightened his grip, his hand reassuring.

"Where are you from?" Shelley asked.

"Small town of Belin, Utah."

Larry'd received some mail from Belin. She'd seen it, but knew better than to open it. Early on she'd felt his wrath when she encroached on what he considered private.

"I'm so sorry." The pain in Shelley's back exploded, and she quickly took a couple of deep breaths. "Larry came home with Ryan on September thirteenth, talking about an unfit ex-wife and taking over parental rights."

"And just like that you believed him?" the woman asked.

"He was my husband. Of course I believed him."

Shelley had questioned. Larry had photos, documents and even a copy of the arrest of one Angela Wagner, his ex-wife, who Shelley had never heard of. Apparently no such person existed. Across from Shelley was Maureen, who'd been married to Larry, only then his name had been Henry Williams.

Another pain, a warm rush. Worst time for labor.

She nudged Oscar and whispered, "My water just broke."

CHAPTER TWENTY-FOUR

"How long have you been in labor?" Oscar asked, helping her stand.

Shelley didn't answer. Instead she said, "Wait. I need to protect Ryan—"

Oscar didn't hesitate. "You need to protect both the baby you're about to have and yourself."

"This is supposed to be the happiest day of my life." Tears started rolling down her face.

He turned and addressed the people in the room. "Look, do the DNA swab at the hospital. We have to go."

Looking at Maureen Peterson, he said, "Ma'am, it's very likely that you and Shelley have a lot in common. You can work together or you can fight. But you've spent the last year searching relentlessly for your son. That makes you a hero in my eyes. I also know and love Shelley Brubaker, who went back to her maiden name, and who has been taking excellent care of—" he paused "—a three-year-old who came into her life unexpectedly. I assure you, the boy has enough Legos to build the Statue of Liberty, enough trains to make it from here to California, every DVD of Curious George, and has been hugged enough to know what it means to be safe."

"It's true," Riley said. "Ryan's had the best of care."

Teary-eyed, Maureen got choked up.

Shelley gripped Oscar's arm tightly.

Oscar didn't waste another minute. He led Shelley from the room and said, "Culpepper, get your car and bring it around front. Riley, you contact Shelley's doctor and tell him we're on our way. Everyone else, this conversation will have to take place at a later date."

Culpepper, shaking his head and muttering something about "never happened before," hurried from the room.

"Larry did it," Shelley told Oscar, leaning into him. He felt her weight but it didn't bother him. If he had to, he'd carry her to the Sarasota Falls Hospital.

"Larry's capable of anything," she said. "You can't stop him."

Oscar felt his heart break. Shelley'd trusted him. He'd let her down.

"I can walk on my own now," Shelley protested.

"Believe me, helping you to the car is the easiest burden I'm dealing with." He marched out the door, waiting only for Lucas to hold it open, and then deposited Shelley in Culpepper's backseat. He followed her in, holding her hand and saying, "Go ahead—squeeze."

She looked away from him, shuddering and moaning.

"Drive!" Oscar ordered.

Culpepper floored it.

The Sarasota Falls Hospital was a ten-minute drive on a good day. Culpepper made it in five and pulled up in front of the main doors. Oscar jumped out, shouting, "I'll get a wheelchair."

There wasn't one, not that he could find.

By the time Oscar got back to the car, Culpepper was helping Shelley out of the backseat, and a nurse was hurrying past him, saying to Shelley, "You'll be fine. Your doctor's on the way. Let's prep you."

Shelley said a four-letter word. The nurse didn't so much as blink, but Oscar and Culpepper shared a look and followed the nurse, who'd amazingly found a wheelchair and was already in the lobby.

"Should we follow?" Culpepper asked.

"I don't think so."

There were no other visitors, and the woman manning the front desk waved them over. "There's a waiting room down the hall, room twelve. If Shelley wants either of you—" she gave Culpepper a *who-are-you?* once-over "—that's where they'll look."

"You don't need to stay," Oscar told Culpepper. "It's not like Shelley's gonna leave without our knowing it."

"You staying?"

"Until it's over." Oscar didn't just mean the birth. He meant until they caught Larry, and until Shelley didn't need him anymore.

He hoped he never had to leave.

He'd let her down.

"I'm heading back to the station, then," Culpepper said. "It's only right that Ms. Peterson be reunited with Billy. It's been about a year since he was taken."

Oscar closed his eyes. As an officer of the law, he had to do what was right, even if it felt all wrong. "And you're one hundred percent sure that Ryan and Billy are the same child? One hundred percent?"

"I'm so sure that I'd lay my badge on the table if anyone argued."

Oscar looked down at his chest, where his badge once more hung.

"Townley's talked a lot about you," Culpepper said. "He said you were one of the bravest men he'd served with. You tell me, honestly. You've seen the photo. Is Ryan Billy?"

Oscar slowly nodded, glad that Shelley wasn't here.

"We'll do the swab to confirm, but—" Culpepper's phone rang. He pulled it from his pocket, checked the number and took the call. Oscar listened to the back-and-forth, even more glad that Shelley wasn't hearing this.

Ryan had been introduced to Maureen Peterson and remembered her. He'd said, "Mommy, lap" before jumping into it.

"Can't even imagine all that's going through your girl's mind," Culpepper said, showing he did have a soft side. "I've got three boys of my own. The minute they grab hold of your heart, there's nothing you wouldn't do for them. I'm also raising a girl from my wife's first marriage." Culpepper raised his left hand so that only the baby finger showed. "See this? She's got me wrapped around hers. Doesn't matter blood. What matters is the heart. I hope we can get Shelley and Maureen working together. It will make it a whole lot easier on Billy."

"Ryan," Oscar corrected him, despite knowing it was wrong.

Culpepper shook his head as he turned and exited the hospital, leaving Oscar alone to walk toward the waiting room.

He was the only one there.

Spotting a chair in the farthest corner, he sat and took out his cell phone, calling Townley, who didn't answer.

Next he called his aunt Bianca, who said she'd be there after she finished checking a family in.

Minutes passed. Oscar skimmed three magazines. Finally a nurse came in, asked if he was here for Shelley and volunteered to tell Shelley he was there.

"She knows I'm here."

"Really? Hmm."

Oscar wasn't sure what the interchange meant except that Shelley wasn't asking for him.

Finally his cell sounded, and he saw Townley's name on his screen. Oscar took the call and asked, "Have you heard of Billy Williams?"

"Yes."

"Why didn't you tell me?"

"There was nothing to tell until today. Culpepper took the call from Maureen Peterson just hours ago."

"How did she trace Ryan to Sarasota Falls?"

"Your girl's been on the television quite a bit. One time, the shot included Ryan—er, Billy. It's a funny thing. As far as we can tell, Larry Wagner didn't defraud anyone in connection to Maureen. He married her, got her pregnant, and a couple of months after the baby was born, he took off. She tried to find him, but no luck. Then, a year ago, Billy disappeared from his preschool. All we had was that a smallish man had been seen in the neighborhood, very little description. We didn't know the whole story until Maureen started unraveling it this morning. She'd seen Ryan on television, Googled Shelley, and found a photo of Shelley and Larry."

"So, why did Larry take Ryan?"

"We're going to find out," Townley promised. "Tell me what's going on down there."

Quickly Oscar filled Townley in on the day's events, ending with the fact that he was at the Sarasota Falls Hospital, waiting for Shelley to have her baby.

"And there's no sign of Larry, LeRoy, Henry, whatever he goes by?" Townley spit.

"No, but the doctor who Shelley uses had an office broken into last night."

"Anything taken?" Townley asked.

"Not a thing, but the computer was messed with."

"I keep trying to find a connection. What brought LeRoy to Sarasota Falls, of all places? It's not a hot spot. He didn't come looking for a woman with an expensive Victorian to sell."

"I agree, and I also agree that his every move has something to do with money."

"It has something to do with Candace," Townley surmised. "I think from even before Shelley met him."

Oscar grimaced. "What makes you say that?"

"He targeted Sarasota Falls. He didn't know anything about Shelley. She's collateral damage. On the other hand, he came back for Candace, which put him in danger. There had to be a strong pull."

"The woman who giggles? She's the only one we don't have a handle on, right?" Oscar said. "If we can figure out who she is, we'll know the answer."

"That doesn't mean we'll find him."

"It's another piece to the puzzle, though." Oscar stood, stretched and paced the room. He was starting to hate this tiny space. He wanted to be with Shelley, holding her hand and promising her he'd take care of everything.

He'd made that promise once before. It hadn't turned out the way he'd expected.

"Was Maureen Peterson able to share anything we didn't know?"

"Yes. She said while they were married, he was taking computer classes at the community college. She says he was on the computer all the time. After he left, she took one of the laptops in for repair, and the tech guy said something to her about being a hacker. Wasn't her. But Larry."

"You think he's gotten into anything important? Police files or—"

"I think he's good. He's managed to get her phone number every time she's changed it. He's used a micro GPS tracker so he'd know where she is. I could go on."

"I have another call," Townley said. "You be careful. Keep me posted."

Oscar signed off, wishing he knew what to be careful of.

Before he had time to put his phone back

in his pocket, it sounded again. "What's happening?" Riley asked.

"I'm in the waiting room. No one else in Sarasota Falls is having a baby. Either that or all their family is in with them. I hear that Ryan and Maureen met each other and there's little doubt."

"Trimble's already sent the swab to the DNA Diagnostic Center in Runyan. The man arranged a court order in less than an hour. It helped that all the paperwork had already been processed. We'll have the proof by tomorrow."

Oscar shook his head. His hometown certainly had more than its share of connections to this case: Candace's hometown, Larry Wagner meeting the giggling woman and now the nearby DNA Diagnostic Center.

"What will happen with Ryan tonight? I know that's going to be Shelley's first question."

Riley didn't answer right away. Oscar said, "Until tomorrow, when the sample is processed, Ryan cannot go with Maureen Peterson."

"A representative from child protective services is on her way. Ryan will spend the night in a temporary foster home."

"Here in Sarasota Falls?"

"Yes."

"Do you know the family?"

"Not yet."

"Can I watch Ryan?"

"No."

"What if Shelley gave permission?"

"Not a possibility. Shelley is not the legal guardian. Any papers she has are probably forged. We don't want to do anything to cause Trimble or Maureen Peterson to start questioning whether or not Shelley had anything to do with the kidnapping."

"Come on. They can't think that."

"What would have happened if Shelley hadn't gone into labor?"

"I don't know."

Oscar hit the off button and then put his phone on mute. He didn't want any more calls. He wanted to be in with Shelley. She shouldn't have been going through any of this alone. A half-dozen times he walked down the hall, wanting to be where she was. A half-dozen times he returned to the waiting room. He was out of his element.

He found another magazine and skimmed through it. Then he went down the hall and got a bad cup of coffee and some chips out of a machine. Returning, he neared the waiting room and heard a distant wail. Shelley had a good set of lungs on her. Leaning against the wall, he waited, feeling half like an intruder and half like the luckiest man on earth. He'd get to be one of the first people to see Shelley's baby. He hoped the little girl looked just like her mother.

Finally it grew quiet. He could hear talking, the doctor giving orders and even Shelley asking a question. One more scream. Then came laughter. Shelley's. Like he'd never heard before. His heart soared. She was all right. He'd not even realized how worried he was.

After a few minutes, the door opened and a hospital bed was wheeled from the room. Shelley looked at him, gave a half smile and looked away.

"She's going to recovery," the nurse said. "We had a few problems with the placenta..." Her words tapered off as she moved. He thought about moving with her down the hallway, but a tiny bed with plastic sides was wheeled from the room. A baby, lungs not quite loud but strong nevertheless, followed her mother. Oscar longed to introduce himself to the baby.

But he knew what Shelley's half smile meant. She was displeased, and he didn't blame her.

The nurse, who knew nothing except he was the man who'd accompanied Shelley on a few doctor visits, came over and said, "She'll be assigned a room in a couple of hours. Go get something to eat. You look ready to collapse."

He nodded and headed to the front of the hospital, his feet slowing because he didn't want to leave. He hesitated at the front door and, instead of walking through it, sat in a visitor's chair, turning his phone back on and checking his messages.

Aunt Bianca had texted that she was on her way. Oscar quickly called her back. "Stop by Shelley's. Get Robert to let you in. I know she has a suitcase packed by the front door. Look on her fridge. She had a list of to-dos written there."

"On my way," Bianca said.

Ten minutes later, Bianca's number again appeared on Oscar's phone, but it was Robert's voice that he heard. "Bianca tells me that Shelley's just had her baby, and I should unlock the door so she can get a suitcase."

"Yes. I'm at the hospital now."

"Something curious I thought I should share. The Sarasota Falls Medical Center called me this morning about their break-in. I swept the system and found something. It's a bit like teenagers when they hack into their school's system and change grades."

"You have my full attention," Oscar said.

"Whoever broke into the medical office, hacked the system, installed hardware that gave them passwords, and did a single change."

"You found one change."

"I did, just about twenty minutes ago. It wasn't easy, but I focused on Shelley. I knew she was a patient, and I know she's the one person in town who's had the most trouble lately."

Oscar grinned. He'd just been shown up by a geek.

"What exactly did the hacker do?"

"Changed the permissions on Shelley's file. They deleted the restraining order Shelley had against her ex-husband. The way the file read before the change, Larry Wagner had no rights and could not enter the area of the hospital where his child was."

"And now?" Oscar was afraid he knew the answer.

"Now the file reads that Larry has the same rights as any involved father would. Why would someone change Larry Wagner's rights?"

Oscar's thoughts came faster than his words.

The only person who might want to give Larry Wagner permission to see Shelley's baby was Wagner himself. He headed for the nursery. His job right now wasn't protecting just Shelley, but also her baby daughter.

CHAPTER TWENTY-FIVE

"HERE, SUCK ON this ice." The nurse handed Shelley a cup. Under a warm blanket, Shelley almost rested, secure, calm. The feeling, though, was an illusion. Since her mouth was dry, she slid her hand out from under the blanket and tipped the cup. Then she closed her eyes. The nurse attending her talked about the weather, traffic and the latest book she was reading. All safe topics.

Lately all Shelley'd talked about was Larry, his threats, Candace Livingston and now Maureen Peterson.

"When can I see my baby?" Shelley asked.

"As soon as we take you to your room, the baby will be brought in. Someone will stop by to discuss breast-feeding."

Shelley closed her eyes, smiling, and thought about the mat of dark hair, the mottled reddish skin and the strong wail. She thought about the pain, about the doctor saying, "Let's take care of this now," and knowing something was wrong. Not with the baby, but with her.

Good.

The nurse had held up the most beautiful baby in the world so she could see. "Over seven pounds," she'd stated.

"Maybe eight," another nurse had said.

Her baby.

She'd do it all again, marry Larry, cope with all of it, just to have this moment. Go through the pain, the complications, just for this baby.

Maureen Peterson had probably felt the same way. What had she called her ex-husband? Oh, yeah, Henry Williams. Shelley wondered where they'd lived and how long Maureen had been married to him. He'd made Ryan disappear twice: once from Maureen and now from Shelley.

Already her heart swelled with love, and she hadn't even held the baby in her arms yet.

Empty arms. For the last year, Maureen had empty arms.

"Do you have a name picked out?"

She'd had a name, but now she needed a new one. The old one wasn't right.

A phone sounded, and the nurse answered. Shelley listened to "Yes, she's down here. No, she's not ready to be moved to her room yet. Oh, that's sweet."

"What?" Shelley asked.

The nurse ended the call and said, "Officer Guzman is sitting in a chair by the nursery."

Shelley frowned. She couldn't shake Oscar Guzman. He frustrated her, angered her and most of all intrigued her. But he'd crossed the line today. He hadn't warned her about Maureen Peterson. She'd felt ambushed, and for some reason, she blamed Oscar for it all. Probably because for the last few weeks, she'd stopped feeling alone because of him.

"We've put on extra security," the nurse said. "For while you're here. We know about your ex-husband."

"Thank you."

"I guess when your boyfriend is an ex-marine, though, you've got permanent security."

"He's not my boyfriend. When can I be taken to my room?"

"We want to monitor your bleeding and blood pressure a little longer."

Shelley lay back, exhausted. She wanted to sleep. She wanted her baby. She wanted Oscar to tell her that everything was okay.

Would that ever be true?

The nurse removed Shelley's blanket and gave her a new, even warmer one. The hum of machines lulled her into closing her eyes, drifting, not that she'd allow herself to fall asleep. Too much to worry about.

When she woke up, she was in her room, and Oscar sat in a chair by the window. The light from the window seemed to hit him like a spotlight. His neck was tilted at an odd angle as he dozed. A bassinet was at his left.

She tried to sit up. Oscar jerked awake, blinked a few times and wheeled the baby over.

"Big surprise, huh?" he said.

"Yeah." She went up on her elbows, surprised by how weak she was.

"Would you like me to hand him to you?"

She nodded.

Oscar walked quietly to the bassinet, peering down somewhat in awe. She watched as his hands disappeared inside. When he lifted the baby, slowly and gently, at first all she could see were Oscar's hands, cupping her son, before he transferred the baby to her waiting arms.

Instantly, Shelley calmed. The feel of her baby's warm, soft body against her chest was unlike any other experience. The wrinkled, red face scrunched up. For a moment, she thought he'd cry, but instead he mewed—that was the only word she could think of to describe it—and relaxed. She'd never thought of scent as being so powerful an emotion. But here she lay, surrounded by a world that wanted to take from her, and she was savoring all this little bundle had to give. Oscar went back to his chair and gave her a moment before saying, "You'll have to return some of the clothes we bought the other day."

"I don't mind, so long as he's safe and healthy."

"How you doing, Shelley?" Riley took one step in the room, shattering the mood and slamming reality back into place.

"All right. Where's…Billy?"

"He's fine. There's no need to worry," Oscar said.

Riley looked at Oscar. "You sure everything is okay here?"

Oscar nodded. "I haven't let the baby out of my sight."

"What's going on?" Shelley asked.

"We figured out what happened during the break-in last night at your doctor's office," Oscar replied. "You can thank your landlord. Robert figured out that someone deleted the restraining-order entry you had against Larry so that it looked like he had a right to come in and see the baby."

"He wouldn't!"

"Hard to imagine," Oscar agreed. "But the head nurse says your original Kardex card went missing."

"Kardex?" Shelley and Riley asked at the same time.

"It's a paper that has your important information on it so that the next shift can know what's going on at a glance."

"Would Larry and the restraining order have been mentioned on the card?"

"Yes," Oscar said. "They've already made a new one, and word of mouth is a powerful thing. Even with me here, and I'm not moving, your nurse has stopped in every five minutes or so."

"How worried should I be?" Shelley asked softly.

Riley said, "We're concerned enough that Officer Stillwater is in the parking lot, Oscar's with you and the hospital has doubled their security."

Shelley looked at her baby, wrapped tightly in a blanket. "I'll keep you safe," she whispered. He pursed tiny lips as if believing her.

"I can't even fathom Larry going through all this in order to punish me," Shelley said. "I mean, I didn't actually see him kill Candace."

"We believe the threat is real," Oscar said. "So do you. Otherwise, why go through all that you did to push us...me...away?"

The baby let out a tiny whimper as if sympathizing with him.

"You're right," Shelley said to Oscar. "I want to be informed from now on about the case, all of it. I need to be informed."

He looked at Riley. "She's right. She deserves to know. Tell us what's going on."

"An undercover cop working in Santa Fe called us an hour ago." Riley gave Shelley a sympathetic look. "Seems the news has already picked up the story of Ryan being Billy and Larry Wagner being a kidnapper along with everything else."

Shelley closed her eyes. She was moving to Timbuktu when this was all over.

"Larry's photo has been displayed prominently on all major stations. Dallas PD got a call and investigated it. Apparently a husband and wife who couldn't have children were negotiating a deal with a couple they met online who didn't want the baby they were about to have."

"A baby broker?" Oscar asked.

"Not a legal one," Riley responded. "They recognized Larry on the television and called the police. They'd already paid him twenty-five thousand dollars with another twenty-five to be paid either tomorrow or the next when Larry—going by a different name, by the way—delivered the child."

"My child," Shelley said.

Shelley didn't kid herself. Larry wasn't the kind of guy to give up on a deal that could net him fifty thousand dollars. If he'd found the first couple, he could find another.

She looked at Oscar. "How does Candace figure in all this?"

"We still don't know."

"But he knows you're here. He knows Maureen Peterson is here. Surely he's going to back off," Shelley said.

"Except for the motel and the restaurant, Maureen hasn't been around town. We're hoping he doesn't know she's here."

"He's known everything else," Shelley pointed out. "He's not one to give up. He'll try something."

"I think you're right," Oscar said. "He's gotten away with his cons for so long that he thinks he's invincible. It's become a game to him. Maybe the game is even more important than the money. But this time, I have a vested interest." He looked at her, something simmering in his expression, making promises she wanted to hear but was afraid to believe.

He whispered, "I'll be waiting."

THE SWAB CAME back positive. Oscar hung up the phone and walked down the hall to Shelley's room. She'd slept most of the night, waking only to nurse the baby. It wasn't working, and she kept switching to bottles of formula so tiny that his hand—when he'd unwrapped one for her—almost fumbled it.

This morning, she looked beautiful sitting up in bed, holding her baby and feeding him.

Oscar couldn't seem to form the words, and Shelley saved him. "Ryan really is Billy Williams."

"Yes."

"What happens next?" Her voice had a dry rasp but was strong, like she was.

"What do you mean?"

"Does she take him outright? Or do I get to say goodbye? Can I send some of his toys and clothes with him? Is there any chance at all that I'll be able to visit him once in a while?"

"I don't know." His voice was raspier than

hers. Being with her, knowing what she was going through, was hard.

"Find out for me, okay? I mean—" she choked a little, looking down, touching her son's forehead reverently "—I mean, if somebody took my son, if I had to wonder for a year where he was, if he was being cared for, loved, I'd…I'd lose it. I'm so sorry for all Maureen Peterson went through. I have to do the right thing."

"I'll find out. I'll call right now."

"Thanks."

Oscar went back in the hallway and pulled out his phone. Then he thought twice and called Leann Bailey instead.

"Sure, I'll stay with Shelley," she said after he shared his idea with her. "You do whatever it takes."

Shelley was dozing when he got back to the room. He peeked in the bassinet to check on the baby, still not yet named.

"How's everything?" Oscar's favorite nurse hustled in and asked.

"Good. The baby's eating a lot."

"They do." The nurse gently woke Shelley to say, "It's time for the full pediatric exam. This will take only about thirty minutes."

"What will you do?" asked Shelley.

"Nothing major. The doctor just looks at his eyes and checks the heart, pulse and umbilical cord." The nurse wheeled the baby from the room. Oscar waited for Leann. When she arrived, he filled her in and then he headed for his motorcycle. At a quiet point during the night, he'd gone to his aunt's for a quick change of clothes and something to eat before returning straight back to the hospital and Shelley's side.

Calling Riley, he asked, "Can you arrange for a meeting between Maureen and—"

"Ryan—I mean, Billy—is on his way here from the temporary foster home. Maureen's also here and about to jump out of her skin. I've never seen a— Oh!"

Oscar could hear noise, happy laughter, and Riley saying, "Be careful."

"I'll be there in a minute," Oscar told him.

Hurrying inside the station, he went to the break room. Ryan was at one of the tables, laughing while Maureen stacked plastic cups so he could knock them down.

"I told Shelley about the swab being a positive match," Oscar said.

No one said anything. They all managed to look uncomfortable.

Ryan slid to the floor, picked up three plastic cups, handed them to Maureen and ordered, "Lap." She picked him back up, never taking her eyes off Oscar.

"Shelley wants to know if she can send some of Ry—Billy's toys with him, clothes too, and say goodbye."

Maureen's head bowed.

"Where's Mom?" Billy asked, which seemed to make everyone even more uncomfortable.

"It might be easier," Riley said, the voice of reason, "to let Ryan see Shelley, let him slowly separate from her instead of feeling ripped away."

Maureen looked at the ceiling, the floor and then Oscar. "I don't know if I can. I've missed a whole year. I don't want to share."

"Look at him," Oscar said. "He's been well taken care of. You may not want to share, shouldn't have to share, but Shelley's going to be hurting exactly the same way you have for the last year, through no fault of her own."

"I'll think about it," Maureen said. This time she, instead of Billy, knocked down the tower of plastic cups. Appeared as if she enjoyed it, too.

"The paperwork is finished," Riley said. "Ms. Peterson and Billy will be leaving as soon as Trimble gets here. So far the media hasn't heard about the threat at the hospital. I want to keep it like that. Otherwise I'm afraid there will be so many faces that something could go wrong in a crowd."

"What threat?" Maureen asked.

Riley frowned. Obviously he'd been talking low and never expected to be overheard. He opened his mouth to answer, but Oscar's phone pinged.

Oscar checked his screen. Leann's name appeared. "Everything all right?" he queried.

"No!"

CHAPTER TWENTY-SIX

SHELLEY DIDN'T CARE that she was in her night-gown. The hospital didn't have that many rooms, and she intended to search each and every one. Behind her, down the hall, she could hear Officer Leann Bailey coordinating with security. They'd already locked down the hospital. No one was getting in or out.

"The bathroom," Leann explained loudly over her cell phone for the hundredth time. "I stepped into the bathroom for a minute."

Shelley didn't know who Leann was talking to and didn't care. She cared only that during that minute, the nurse returned the baby and someone shouted as if in pain. The nurse turned away, and when she looked back, the baby was gone.

That was all it took. By the time Leann had the bathroom door open and Shelley shot out of bed, it was too late. The room across from Shelley's was empty and had a window open. It looked like the abductor had escaped.

"Shelley—" Leann came in the room as Shelley finished searching the bathroom "—you need to get back to bed. You look ready to fall down. When we find the baby, you'll need your strength because—"

"You've got to be kidding," Shelley said. "You really think I'm going to bed? I'm searching all the rooms on this side. All of them. You look on that side."

"It could be dangerous. You're not qualified…"

"Don't even go there." Shelley didn't so much as pause. She went into the room next to the one she'd just searched and walked into the bathroom. Should she encounter Larry, she'd take him on with her bare hands.

"Shelley!" Oscar called to her.

"He didn't leave by that window," she told him, poking her head out of the bathroom. "But the one on the right has an open window. The grass is a bit trampled. I don't know if that means anything or not."

"Riley's looking at the footage of who's come into the hospital in the last twenty-four hours. Lucas, Culpepper and Trimble are driving a grid. I'll tell Culpepper about the grass. A helicopter's on its way from Runyan."

She turned, hitting the ground with her knees and looking under the hospital bed.

"I'll do the next room," Oscar said.

"And I'll do the one next to it." Maureen Peterson was at the door, and for Shelley, who'd been holding back the tears, it was this woman's appearance who broke the dam.

"Thank you."

"No," Maureen said, "thank *you*."

THE MINUTES TICKED BY. Shelley and Oscar checked every empty room. The security team was at their heels, ready with keys or whatever else they needed.

Oscar's phone trilled. He took the call and listened. When he hung up, he told them, "Riley says that no one remotely matching Larry has entered the hospital."

"What next?" Maureen asked.

"Riley and two other officers are combing through the basement, the control room and the cafeteria. They want you to get out of sight."

Shelley started to argue, "But—"

"Wagner knows how to play both of you. We need our attention on getting the baby back, not on…" Oscar's voice tapered off as he heard a sound come from one of the rooms that had a patient. A giggle. For some reason, he stopped breathing. Something nudged his memory.

Riley talked about interviewing a motel clerk about one of the women Larry was having an affair with. No name. But she giggled enough that the clerk remembered.

The waiter in Runyan, too, had remembered Larry's date, a woman who giggled.

It was a long shot. Everyone giggled. Even Oscar had been known to let one loose.

But now was not the time to giggle, and some people giggled when they were nervous.

Oscar put a finger to his lips, looked at the closed door two down from where he was standing and then at the guards.

"Marvin Templeton," the chief security guard whispered. "Had gallbladder surgery this morning. Got ten children. They've all been in and out to see him."

"In your hospital room," Oscar ordered Shelley and Maureen in a hushed voice.

They both shook their heads.

He looked at Shelley and mouthed, *I promise I'll get your son back. Trust me.* He'd asked her to do that once before. She hadn't been able to do it.

Maureen pulled on Shelley's arm. "Come on. They're right. We're in the way."

The giggle came again. He knew that giggle. Something else nudged at Oscar. It all came together, wildly, but together.

No.

Yes.

Maybe.

Didn't matter.

Maureen pulled Shelley into the room she'd been searching while Oscar walked up to Marvin Templeton's door, reaching down, turning the knob and slowly opening it.

Guiltily, Tiffany Little, Candace's step-mother, glanced up.

"Where's the baby?" Oscar asked.

"Oscar," Tiffany said, cool and calm, with mock surprise. "What's going on? There's so much noise. Is something happening with Shelley? I've been afraid to leave Marvin. He's a distant cousin. Is there a problem I should know about?"

Her eyes worried him. No feeling. None. Marvin slept. Oscar noted the sheet rise and fall.

"I'll escort you out," Oscar said.

"Thank goodness," Tiffany breathed. "I've been so scared. Let me get my purse." She stood, flowing royal blue shirt, white pants, silver sandals. She picked up a good-size tote bag, yarn spilling out.

"This way." Oscar beckoned, and Tiffany came toward him. When she got to him, he held the door open wide. She peeked out, saw the empty hallway and smiled.

"I'll tell Jack how helpful you were."

Four moves, maybe taking three seconds. He grabbed her right hand, the one holding the tote, and before she could even open her mouth to protest, he squeezed, relieving her of the bag. He had her handcuffed when she finally mouthed the word *noooo*.

Shelley stepped into the corridor from the room nearby, big eyes, breathing in and out loudly to hold back tears. He knew this woman. Knew what she was thinking, feeling, what she wanted.

Oscar turned Tiffany over to the security team and cautiously reached into the tote. Shelley was right there beside him as he lifted her son from the soft cushion of yarn. Her hands entwined with his.

"Oscar," she whispered, her hands roaming over her son, checking everything from downy hair to ten tiny fingers.

He'd do anything for her: give her the

moon, rescue her son, give up the FBI. He was that in love.

She was gazing down at her son.

That was when he realized she wasn't talking to him. She was talking to her son.

Calling the little boy Oscar.

CHAPTER TWENTY-SEVEN

"Larry Wagner's singing like a canary," Riley said from his desk at the station. "He didn't mean to kill Candace Livingston and he's afraid of what'll happen next."

"He should be afraid," Oscar growled. They'd found Wagner at a motel the next town over. When Tiffany hadn't returned by the designated time, he'd called. Come to find out, Wagner wasn't the only one good at tracing.

Oscar stared at the two photos Riley'd hung on the corkboard in the interrogation room. One of Larry Wagner, the other of Tiffany Little. Not their real names.

"I still can't believe it," Riley said. "Man had six aliases and four ex-wives. Of course, they weren't really wives since he wasn't legally married to any of them. Apart from Tiffany."

"I can't stop thinking of him as Larry Wagner instead of LeRoy Saunders. Imagine, Tiffany Saunders." Oscar snatched Tiffany's photo from Riley's hand. "She's still claiming that Larry forced her into entering the hospital and taking the baby."

"They're quite a pair." Culpepper had driven in this morning and planned to stay only the day in order to tie up loose ends. The FBI wanted to stamp this one closed. "All this to cover gambling debts and ridiculous jet-setting. Did you see the report on how much he'd paid to rent a house next month in Saint Thomas? Makes no sense."

Riley shuffled the report he held and said, "It would be their third visit, and it wasn't a house but a mansion."

"I can't believe they got away with this for so many years."

Oscar shook his head, thinking about Tiffany and her need for things.

Tiffany, if the history they'd pieced together for her was correct, had understood the value of selling to the highest bidder. She'd been raised in Surprise, Arizona, and had a baby when she was just seventeen.

There wasn't a father's name on the birth certificate, and there was no evidence that Tiffany had raised a baby. She claimed that a relative had raised the little girl, but the relative she named didn't seem to exist, and Tiffany hadn't seen or heard from her in years. Tiffany's family, too, seemed to have died off.

There was, however, evidence that three days after Tiffany delivered and left the hospital, she and Larry had made their first trip to a different country and stayed for a few months.

"She sold that baby," Culpepper said. "I doubt we'll be able to find the little girl."

"They conned people and came up with these moneymaking schemes so they could keep a certain lifestyle," Oscar said, amazed. "That's hard work. It seems so unlike them. And what kind of mother sells her child?"

He didn't understand Tiffany at all, but then, he had a mother who'd put her children before everyone. Shelley was the same way.

"The kind who loves money more than anything else," Riley said.

"I blame her for Candace's death," Oscar admitted. "More than I blame Wagner, even though he did the pushing."

The police had found in Tiffany's belongings a certified letter, from a law firm in Nebraska, addressed to Candace. A relative on Candace's mother's side had passed away, and

Candace was in the will for more than a million dollars.

Which Tiffany intended to get ahold of.

"She'd married Jack for money. She was bilking him and it was time to leave, but she'd wanted more. Pretending to be Candace and getting an inheritance that neither Jack nor Candace knew about must have seemed too easy."

"I bet Wagner was ticked that the letter came after he'd burned his bridges in Sarasota Falls. It would have been easier for him had he been able to walk around freely."

"Why didn't Tiffany just look for the birth certificate?" Culpepper pointed out. "She was a somewhat frequent visitor at the Livingstons' home."

"Never alone long enough to search," Riley replied.

Tiffany was facing charges for more than a dozen crimes, from petty ones to felonies, the most serious of which was accomplice to murder.

She was no longer giggling.

"Amazing how she went about it," Riley said. "If only the certified letter had gone to Candace's residence instead of Jack's."

"If only Candace hadn't interrupted Wagner when he was looking for her birth certificate. It makes me mad. Someone with his devious mind and computer skills could have made a fake birth certificate easily."

"Too easily," Riley agreed. "He liked the game, wanted to play, and Candace got in the way."

"I've never had two criminals provide such a puzzle concerning their activities," Culpepper said. "And I've been an agent for thirty years."

Riley and Oscar could only nod.

Culpepper was glued to his laptop, typing a million words a minute. "It seems Larry came here to scam the town while Tiffany began taking Jack for everything he had."

"He'd done the home-liquidator method before, and it worked well for him," Riley added.

"Why marry Shelley, though?" Oscar asked.

"Easier to gain the trust of the townspeople," Riley supplied.

"I still can't figure out why Larry kidnapped Billy from Maureen when he did," Culpepper groused.

Shelley and Maureen walked into the room. In one hand Shelley was holding little Oscar in his carrier, and in the other hand a basket of chocolate muffins. "I think Maureen and I have that figured out."

She set the baby on the chief's desk, pushing Riley aside in the process. The muffins she plunked down next to the carrier. She amazed Oscar. She had to be the strongest, bravest woman he knew. She and Maureen had met at the Station, eating Jimmy Walker's chicken-fried steaks, and agreed to be friends. After all, they'd shared a heartache, and both had come away with the only good part of Larry.

Children.

Maureen was living with Billy in a duplex near the police station. Shelley and little Oscar had moved into Bianca's Bed-and-Breakfast until Shelley figured out what she wanted to do next. Right now, she was a media darling. If she took one or two of the deals offered to her, she just might be able to pay back her friends who'd been ripped off by her ex-husband.

Another bonus was Peeve taking on the role of little Oscar's faithful protector.

"Go ahead," Riley encouraged. "Fill us in."

"Billy was a preemie," Shelley said. "He was born at thirty-one weeks and was in the neonatal intensive care unit, unable to breathe or eat on his own. He almost didn't make it. I thought he was three. He's really four, but small for his age."

"That doesn't answer my question," Culpepper said.

Shelley explained, "Maureen thinks that Larry held off taking Billy until he was healthy. People paying upwards of fifty thousand dollars to buy a baby want a healthy one."

Culpepper frowned. "Even though Billy's no longer a baby?"

"Billy's still very young, and he's both gorgeous and sweet," Shelley said as she checked on little Oscar, sound asleep.

"Larry always said Billy was the prettiest baby he'd ever seen. He was beside himself that Billy was so sick those first few months. And to think I thought it was a father worrying," Maureen told them.

"Listen, the FBI could use you and Shelley in the field to figure out cases like this," Culpepper said, pointing at the two women.

"Not a chance," Shelley replied. "I've got a job that will last at least eighteen years, not to mention all that baking."

"Then I guess it's up to you," Culpepper said to Oscar. "We do need dedicated people in the field. Townley was right. I'll be sure to pass on how fine a job you did here in Sarasota Falls. Of course, I can't promise you'll be based in New Mexico. You'll go where you're needed."

Oscar didn't respond.

"How's Jack holding up?" Riley asked.

"He sold the home that he bought for himself and Tiffany. He's moved into my mother's neighborhood in Runyan. She's practically moved in with him." Oscar smiled and held up a hand. "No, not like that."

A call came in. Riley took it and headed out the door. Maureen followed him, saying something about picking Billy up from preschool. Culpepper shut down his laptop, gathered his papers and said, "I'm leaving shortly. My job here is done. Oscar, if I don't see you before I leave, look me up next time you come to Albuquerque."

"Have a safe trip," Oscar said.

Then it was only Oscar and Shelley in the chief's office, with little Oscar as a chaperone.

Shelley smiled and shared, "Your aunt watched little Oscar, and I baked all morning. I love her kitchen, but wish I had one of my own, the same size. Then I took little

Oscar and we went over and helped Robert with a few financial spreadsheets. I think he's going to expand his business."

"What are you doing for the rest of the day?" Oscar perched on the table, scooted little Oscar's carrier over and pulled Shelley in close.

"I'm going to visit my dad."

"How about when I get off shift, I meet you there and we have dinner after?"

It felt weird, these little moments, so intimate, yet never crossing the line to commitment. Since the capture of LeRoy and Tiffany Saunders, their time had not been their own. Oscar was filling out reports for both Sarasota Falls and the FBI while Shelley was dealing with the press, baking and taking care of a newborn.

"I can't believe he's two weeks old already," Shelley said. She didn't move from Oscar's arms, but she extended a hand to caress her son's hair. "He looks a lot like Billy."

"Will Maureen stay awhile?"

"I don't know. Larry picked women who didn't have family, or who didn't have family who might interfere. She doesn't have anyone in Utah. I think she'd stay if a job came her way."

"Jobs are important," Oscar said.

She closed her eyes, leaning against him. "Albuquerque's not so far away. I know Culpepper said he couldn't promise, but…"

"I don't want a long-distance relationship," Oscar said.

"Until my dad—"

"I don't want to work for the FBI, either."

She opened her eyes, looking up at him, searching. "What do you mean?"

"I love working for the Sarasota Falls Police Department. I love community policing. If I stay here, not only do I get to bug Riley every day, but maybe, if you say yes, I could come home to you at the end of every shift."

"You don't bug me!" Riley called from down the hall.

"Of course," Oscar said, "in a small town, everybody knows everything."

"What do you mean, come home to me?" Shelley asked.

"It's a strange thing, but I've worked since I was eighteen. I was trying to hunt down the memory of my father. In the last few weeks, I found out that while I am a lot like him— love adventure, want to do what I can for the world—I'm also a whole lot like my mother and my uncle Rudy. I want family, forever."

Shelley reached out, touched his cheek. His throat went dry, but he kept talking. "The military housed me. Even when I attended college. Here I live with Bianca. I tried paying rent and she kept sticking money in my shoes in order to give it back to me."

"What do you mean, come home to me?" Shelley repeated.

"I bought a house today."

"What!"

"For after we get married. I'm in love with you, Shelley."

"Don't you think I should help pick—"

"Does that mean yes?" Oscar interrupted.

"No, I want some say-so in picking out the house."

"I bought your house. The one your parents owned and you had to sell. I want to fill it with children and laughter. Your father can visit. And—"

"Yes."

"Your father can visit?"

"Yes, but that's not what I'm yessing. I'm yessing you. I'll marry you. I love you, Oscar."

Oscar'd spent the last fifteen years thinking he needed to save the world.

His whole world stood in front of him now.

"Kiss her already!" Riley yelled.

So Oscar did.

* * * * *

Be sure to check out the rest of
Pamela Tracy's compelling
Harlequin Heartwarming romances:
THE MISSING TWIN,
SMALL-TOWN SECRETS,
THE GREATEST GIFT,
WHAT JANIE SAW and
KATIE'S RESCUE!
Available at Harlequin.com.

Get 2 Free Books,
Plus 2 Free Gifts—
just for trying the Reader Service!

Get 2 Free Books,
Plus 2 Free Gifts—
just for trying the Reader Service!

Get 2 Free Books,
Plus 2 Free Gifts—
just for trying the
Reader Service!

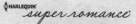

Get 2 Free Books,
Plus 2 Free Gifts—
just for trying the *Reader Service!*

YES! Please send me 2 FREE Harlequin® Heartwarming™ Larger-Print novels and my 2 FREE mystery gifts (gifts worth about $10 retail). After receiving them, if I don't wish to receive any more books, I can return the shipping statement marked "cancel." If I don't cancel, I will receive 4 brand-new larger-print novels every month and be billed just $5.49 per book in the U.S. or $6.24 per book in Canada. That's a savings of at least 19% off the cover price. It's quite a bargain! Shipping and handling is just 50¢ per book in the U.S. and 75¢ per book in Canada.* I understand that accepting the 2 free books and gifts places me under no obligation to buy anything. I can always return a shipment and cancel at any time. Even if I never buy another book, the 2 free books and gifts are mine to keep forever.

161/361 IDN GLQL

Name _____ (PLEASE PRINT) _____

Address _____ Apt. # _____

City _____ State/Prov. _____ Zip/Postal Code _____

Signature (if under 18, a parent or guardian must sign) _____

Mail to the **Reader Service:**
IN U.S.A.: P.O. Box 1867, Buffalo, NY 14240-1867
IN CANADA: P.O. Box 611, Fort Erie, Ontario L2A 9Z9

Want to try two free books from another line?
Call 1-800-873-8635 today or visit www.ReaderService.com.

* Terms and prices subject to change without notice. Prices do not include applicable taxes. Sales tax applicable in N.Y. Canadian residents will be charged applicable taxes. Offer not valid in Quebec. This offer is limited to one order per household. Books received may not be as shown. Not valid for current subscribers to Harlequin Heartwarming Larger-Print books. All orders subject to credit approval. Credit or debit balances in a customer's account(s) may be offset by any other outstanding balance owed by or to the customer. Please allow 4 to 6 weeks for delivery. Offer available while quantities last.

Your Privacy—The Reader Service is committed to protecting your privacy. Our Privacy Policy is available online at www.ReaderService.com or upon request from the Reader Service.

We make a portion of our mailing list available to reputable third parties that offer products we believe may interest you. If you prefer that we not exchange your name with third parties, or if you wish to clarify or modify your communication preferences, please visit us at www.ReaderService.com/consumerschoice or write to us at Reader Service Preference Service, P.O. Box 9062, Buffalo, NY 14240-9062. Include your complete name and address.